the perfect scandal

(a jessie hunt psychological suspense—book 23)

blake pierce

Blake Pierce

Blake Pierce is the USA Today bestselling author of the RILEY PAGE mystery series, which includes seventeen books. Blake Pierce is also the author of the MACKENZIE WHITE mystery series, comprising fourteen books; of the AVERY BLACK mystery series, comprising six books; of the KERI LOCKE mystery series, comprising five books; of the MAKING OF RILEY PAIGE mystery series, comprising six books; of the KATE WISE mystery series, comprising seven books; of the CHLOE FINE psychological suspense mystery, comprising six books; of the JESSIE HUNT psychological suspense thriller series, comprising twenty six books; of the AU PAIR psychological suspense thriller series, comprising three books; of the ZOE PRIME mystery series, comprising six books; of the ADELE SHARP mystery series, comprising sixteen books, of the EUROPEAN VOYAGE cozy mystery series, comprising six books; of the LAURA FROST FBI suspense thriller, comprising eleven books; of the ELLA DARK FBI suspense thriller, comprising fourteen books (and counting); of the A YEAR IN EUROPE cozy mystery series, comprising nine books, of the AVA GOLD mystery series, comprising six books (and counting); of the RACHEL GIFT mystery series, comprising ten books (and counting); of the VALERIE LAW mystery series, comprising nine books (and counting); of the PAIGE KING mystery series, comprising eight books (and counting); of the MAY MOORE mystery series, comprising eleven books (and counting); the CORA SHIELDS mystery series, comprising five books (and counting); of the NICKY LYONS mystery series, comprising five books (and counting), and of the new CAMI LARK mystery series, comprising five books (and counting).

An avid reader and lifelong fan of the mystery and thriller genres, Blake loves to hear from you, so please feel free to visit www.blakepierceauthor.com to learn more and stay in touch.

Copyright © 2022 by Blake Pierce. All rights reserved. Except as permitted under the U.S. Copyright Act of 1976, no part of this publication may be reproduced, distributed or transmitted in any form or by any means, or stored in a database or retrieval system, without the prior permission of the author. This ebook is licensed for your personal enjoyment only. This ebook may not be re-sold or given away to other people. If you would like to share this book with another person, please purchase an additional copy for each recipient. If you're reading this book and did not purchase it, or it was not purchased for your use only, then please return it and purchase your own copy. Thank you for respecting the hard work of this author. This is a work of fiction. Names, characters, businesses, organizations, places, events, and incidents either are the product of the author's imagination or are used fictionally. Any resemblance to actual persons, living or dead, is entirely coincidental. Jacket image Copyright Volodymyr TVERDOKHLIB, used under license from Shutterstock.com.
ISBN: 978-1-0943-8014-8

BOOKS BY BLAKE PIERCE

CAMI LARK MYSTERY SERIES
JUST ME (Book #1)
JUST OUTSIDE (Book #2)
JUST RIGHT (Book #3)
JUST FORGET (Book #4)
JUST ONCE (Book #5)

NICKY LYONS MYSTERY SERIES
ALL MINE (Book #1)
ALL HIS (Book #2)
ALL HE SEES (Book #3)
ALL ALONE (Book #4)
ALL FOR ONE (Book #5)

CORA SHIELDS MYSTERY SERIES
UNDONE (Book #1)
UNWANTED (Book #2)
UNHINGED (Book #3)
UNSAID (Book #4)
UNGLUED (Book #5)

MAY MOORE SUSPENSE THRILLER
NEVER RUN (Book #1)
NEVER TELL (Book #2)
NEVER LIVE (Book #3)
NEVER HIDE (Book #4)
NEVER FORGIVE (Book #5)
NEVER AGAIN (Book #6)
NEVER LOOK BACK (Book #7)
NEVER FORGET (Book #8)
NEVER LET GO (Book #9)
NEVER PRETEND (Book #10)
NEVER HESITATE (Book #11)

PAIGE KING MYSTERY SERIES
THE GIRL HE PINED (Book #1)
THE GIRL HE CHOSE (Book #2)

THE GIRL HE TOOK (Book #3)
THE GIRL HE WISHED (Book #4)
THE GIRL HE CROWNED (Book #5)
THE GIRL HE WATCHED (Book #6)
THE GIRL HE WANTED (Book #7)
THE GIRL HE CLAIMED (Book #8)

VALERIE LAW MYSTERY SERIES
NO MERCY (Book #1)
NO PITY (Book #2)
NO FEAR (Book #3)
NO SLEEP (Book #4)
NO QUARTER (Book #5)
NO CHANCE (Book #6)
NO REFUGE (Book #7)
NO GRACE (Book #8)
NO ESCAPE (Book #9)

RACHEL GIFT MYSTERY SERIES
HER LAST WISH (Book #1)
HER LAST CHANCE (Book #2)
HER LAST HOPE (Book #3)
HER LAST FEAR (Book #4)
HER LAST CHOICE (Book #5)
HER LAST BREATH (Book #6)
HER LAST MISTAKE (Book #7)
HER LAST DESIRE (Book #8)
HER LAST REGRET (Book #9)
HER LAST HOUR (Book #10)

AVA GOLD MYSTERY SERIES
CITY OF PREY (Book #1)
CITY OF FEAR (Book #2)
CITY OF BONES (Book #3)
CITY OF GHOSTS (Book #4)
CITY OF DEATH (Book #5)
CITY OF VICE (Book #6)

A YEAR IN EUROPE
A MURDER IN PARIS (Book #1)
DEATH IN FLORENCE (Book #2)

VENGEANCE IN VIENNA (Book #3)
A FATALITY IN SPAIN (Book #4)

ELLA DARK FBI SUSPENSE THRILLER
GIRL, ALONE (Book #1)
GIRL, TAKEN (Book #2)
GIRL, HUNTED (Book #3)
GIRL, SILENCED (Book #4)
GIRL, VANISHED (Book 5)
GIRL ERASED (Book #6)
GIRL, FORSAKEN (Book #7)
GIRL, TRAPPED (Book #8)
GIRL, EXPENDABLE (Book #9)
GIRL, ESCAPED (Book #10)
GIRL, HIS (Book #11)
GIRL, LURED (Book #12)
GIRL, MISSING (Book #13)
GIRL, UNKNOWN (Book #14)

LAURA FROST FBI SUSPENSE THRILLER
ALREADY GONE (Book #1)
ALREADY SEEN (Book #2)
ALREADY TRAPPED (Book #3)
ALREADY MISSING (Book #4)
ALREADY DEAD (Book #5)
ALREADY TAKEN (Book #6)
ALREADY CHOSEN (Book #7)
ALREADY LOST (Book #8)
ALREADY HIS (Book #9)
ALREADY LURED (Book #10)
ALREADY COLD (Book #11)

EUROPEAN VOYAGE COZY MYSTERY SERIES
MURDER (AND BAKLAVA) (Book #1)
DEATH (AND APPLE STRUDEL) (Book #2)
CRIME (AND LAGER) (Book #3)
MISFORTUNE (AND GOUDA) (Book #4)
CALAMITY (AND A DANISH) (Book #5)
MAYHEM (AND HERRING) (Book #6)

ADELE SHARP MYSTERY SERIES

LEFT TO DIE (Book #1)
LEFT TO RUN (Book #2)
LEFT TO HIDE (Book #3)
LEFT TO KILL (Book #4)
LEFT TO MURDER (Book #5)
LEFT TO ENVY (Book #6)
LEFT TO LAPSE (Book #7)
LEFT TO VANISH (Book #8)
LEFT TO HUNT (Book #9)
LEFT TO FEAR (Book #10)
LEFT TO PREY (Book #11)
LEFT TO LURE (Book #12)
LEFT TO CRAVE (Book #13)
LEFT TO LOATHE (Book #14)
LEFT TO HARM (Book #15)
LEFT TO RUIN (Book #16)

THE AU PAIR SERIES
ALMOST GONE (Book#1)
ALMOST LOST (Book #2)
ALMOST DEAD (Book #3)

ZOE PRIME MYSTERY SERIES
FACE OF DEATH (Book#1)
FACE OF MURDER (Book #2)
FACE OF FEAR (Book #3)
FACE OF MADNESS (Book #4)
FACE OF FURY (Book #5)
FACE OF DARKNESS (Book #6)

A JESSIE HUNT PSYCHOLOGICAL SUSPENSE SERIES
THE PERFECT WIFE (Book #1)
THE PERFECT BLOCK (Book #2)
THE PERFECT HOUSE (Book #3)
THE PERFECT SMILE (Book #4)
THE PERFECT LIE (Book #5)
THE PERFECT LOOK (Book #6)
THE PERFECT AFFAIR (Book #7)
THE PERFECT ALIBI (Book #8)
THE PERFECT NEIGHBOR (Book #9)
THE PERFECT DISGUISE (Book #10)

THE PERFECT SECRET (Book #11)
THE PERFECT FAÇADE (Book #12)
THE PERFECT IMPRESSION (Book #13)
THE PERFECT DECEIT (Book #14)
THE PERFECT MISTRESS (Book #15)
THE PERFECT IMAGE (Book #16)
THE PERFECT VEIL (Book #17)
THE PERFECT INDISCRETION (Book #18)
THE PERFECT RUMOR (Book #19)
THE PERFECT COUPLE (Book #20)
THE PERFECT MURDER (Book #21)
THE PERFECT HUSBAND (Book #22)
THE PERFECT SCANDAL (Book #23)
THE PERFECT MASK (Book #24)
THE PERFECT RUSE (Book #25)
THE PERFECT VENEER (Book #26)

CHLOE FINE PSYCHOLOGICAL SUSPENSE SERIES
NEXT DOOR (Book #1)
A NEIGHBOR'S LIE (Book #2)
CUL DE SAC (Book #3)
SILENT NEIGHBOR (Book #4)
HOMECOMING (Book #5)
TINTED WINDOWS (Book #6)

KATE WISE MYSTERY SERIES
IF SHE KNEW (Book #1)
IF SHE SAW (Book #2)
IF SHE RAN (Book #3)
IF SHE HID (Book #4)
IF SHE FLED (Book #5)
IF SHE FEARED (Book #6)
IF SHE HEARD (Book #7)

THE MAKING OF RILEY PAIGE SERIES
WATCHING (Book #1)
WAITING (Book #2)
LURING (Book #3)
TAKING (Book #4)
STALKING (Book #5)
KILLING (Book #6)

RILEY PAIGE MYSTERY SERIES
ONCE GONE (Book #1)
ONCE TAKEN (Book #2)
ONCE CRAVED (Book #3)
ONCE LURED (Book #4)
ONCE HUNTED (Book #5)
ONCE PINED (Book #6)
ONCE FORSAKEN (Book #7)
ONCE COLD (Book #8)
ONCE STALKED (Book #9)
ONCE LOST (Book #10)
ONCE BURIED (Book #11)
ONCE BOUND (Book #12)
ONCE TRAPPED (Book #13)
ONCE DORMANT (Book #14)
ONCE SHUNNED (Book #15)
ONCE MISSED (Book #16)
ONCE CHOSEN (Book #17)

MACKENZIE WHITE MYSTERY SERIES
BEFORE HE KILLS (Book #1)
BEFORE HE SEES (Book #2)
BEFORE HE COVETS (Book #3)
BEFORE HE TAKES (Book #4)
BEFORE HE NEEDS (Book #5)
BEFORE HE FEELS (Book #6)
BEFORE HE SINS (Book #7)
BEFORE HE HUNTS (Book #8)
BEFORE HE PREYS (Book #9)
BEFORE HE LONGS (Book #10)
BEFORE HE LAPSES (Book #11)
BEFORE HE ENVIES (Book #12)
BEFORE HE STALKS (Book #13)
BEFORE HE HARMS (Book #14)

AVERY BLACK MYSTERY SERIES
CAUSE TO KILL (Book #1)
CAUSE TO RUN (Book #2)
CAUSE TO HIDE (Book #3)
CAUSE TO FEAR (Book #4)

CAUSE TO SAVE (Book #5)
CAUSE TO DREAD (Book #6)

KERI LOCKE MYSTERY SERIES
A TRACE OF DEATH (Book #1)
A TRACE OF MURDER (Book #2)
A TRACE OF VICE (Book #3)
A TRACE OF CRIME (Book #4)
A TRACE OF HOPE (Book #5)

PROLOGUE

Jessie was cold.

There wasn't anything she could do about it. Not while she was lying on her side in the back seat of an old sedan, handcuffed, as the car she was in raced along a freeway, heading into the night and away from Los Angeles to an unknown destination.

Just a few hours ago, she had been about to marry the man of her dreams—her partner Detective Ryan Hernandez—in a sunset wedding at an oceanside resort with a small coterie of friends and family in attendance. But then her longtime nemesis, Andrea "Andy" Robinson, had slipped into the bridal suite, drugged her, and snuck her out a side exit before anyone knew she was gone. Now Andy, currently in the driver's seat of the sedan, was claiming the two of them were going off to live some kind of new life together.

"We're going to find our tiny, shared universe," were the particular words that stuck in Jessie's head out of the many that Andy said. It was yet more proof that Andy Robinson was dangerously disturbed, not that more proof was needed. After all, this was a woman who had murdered at least one person, tried once to kill Jessie, and coordinated the killings of multiple other innocent civilians.

Andy's blonde hair was whipping wildly about her face as the wind shot through the open window. She glanced back and Jessie caught a glimpse of her face in the rearview mirror via a freeway light. It wasn't quite maniacal. If someone else driving by looked over at her, they might not notice anything amiss.

But Jessie Hunt knew better. She recognized the too-wide grin, the strained neck muscles, and most of all, the blazingly blue eyes that somehow seemed even more intense than usual. Andy Robinson was well-practiced at hiding the sickness lurking just below the surface, but the cracks seemed to be showing more now. At the rate she was deteriorating, even people who weren't trained as criminal profilers would be able to sense that they were in the presence of danger.

"Don't worry," Andy said. "We'll make a stop at some point soon. I know you must be getting chilly back there. I can't uncuff you just yet, but I have a blanket in the trunk that I can tuck around you to keep you warm."

Or you could just roll up the windows, Jessie thought. She would have said it out loud, but she knew it wouldn't have done any good. Andy enjoyed the discomfort of the cold and though she would never admit it, she took pleasure in making Jessie uncomfortable and then being the one to offer her a salve for that discomfort. It was a way of maintaining power over her. If Jessie asked for the windows to be rolled up, it would be a sign of weakness and a concession that she had no control over what happened to her.

She didn't know what Andy's plan was, but she did know one thing. If she was going to get out of this alive, she needed to maintain her captor's respect. It was clear that whatever Andy intended, it wasn't just to kill Jessie and drop her body in the desert. She longed for something more: some kind of connection, and the harder Jessie made her work to get it, the better chance she had of finding some way out of this nightmare.

So, Jessie Hunt suffered through the cold in silence.

CHAPTER ONE

EIGHT HOURS EARLIER
7:42 p.m., Saturday night

Honey Potter had seen a lot of unusual things in her career as a lovemaking coach, but she'd never encountered anything like this. The Peninsula Resort and Spa, where she worked, was in chaos.

She'd been expecting to attend the nuptials of Jessie Hunt and Ryan Hernandez, who she'd helped with an investigation here at the resort a little while back. Instead, she appeared to be a witness to a crime scene. Just a few minutes ago, a woman in a white dress had walked down the aisle, pulled back her veil to reveal that she was not Jessie, and started laughing crazily. Then all hell broke loose.

The woman tried to run toward the oceanside cliff and throw herself onto the rocks below, only to be tackled by two female guests, one in an evening gown and another in a cocktail dress. Honey later learned that they were both coworkers of Jessie's, one a detective named Susannah Valentine and the other a police researcher named Beth Ryerson.

As she was processing the fact that the real bride had gone missing, a crowd of law enforcement surrounded the fake bride. Honey couldn't hear what was being said but the imposter continued to cackle madly until Jessie's friend, who Honey knew went by Kat, started to pummel her into submission. The cackling stopped. By the time the others pulled Kat off the woman, she was curled up into a whimpering ball.

"Take a walk, Gentry!" ordered an older man Honey knew to be Captain Roy Decker, Jessie's boss, who was supposed to give her away. "You're lucky I don't have you arrested."

Kat Gentry stormed off angrily in the direction of the bridal suite, followed closely by a youngish woman probably not more than twenty, tall, blonde, and skinny but with a purposeful stride well beyond her years.

Honey looked around for Ryan to offer to some words of support but couldn't find him. It would have been hard to miss Detective Ryan

Hernandez. With his dark hair, square jaw, and muscled frame, he stood out in most crowds. But it was his high wattage smile and warm, brown eyes that had made even a veteran of the world of lust like her a little weak-kneed when she first met him.

After a moment, Honey realized that it made sense that he was gone. He would have been far less interested in beating answers out of the woman who took his fiancée's place at the alter than in finding the woman he loved. He was probably already up at the bridal suite looking for her.

This wasn't Honey's area of expertise. She was used to helping couples rediscover ways to connect with each other or explore new erotic avenues to keep things exciting. She used to do it as an adult film actress. Now she did it as a licensed sex therapist with a very particular specialty. She was way out of her depth in this situation.

As if to reinforce her self-doubt, Captain Decker, a weathered, slouchy man in his sixties with intermittent clumps of gray hair and glasses, began barking orders at the remaining guests assembled near the gazebo where the ceremony was to have taken place.

"Detectives Valentine and Bray," he instructed the two female detectives closest to him, "I need one of you to catch up to Hernandez. He went straight to the bridal suite, but I'm worried he that he might be in shock. I don't want to miss an important clue because he's thinking like a man whose fiancée is missing rather than a detective. Whoever stays here, take this imposter into custody. Read her rights but don't start questioning her yet. I want to be there for that."

Honey watched as the two detectives snapped into action. The one in the evening gown who had helped tackle the imposter bride—a gorgeous, curvy brunette in her late twenties who looked more like a swimsuit model than a detective—hurried up to the bridal suite. The other detective, in her late thirties with dirty blonde hair and an unflappable air of professionalism, walked over to the handcuffed woman, still in the fetal position on the ground, knelt and began whispering quietly in her ear. Honey couldn't hear what she said because Decker's voice drowned her out.

"Winslow and Ryerson," he said, pointing at a slightly built, young, African American man and the towering brunette next to him in the cocktail dress who'd helped tackle the imposter bride before she could throw herself off the cliff, "time to earn your field stripes as police researchers. Work with hotel security. I want you to go through every snippet of footage from the last half hour. Look for anything that indicates how this woman got into the resort and where the hell Jessie Hunt went."

"I can help with that," said Hugo Cosgrove, Peninsula's head of security, waving at them from the top of the path. "I'll take you to our security office control center. Also, we've already shut down all the roads out of the resort and are having security search each vehicle. It might already be too late at this point, but we figured it can't hurt."

"Thank you," Decker said, before turning his attention to the remaining people standing nearby. "As for the rest of you, I'm looking around and I see people who came here as guests, hoping to help Ryan and Jessie celebrate their special day. Not only do we have almost every member of Homicide Special Section, the elite investigative unit they worked in together, here right now, but I also see representatives of Los Angeles divisions of the FBI, the U.S. Marshals Service, the County Sheriff's Department, not to mentioned retired LAPD detectives and criminal profilers. One of our own is missing. I plan to set up a command center and utilize every resource at our disposal to find Jessie Hunt. And while it's not official. I think we can all guess who's responsible for this: Andy Robinson. I'm guessing that if we find her, we find Jessie. Let's move up to the security office and reconvene there. I could use all your help."

A slew of people followed Decker back up the hill. A middle-aged, chunky man that Honey guessed was one of the retired detectives, stayed back to help the dirty-blonde-haired detective corral the imposter bride. Honey noticed only one other person—besides herself—who didn't seem to have an assigned job. An attractive black woman, maybe thirty, sat in one of the ceremony folding chairs, with her head in her hands. She was sobbing softly.

Honey had heard that Jessie had a half-sister who was here tonight and wondered if this might be her. Perhaps in the rush to rescue her, no one had thought to console her sibling. Honey couldn't solve crimes, but maybe she could at least help with this. She walked over and sat down next to the woman.

"How are you doing?" she asked softly.

The woman looked up. Even the tears streaking down her face couldn't hide her beauty.

"I've been better," she muttered.

"Are you Jessie's sister, Hannah?" Honey asked.

That almost seemed to make the woman laugh.

"No," she said. "Hannah was the tall, blonde teenager who barreled up the hill a minute ago, ready to kill whoever did this to her big sister. I'm Lacy, a friend of Jessie's from college. We were super close until a few years ago. Then we had a falling out over something stupid. I moved to Europe, and we just never really patched things up. I hoped tonight might change that. And now I'm worried that I might never get the chance."

Honey put her hand on Lacy's shoulder and gave a gentle squeeze. She might not be a detective, a police researcher, or an FBI agent, but this she could help with.

"Don't worry, Lacy," she said quietly, "you heard the captain. The resources of the entire law enforcement community of Southern California are being brought bear to find Jessie. You'll see her again. You'll patch things up. You'll have a drink, years from now, talking about how crazy this night was."

Lacy nodded. She seemed to believe it. And Honey wanted to as well. After all, Jessie Hunt was more than just a criminal profiler. To many in this city, she was a symbol of justice and fortitude, someone who had suffered terrible personal tragedies yet still fought to keep its residents safe. If they lost her, it would be devastating to more than just the people here tonight. Besides, what she said was true. LAPD, Sheriff's Department, FBI, U.S. Marshals—there was an army of investigators on site, all of whom were personally invested in Jessie's safe return.

And yet, something gnawed at Honey. Even though her experience in the adult film industry had been mostly positive, largely because she insisted on total control of everything she did and with whom, she saw a lot of ugliness. Many women fell through cracks, a lot disappeared, even really famous ones with teams of people whose prosperity depended on them being found. It was scary out there, even for a criminal profiler who had an army of supporters looking for her.

But Honey didn't say any of that to Lacy. She just sat with her, not speaking, a silent source of support if she was needed.

CHAPTER TWO

4:57 a.m., Sunday morning

Jessie could feel her muscles start to cramp up.

She tried to ignore it, not wanting to give any indication of weakness. But she was almost to the point where she wouldn't be able to mask the sound of the occasional whimper escaping her lips.

By now she knew they were heading east into the desert. In Los Angeles, the last few nights had been in the high fifties but it was easily ten to fifteen degrees colder than that here. She guessed that they were either in California's Mojave desert or maybe as far east as Nevada or Arizona.

"I haven't forgotten about that blanket," Andy said from the front seat, seeming to read her mind. "There's a rest stop at the next exit. Assuming there's no one else there, we'll pull over."

"How generous of you," Jessie replied snarkily, refusing to allow herself to sound sincerely grateful to her abductor.

"I know you're frustrated," Andy told her with a smile on her face. "You probably didn't have 'get kidnapped on my wedding day' on your Bingo card when you woke up this morning. But believe me, I saved you from a bunch of hassles. Now you don't have to worry about the inevitable divorce in a couple of years, the little sister living off you even though she's supposed to be off at college or—what is it these days—culinary school? The annoying friend who keeps using your inside access with the LAPD to keep her struggling detective agency afloat. You're in the clear on all of all that. And no one will blame you. I take the hit and you get the freedom. It's a win-win scenario for you. I know you don't see it that way yet, but you'll get there."

Jessie didn't reply. Was she really expected to respond to the warped logic that Andy using to make her argument? There was no point in that. Almost more concerning than her unhinged reasoning was the specificity of her knowledge.

How had she learned that Hannah was applying to culinary schools? How did she know that Jessie occasionally passed on LAPD tips to Kat to help with her private eye cases? Until a week ago, Andy Robinson had been incarcerated. Had she known all this while being held in the Western Regional Women's Psychiatric Detention Center? Or did she learn all of it in the week since her release?

And what else did she know? Clearly, she'd discovered enough to infiltrate Jessie's wedding, despite supposedly being watched round the clock. And even with a dozen law enforcement members as wedding guests, she managed to sneak into the bridal suite with an accomplice, incapacitate the bride, and sneak her out of the resort without being noticed.

That wasn't a plan constructed on the fly. While Andy clearly viewed it as some kind of *Thelma & Louise* sequel, it had been meticulously planned by someone who, while disturbed, was also, brilliant. If Jessie was going to uncover the woman's plan and find a way out of this situation, she needed to know what she was dealing with. And that meant engaging with Andy, even if the idea made her slightly ill.

"You seem awfully sure of yourself," she finally allowed. She knew that any overt pleasantry would be met with suspicion, so she went with a reluctant, skeptical, compliment.

"Maybe you've forgotten who you're dealing with," Andy replied tartly. "I'm not one of your clumsy serial killers whose every choice is beholden to their violent impulses. It's so easy to profile them, isn't it, Jessie? They're all at the mercy of their desires. Understand their desires and you can predict their actions. But I don't work that way."

"I didn't suggest that you did," Jessie told her, sensing the car veer right and slow down, indicating that they'd pulled off the freeway. "But you'd acknowledge that drugging me and sneaking me out of my own wedding isn't exactly embracing the sisterhood. What happened to supporting each other's choices, even if we don't agree with them?"

"I'm not a sophomore at liberal arts college, Jessie. My job isn't to enable your bad decisions. I'm rescuing you."

"What if I don't want to be rescued?" Jessie shot back as the car rolled to a stop. "Do you really expect me to thank you for putting me in a situation that required tying me up? You do see that this isn't a great way to build trust, right?"

"Desperate times call for desperate measures," Andy replied as she put the car in park. "You'll get there eventually. Now do you want that blanket or not?"

"Would you at least untie me, as a gesture of good faith?"

Andy turned around in her seat and offered a sympathetic smile.

"But Jessie," she said sweetly, "you just told me that you didn't want to be rescued by me. Considering that, it would be awful foolish of me to untie you, don't you think?"

"How do you expect to ever win me over if you do everything by force?" Jessie challenged.

Andy smiled. Jessie wanted punch her in the face.

"It won't always be this way," she assured her. "When I'm more confident that you won't try to make a run for it the second that I give you a little autonomy, then we'll loosen those bonds a little bit. Ironic, right? We have to strengthen *our* bonds in order to loosen yours. Anyway, enough chitchat for now. Let me get you that blanket and then we'll get back on the road. After all, we've still got a ways to go, and that head start we got won't last forever."

She got out of the front seat and headed to the back of the car. Jessie looked at the cuffs holding her in place, one on her wrist and one on her ankle, both attached to the metal frames of the backseat. She waited until she saw the trunk pop before she started tugging on the cuffs with her arms and legs, hoping for some give in the frames or the cuffs. But there was none.

Worse, the effort caused a rippling, stinging pain in her wrist and ankle. She didn't know if it was being in one position for so long, the lack of circulation, or the cold, but the effort to yank free made her extremities feel like they'd been attacked by dozens of bees. The trunk slammed shut and Andy reappeared. Jessie gulped hard, hoping to mask the pain she felt.

"Thirsty?" Andy, asked, misinterpreting the swallowing motion, and pulling out a bottled water.

"How do I know it's not drugged?" Jessie asked through gritted teeth.

"You don't," Andy replied casually, "but it's not. I can't promise I won't knock you out again but there's not really any need for it right now, in the middle of the night, with you tied up like this."

She gave Jessie several glugs, then tucked the blanket in around her. It was thick and, despite being a little scratchy, started to warm her up right away. Andy got back in the front seat and turned the car back on.

"You know, I was thinking about your people back at the resort," she mused amiably. "They're probably moving heaven and Earth to find you by now, not that it'll do them much good. To be honest, that's part of the fun of this for me—knowing that all those big important, folks are going to bring their power to bear in the search for you, and in the end, it won't matter. You know why?"

"No," Jessie said, deciding to play along for now. "Why?"

"Because we're going somewhere very special," Andy said, sounding borderline giddy, "someplace they'll never find us, no matter how hard they look, or for how long. And when we get there, I think you'll be surprised to find that you're going to love it. I promise."

CHAPTER THREE

7:46 p.m., Saturday night

At first Ryan Hernandez couldn't think.

He'd been in something like shock when the woman in front of him at the wedding pulled back her veil, started laughing maniacally, took off in in the direction of the oceanside cliff, and was tackled by Susannah Valentine and Beth Ryerson just before she could jump.

He was still in a semi-stunned stupor, not fully processing that Jessie wasn't there when people began interrogating the imposter. It was only when Kat Gentry started pummeling the woman that his brain clicked back on. There were more than enough people to deal with the crazy fake bride. He needed to know where Jessie was.

That's why he had gone up to the bridal suite. That's why he had forced himself to take several slow, deep breaths once he was sure she wasn't there. The suite was now a crime scene, and he couldn't let his panic and emotion corrupt it and possibly prevent the discovery of some crucial piece of evidence.

He had stepped back outside just as Kat Gentry and Hannah Dorsey came running up.

"She's not in there," he said quickly. "Don't go in. CSU is going to have to process the scene and they don't need us muddying it up."

Kat and Hannah, both out of breath, nodded.

"Did the woman say anything?" he asked. "The one in the wedding dress?"

Kat, a former Army Ranger, and Jessie's best friend, shook her head.

"My fists got her to stop laughing but she shut up completely after that," she said. "Captain Decker sent me packing."

"You're lucky that's all he did," Ryan said.

"Believe me," she replied, "if it was just me and her, that interrogation would still be going on and she'd be talking."

Ryan wasn't inclined to doubt her. Katherine "Kat" Gentry wasn't to be trifled with. Even if one didn't know about her military background, her powerfully built, muscular frame, along with the multiple facial burn marks and a long scar that ran vertically down her left cheek from just below her eye should have been enough to tell people not to screw with her. But it was moot now.

"That's spilled milk," Ryan told her. "We have to assume we won't get anything out of her. How are we going to find Jessie?"

"By finding Andy Robinson," Hannah said, speaking up for the first time.

"What do you mean?" Ryan asked.

"We didn't have time to get into it earlier, with everybody rushing around before the ceremony," Hannah explained, "but I recognize the woman in that dress. She's the same woman who tried to mow Kat down earlier today when we were running wedding errands for you guys. That's not a coincidence. I bet that if we put her face and prints into the system, we'll find that this imposter bride was one of Andy's acolytes and that she helped her with this whole plan."

Ryan immediately knew what she was referencing. While in the Female Forensic In-Patient Psychiatric Unit of the Twin Towers Correctional Facility, where Andy Robinson had been held prior to her transfer, she had cultivated a group of minions, a cult-like collection of followers. Some of those women, after being released, committed heinous murders on her behalf. Others, like this fake bride, were apparently part of sleeper cells, leading seemingly normal lives but ready to be activated on Andy's command.

"I'll have Jamil Winslow plug her into the system," Kat said. "Once we get a name, we can find out exactly how she's connected to Andy. Maybe that will give us a way to go at her."

She dashed off, leaving Ryan alone with Hannah. He looked over at the half-sister of the woman he was to have married less than five minutes ago. They were similar in so many ways. Both were tall, though at five-foot-ten, Jessie had an inch on her little sister. They shared the same penetrating green eyes. Both had lean, athletic frames, although Hannah's veered more toward pure skinniness. Jessie's hair was brown, and Hannah's was blonde, but they each wore it just below the shoulders. Both were stubborn and driven and unrelenting in pursuit of their goals.

But Jessie was an adult. The person in front of Ryan was still a few weeks shy of her 18th birthday and right now, she looked it. He realized that she'd been putting on a brave face, doing all she could to stay strong in order to help with the search. But now, alone with him, the veneer seemed to be cracking and she looked like a lost little girl.

"Hey," he said softly, "it's going to be okay. "We're going to find her."

Hannah looked up at him. Her eyes were damp, but her gaze was steely.

"You don't have to sugarcoat it for me, Ryan," she said. "We both know what Andy Robinson is capable of. There's a real chance I may never see my sister again. When we re-join everyone, I'll put that thought out of my head and focus all my energy on getting her back. But right now, in this moment, let's be honest with each other and allow for the possibility that she might be gone for good."

Ryan shook his head.

"I know I should say something right now to validate how you're feeling," he told her, "But that's not how I operate. I'm going to grind every second until we get her back and deal with everything else afterward. And I'm going to share a little secret with you, Hannah. We need you. You are incredibly smart. You know Jessie well. If she's able to leave us any clues as to her whereabouts, you're just as likely to pick up on them as anyone else. But not if you're in 'never see her again' mode. There will be time for grief and self-pity later."

Hannah's eyes got wide at that last comment, but she didn't object. He kept going.

"Listen, I know you're still technically a minor and Jessie is your guardian. But right now, I need you to be hers. I need you focused. I need you to be an asset and not a little sister who requires taking care of. I know it's not fair to ask that of you but I'm asking it all the same. You can say yes, or you can go home. Which is it going to be?"

She didn't need to speak for him to know her answer. When they headed out, her eyes were dry.

*

"Her name is Corinne Bertans," Jamil Winslow said ten minutes later.

Ryan studied the image of the woman on the screen, as they all crowded around the monitor in the hotel security office where Captain Decker had set up the temporary command center. The woman being discuss was locked in a holding cell just a few feet away, staring blankly into space, seemingly oblivious to the chaos she'd caused.

"As suspected," Jamil continued," she was a prisoner at Twin Towers where her incarceration overlapped with Andrea Robinson's. She was released eight months ago. Since then, she's been leading an unremarkable existence. Like most of the women connected to Robinson, there was no way to discern that they were in her thrall until after they did something on the outside."

"What was she in Twin Towers for in the first place?" asked Dr. Janice Lemmon, a sixty-something woman with thick glasses and frizzy hair who was the personal therapist to both Jessie and Hannah. She was also previously a criminal profiler for the LAPD and FBI before turning her focus exclusively to private patients.

"According to her paperwork," Beth Ryerson volunteered, "she liked going the wrong way."

"What does that mean?" asked Decker.

"Driving the wrong way down one-way streets. Riding bikes into oncoming traffic on bike paths. Running directly into people on running tracks. The thing that got her locked up this time was going to a bowling alley and walking down near the pins, then flinging her ball up the lane where people were standing. She hit a little kid in the leg and crushed his knee."

"But she's done nothing since she got out?" Dr. Lemmon asked.

"Nothing that got in the system," Jamil said.

"Okay, I'm going to have a chat with her," Decker said, starting toward the door.

"Not me, Captain?" Ryan pressed.

"Don't you think you're a little too personally invested in this to conduct an objective interrogation, Hernandez?'

"That's exactly the point," Ryan countered. "This isn't a traditional interrogation. Do you really think she's going to respond to standard questioning? Andy Robinson selected Corinne Bertans to be behind that veil because she had the same general physical characteristics as Jessie. Bertans must have studied her. She probably saw photos of me too. I'm hoping that being in that room together will throw her off, get her to let her guard down a little, maybe reveal something. No offense, Captain, but do you really think she's going to open up to you?"

Decker looked over at Dr. Lemmon, who shrugged.

"It's worth a shot," she said. "If it doesn't work, you can always go the more traditional route."

Decker nodded and Ryan walked into the room. Corinne was facing away from him. Her hair was matted with leaves and her white dress was smeared in mud from where she'd been tackled as she tried to get to the cliff.

"Hi Corinne," he said softly, sitting in the chair across from her.

She glanced over at him. There was recognition in her eyes, but she said nothing. He continued anyway.

"So, from what happened out there, I gather you didn't expect to be in this room now. It looked to me like your plan was to surprise me, which you did, and then throw yourself into the ocean. That part didn't work out so great."

All he got in response was a shrug. He debated how best to proceed. There was no point in making threats. Corinne thought she'd be dead by now. It wasn't like she had anything to lose. Although the more he thought about it, that wasn't quite true.

"How do you think Andy's going to react when she finds out you didn't complete your mission?" he asked simply.

That got her attention. She looked up. Her expression wasn't one of fear but rather shame.

"I'm guessing she'll be pretty disappointed in you," he suggested sympathetically. "Your job was to stun all of us and then kill yourself, leaving everyone with unanswerable questions. By the time we fished out your body, she and Jessie would be so far away that we wouldn't have a chance of finding them. But that's already falling apart, Corinne. We know who you are. We know all about your connection to Andy. Our people are tracking your movements since you left Twin Towers and soon, we'll have a record of every time you interacted with Andy. When she gets caught, she's going to hold you responsible, all because you couldn't complete your one simple task."

Corinne lowered her head without a word.

"But we can help with that," he told her. "We can make it so that she never knows you failed. All you have to do is tell us what you know, and we'll help you out, I promise."

To his surprise, Corinne started laughing again, the same crazy cackle that had escaped her lips when she lifted back the veil. Ryan wasn't sure what to make of it. He thought he'd reeled her in. But somewhere along the line, he'd screwed up badly. He heard a click behind him and turned around to see that Dr. Lemmon had come in the room. She walked over and put her hand on his shoulder.

"May I have a word with Corinne?" she asked quietly.

"Of course," he said, starting to stand up.

"You don't need to leave," Lemmon said. "This will just take a second."

She leaned over and whispered something in Corinne's ear. The younger woman stopped laughing and her spine straightened. Lemmon whispered something else. Corinne looked her in the eyes and nodded. Then she closed her eyes tight and moaned two words: "All mine!"

She repeated them over and over, getting louder and more baleful each time. Lemmon indicated that Ryan should leave the room. As he did, she whispered one more thing to Corinne and she went silent again.

Once they were both in the outer security office again, Susannah Valentine asked what everyone was wondering.

"What the hell was that?"

"I asked if Andy ever said where she planned to take Jessie. That was her answer. Make of it what you will."

"Could it be some kind of riddle?" asked FBI agent Jack Dolan, another wedding guest who had been silent up until now.

"Maybe for Andy," Lemmon said, "but I don't get the sense that Corinne is the game playing type. I suspect that those are the exact words she was told."

"Maybe it's as straightforward as it sounds?" offered Kat's boyfriend, Riverside County Sheriff's Deputy Mitch Connor. "Jessie would be 'all hers' back at her house."

"But why would Andy go to all the trouble to kidnap her from her wedding just to take her back to a place where we can easily access her?" U.S. Marshal Patrick "Murph" Murphy wondered.

"It's actually not that crazy an idea," noted Brady Bowen, Ryan's best man and former partner, now a detective with West L.A. Division. "Some suspects I searched for went back to the place where they were first busted because they figured cops would assume they'd never go back there again."

"Plus," added Detective Karen Bray, "Don't forget that her mansion is in Hancock Park."

"Why is that significant?" Murphy asked.

"I got called to a lot of incidents in that neighborhood back in my Hollywood patrol days and one thing I learned was that a bunch of those houses were built pre-prohibition. Many owners back then had whole sections tunneled out below the homes to hide barrels of illegal hooch. If her place is like that, she could have turned the whole lower level into a livable panic basement, and no one would know."

"I could check the city's zoning and building records to see if she had any alterations made," Jamil offered.

"You could," Bray told him, "But some contractors will build that stuff off the books if they get paid enough, so it might not even be on file. The whole point is to keep it secret."

"Sounds like it's at least worth checking out," Decker said. "Bray, use those Hollywood connections to get a warrant ASAP. In the meantime, I'm going to move our command center to Central Station, where we have access to more resources."

"I want to run point on that home search as soon as the warrant comes through," Ryan told him.

"That's fine," Decker said, before pulling him aside and adding under his breath, "But take Valentine with you."

"Why her?" Ryan asked equally quietly.

"Because she's never afraid to go in guns blazing and if someone has to take Robinson down, it'll be easier for me to defend her shooting the suspect than the kidnap victim's fiancé."

Before Ryan could reply, Decker had spun around and was barking instructions at Jamil and Beth, who were furiously taking down notes. Everyone mulled about the security officer except for Dr. Lemmon who stepped quietly outside, using the cane she'd recently started relying on. Ryan followed her.

He joined her in a secluded area where they could hear the waves crashing in the distance but not the voices inside the office.

"I have to ask," he said. "What did you whisper to Corinne to get her to talk?'

Dr. Lemmon smiled. Her thick glasses glinted in the moonlight, and she leaned over to him, her tiny body dwarfed by his.

"I told her that if she helped us, I'd make sure she got to jump off that cliff into the ocean."

Ryan sat with that for a moment, a little surprised. He didn't think therapists were allowed to engage in such deceptions.

"So, you lied to her," he said.

"Says who?" Lemmon replied noncommittally.

"What, are you going to bust her out so she can make a break for the cliff?"

Lemmon smiled again.

"Detective Hernandez, I don't mean to tell you your business, but shouldn't you be headed to Andy Robinson's mansion so you're ready to bust in there the second that warrant is approved?"

She was dissembling, but she was also right. He needed to go—now.

CHAPTER FOUR

8:52 p.m., Saturday night

Kat didn't even notice that she was speeding.

She was going thirty miles over the speed limit when Hannah pointed at the speedometer. They were headed north on Highland Avenue toward Jessie's house. Hannah was in the passenger seat beside her, lost in her own thoughts. Kat didn't speak either, trying to hide her frustration.

Even though she didn't work for the LAPD, she had been given a direct assignment by Captain Decker: get Hannah safely home and stay with her until further notice. He was concerned that Andy's plan's might not be limited to abducting only Jessie. Retired detective Callum Reid had agreed to follow them back, keeping an eye out for any tails, and staying with them until further notice as an extra precaution.

As she drove, Kat silently seethed. She couldn't help but wonder what additional information they might have gleaned if Decker would have allowed her to question Corinne Bertans her way. Back in Iraq and Afghanistan, she'd never been part of the interrogation teams, and to be honest, she found their tactics to be generally objectionable. But she'd taken mental note of them and was more than willing to give them a shot if they offered even a glimmer of hope of finding Jessie.

On the other hand, some part of her was relieved that the others had pulled her off Bertans back at Peninsula. She'd been so filled with blind rage at this woman in the wedding dress, laughing wildly as she tried to throw herself off a cliff, that she wasn't sure if she would have ever stopped punching her.

The thought scared her a bit. The last time she remembered feeling such unquenchable fury had been years ago, after the IED that exploded, killing several of her compatriots and wounding her. It had taken her a long time and lots of counseling to get back from that dark place. She didn't want to return to it again.

She shook that thought off and focused on a more constructive one. Instead of beating the woman, they were working with what Dr. Lemmon had gotten from her—one phrase: "all mine." Everyone seemed hopeful that the phrase suggested Andy was holding Jessie at her Hancock Park mansion. The theory made sense to Kat too, except for one thing.

"Can you check something for me?" she asked Hannah, speaking aloud for the first time in several minutes.

"Sure," Hannah answered, after looking briefly startled.

"Do you remember how I told you yesterday that once I knew Andy was going to be released from prison, I 'invited' myself into her house and set up several hidden cameras to keep track of her movements?"

"Of course," Hannah said. "You weren't confident that she wouldn't slip past the cops, so you created your own tracking system."

"Right," Kat said, handing over her phone, "And obviously mine wasn't foolproof either. But one thing it's pretty good at is tracking motion on any of the cameras. The system sends me an alert any time someone passes though the frame. I haven't gotten any alerts in the last couple of hours, since before we arrived at Peninsula for the wedding."

"Shouldn't you have gotten some, at least for her house staff?" Hannah asked.

"She usually has them all leave by five," Kat said, "So the only movement after that would come from her. Check the logs, but I don't think there's been any in the last few hours."

Hannah scrolled through the phone.

"I don't see anything."

Kat frowned.

"Doesn't that seem odd?" she asked. "Unless Andy Robinson has some secret Wayne Manor/Batman-style entrance to her home, at least one of these cameras should have been triggered if she returned home."

"What are you suggesting," Hannah asked, "that everybody has it wrong and that Andy took Jessie someplace else entirely?"

"Is that such a crazy proposition?"

"No, actually," Hannah said. "Everyone jumped to the same assumption. It was groupthink in action. But just because Dr. Lemmon didn't think that Corinne was playing games with us, that doesn't mean people drew the right conclusion about what she was saying. What if when she said, 'all mine,' she was wasn't referencing Andy's place. Maybe it was simpler than that. Maybe she was talking about her own."

Kat pulled over to the side of the road and motioned for Callum Reid, in the car behind them, to stop as well.

"What are you doing?" Hannah asked. "We're only a few blocks from home."

"We're following up on your lead," Kat explained. "But we're going to need the help of our retired detective friend back there."

"What do you mean?"

"First of all, he's riding with us from now on," Kat said. "It'll save time. More importantly, who do you think senior police researcher Jamil Winslow is more likely to share information with: you and me or a beloved detective emeritus from his unit? That's why Reid is going to ask Jamil for Corinne Bertans's last known address. And once we get it, that's our next stop."

*

Kat made Hannah wait in the car.

She was glad when the younger woman didn't balk. That was part of the deal. If she wanted to come along, she had to agree to stay put when told. The alternative was to be dropped off at the house. Kat knew there was no way Hannah would go for that. She agreed to the terms immediately.

Still, considering the circumstances and the neighborhood, one last reminder was in order. As Callum Reid got out of the passenger seat, Kat looked over her shoulder into the back seat.

"I'm locking the door. I want you to lie on your side so no one can see that you're in here. I already gave you pepper spray. Between that and your phone, you should be good. Text me if you see anything suspicious. Call if you feel threatened."

Though she looked like she wanted to say something, Hannah simply nodded. Kat got out, locked the door, and looked over at Callum Reid. Considering that he was her only backup, she hoped that he was up to the task.

Jessie always spoke highly of the guy, but the man was retired for a reason. He'd been diagnosed with a serious heart condition that made chasing suspects down alleys inadvisable. Otherwise, he looked the part of a later-years detective. In his mid-forties, he had a bit of a belly. His brown hair was beginning to recede, and he wore black-framed glasses that wouldn't have looked out of place on *Dragnet*. He pulled out his weapon and checked it.

"Not department issued, I gather?" Kat said.

"Nope," Callum replied, holstering the gun. "I'm a civilian, just like you. But my new security consultant gig makes this a business expense. Shall we go check out Corinne's digs?"

"Let's," Kat agreed. "The apartment is 4F in that building on the corner, according to Jamil. Thanks for convincing him to spill, by the way."

"It wasn't that hard," Callum said. "He knows the squad is spread thin and any lead, no matter how questionable, is worth checking out."

"You think Decker will be pissed that he's sharing information with civilians?"

"Only if one of us dies," Callum said, "which seems like a real possibility in this neighborhood."

He was right. As they approached the building, Kat took notice of the fact that almost all the streetlights had been knocked out. Garbage lined the gutters. Every third vehicle was burned out. They were in the Westlake area, just east of MacArthur Park, which was notorious for drug dealing, even in broad daylight. At night, it was often a war zone.

They pushed through the broken exterior gate outside Corinne's building and Kat jimmied the interior door of the complex. The building was six stories high, and they didn't dare take the elevator, instead opting for the stairs.

Kat led the way, using the flashlight on her phone to illuminate the otherwise darkened stairwell. It was now 9:26 p.m., prime time on a Saturday night, but they didn't encounter a single person as they made their way up to the fourth floor, which Kat found odd.

"Wouldn't you expect more foot traffic around here right about now?" she whispered to Callum.

"Not necessarily," he muttered back. "Everyone who wants to cause trouble is out and about somewhere more interesting. Everyone who wants to stay safe is locked up tight."

It made sense once he said it. Kat hoped it stayed that way. If they could avoid any confrontations other than one in which they hopefully found and surprised Andy Robinson, that would be ideal.

They stopped outside apartment 4F. In moments like this, Kat was glad that, as private citizens, she and Callum weren't constrained by entanglements like search warrants. Callum motioned that he would deal with the lock while she covered him. Kat pulled out her gun and waited, feeling the same tingle she got back in her Ranger days, just before they would breach the compound of a suspected enemy combatant. Callum nodded that it was done and moved to the side.

Kat knew there might still be a chain lock, so she entered leg first, kicking hard. There was no chain lock, and the door shot open. A small shard of wood flew into her arm, but she ignored it. She stepped into the darkened room, eyes scanning the space, looking for any movement as well as any sign of wires along the ground that might act as booby traps. She wouldn't put anything past Andy Robinson.

But after five minutes of careful searching, it became clear that the tiny apartment was empty. Callum closed the front door and turned on the lights while Kat texted Hannah the bad news and to let her know they'd be coming back down soon.

"This place is pretty spartan," Callum said.

"Yeah," Kat agreed. "It's like she's barely been living any real life of her own. I get the sense that this was just a way station, that she was just biding her time until Andy called on her."

"We should head back down," Callum said. "I don't love the idea of leaving Hannah alone down there any longer than necessary."

"Me either," Kat said. "Just give me one second."

She went into the bathroom, pulled out the little sliver of wood that had embedded in her forearm when she kicked the door open, and ran the bloody area under the water from the sink faucet. She grabbed a couple of tissues to dab the blood and was just tossing them in the trash when she noticed the medicine cabinet was slightly ajar. For some reason she couldn't explain, she opened it the rest of the way.

It was immediately clear why it wouldn't completely close. Corinne had glued a small whiteboard to the inside of the cabinet, and it was just slightly too big at the edges for the door to completely shut. Written on the board were several numbers and letters that made no sense to Kat. But others were instantly understandable. They were references to Andy Robinson's acolytes.

Next to the letter "L," which she suspected stood for Livia, was the date that Livia Bucco had hacked a law student to death with a machete in a YWCA shower. Under that, next to the letter "R," likely for Roth, was the date that Eden Roth had smeared a liquid poison on multiple people in California Plaza, killing five. On the line below that was today's date—the date of Jessie's wedding—with the letter "C" next to it, almost certainly meaning Corinne.

There was one more line below that, with question marks where the date should be. But next to it was the letter "B." If the pattern followed, Kat imagined that it might be the first initial of the next acolyte's last name.

Of course, Corinne's last name started with a "B" too, but Kat doubted it was her, as she was supposed to have died jumping off that cliff earlier tonight. That meant there was at least one more member of

Andy's cult out there, waiting for go-ahead to inflict some kind of horror on the world. But who was it, what was their task, and when was it supposed to happen?

All those were relevant questions, but unfortunately, none of them were helpful with the most pressing question of the moment: where had Andy Robinson taken Jessie? And on that front, it looked like this place was a bust.

Still, it was worth getting CSU in here to pore over the apartment. Maybe they'd discover something useful. And there was other stuff written on the whiteboard—number and letter combinations that were incoherent to Kat. Maybe Jamil and Beth could crack the code of what it all meant and determine if it could help find Jessie.

One thing was clear. All the information on this board alone would be enough to prove that Andy had, in fact, been operating a secret cult of personality from within the confines of the Twin Towers. There were initials, dates, and even what looked to be cell numbers.

This was evidence that Andy had not been, as she claimed, helping the authorities to solve these horrible crimes committed by former fellow inmates. Rather, it showed that she had been pulling the strings all along, manipulating these vulnerable women and setting them on their violent paths, then using their crimes as a way to bargain for her own release from custody.

It had worked. First, she had manipulated Detective Susannah Valentine. Then she'd played Police Chief Richard Laird, and ultimately, she'd even tricked the Governor into granting her parole. Now there was a mountain of proof to send her back behind bars. There was only one problem. No one could find her.

It seemed that every break they got only helped them after the fact. Everything they learned would help, later, down the line, at trial. But it did them no good right now, as they searched for their missing friend.

Corinne Bertans's apartment was a gold mine for getting a conviction. But in terms of helping Jessie, it was a dead end.

"Let's go," she said called out to Callum. "We're wasting time."

CHAPTER FIVE

6:28 a.m., Sunday morning

Even from her awkward position lying on the backseat, Jessie could see the sun rising in the east.

Considering that just twenty-four hours ago, she was awake to watch the sun rise as she stood outside the Pacific Division Police Station in Culver City, trying to come up with a way to solve a serial stabbing case, she estimated that it was about 6:30 right now. The sun would be fully up in another fifteen to twenty minutes.

She did her best to ignore the low churn of panic in her gut and did a little mental math in her head. The wedding last night was supposed to have taken place at sunset, a little after 7 p.m. But just prior to that, Andy and her accomplice—the one she called Corinne—had drugged her and dumped her in a laundry cart. So, it had been almost twelve hours since she was abducted. The question was: how far had they traveled in that time and where were they now?

The last thing she remembered seeing before slipping into unconsciousness in that bridal suite was Andy in a housekeeping uniform. That explained how she planned to move around the resort without drawing suspicion. But no matter how confident she was, Andy couldn't have just rolled a cart of laundry out to the parking lot while wearing a maid's uniform, dumped its contents in the trunk of a private car, and driven off without attracting attention. It would have been too risky.

That likely meant that Andy had pushed her in the cart to a waiting laundry truck, probably in a garage, which would have driven her off the property. Had she switched uniforms and driven the truck out of the resort herself? It was possible but that would require access to an additional uniform and the truck keys.

It was one thing to knock out a single housekeeper, tie her up, and take her outfit. But commandeering a second uniform and keys to a vehicle was more complicated. Plus, what if security at the resort exit knew the laundry truck drivers? What if there was a sign-out process?

Would they question her? It wasn't enough to just get off the property. Andy needed to get away without arousing suspicion or tipping off those who would come looking for her as to the vehicle she was in. Therefore, driving the truck herself was also too big a risk.

That left only one option. Andy would have had to load Jessie's unconscious body into the truck, then hide there with her, under piles of laundry, until the truck left the resort. That was still taking a chance, as she was dependent on the driver to leave at their assigned time. If the driver was too leisurely about it, they might get stopped when security shut the whole resort down, as they inevitably would once it became clear that the bride was a fake and the real one had gone missing.

Whatever the timing was, it had worked, because Jessie was currently handcuffed to the rear seat of this car. She closed her eyes, trying her best to back time it, imagining how it would have played out: she gets drugged. Guests wait politely, thinking she's just doing last minute touch-ups. The fake bride stalls. At some point the truth is revealed. Chaos ensues.

Hopefully pretty fast, considering all the law enforcement minds on the scene, someone thinks to shut down exits from the resort. The order goes out. She guessed that the laundry truck would have had about fifteen to twenty minutes to leave the premises before the lockdown kicked in.

But it's not like the truck would have made a beeline for the California desert right after that. Andy would have had to let the driver get a good distance from the resort before doing anything, certainly get past any police cars that might be zipping by in the other direction with sirens blaring. She'd know where the truck was headed and want to be sure it was well outside the perimeter that law enforcement would cordon off.

Only then would Andy quietly slip out from under whatever comforters had to be restitched, sneak up on the driver, and press her gun against his temple. She'd direct him to wherever she'd left the old sedan they were in now, likely some darkened, out-of-the-way strip mall without working security cameras, probably in a bad neighborhood.

Jessie wondered whether she would have killed the driver, or hopefully just drugged him, tied him up, and left him in the back of his own truck. She was counting on Andy being more pragmatic than malicious. After all, she had to know that at some point, the authorities would figure out the laundry truck trick, if only when the driver didn't show up at the warehouse. Letting him live wouldn't impact her head start. But counting on Andy Robinson's sense of goodwill was never a smart bet.

Jessie set that aside, trying to stay focused. She readjusted herself on the seat and noticed something that she was embarrassed to acknowledge she hadn't registered until just this moment. She was no longer in her wedding dress.

Instead, she was wearing loose gray sweatpants and a thin, long-sleeved, oversized shirt that read "Manilow's Mob" and had a silhouetted image of Barry Manilow below it. At least Andy had let her keep the white, strappy sandals from the wedding, probably because she didn't have an alternative. She also saw what looked like a black wig on the floor, likely worn by Andy as a disguise until she felt they were far enough out of the city to take it off.

Now that daylight was starting to peek out over the horizon and she could see better, she also caught a glimpse of her own hair out of the corner of her eye and realized that it was no longer its normal light brown but rather a severely dyed, platinum blonde.

She took a long, slow, deep breath and exhaled, trying not to verbalize her sense of violation. It didn't set well with her that Andy had been playing stylist with her while she was unconscious. If she'd done that, what other changes had she made to her?

As troubling as that thought was, she set it aside for now to focus on a more immediate point. In order to do all this, Andy would have required a hotel room, and time—at least three hours and maybe more.

Jessie tried to add it all up. Between the laundry truck hijacking and the hotel makeover, they probably wouldn't have hit the road until after midnight. Andy probably would have taken extra precautions on the drive, getting off the freeway and taking surface streets whenever she saw a potential threat. And considering the age and limitations of the clunker they were in, she doubted it could get over 50 miles per hour.

Calculating all that, Jessie guessed that they'd probably gone somewhere in the range of 200 to 300 miles. Unfortunately, that still left a huge potential area. She knew they were heading generally east because of the flat desert terrain and the chilly temperature. But based on her mileage estimate, they could still be anywhere from the western edge of Joshua Tree or the Mojave Desert to eastern portions of Arizona or Nevada.

"We're here," Andy said, snapping her out of her deliberations.

"Where?"

"Don't get too excited," Andy warned. "We're not at our final destination just yet. This is just a little snack spot. Are you hungry?"

The second Andy asked the question Jessie realized just how famished she was. She hadn't had anything substantial to eat in over eighteen hours. Still, she tried to contain herself as she replied.

"I could eat."

"I figured," Andy said. "So, we're going to pull over. But I need to remind you not to try anything foolish. There are going to be other human beings in the vicinity, and I know you're going to have the urge to make some effort to communicate with one of them somehow, maybe even try to escape. But I have to warn you Jessie. That's a bad idea. It will only lead to bloodshed and guilt—their blood, your guilt. So, I need your word that you're going to behave like a good girl. Do I have it?"

Jessie nodded.

"I'm going to need verbal confirmation on this one," Andy said.

"You have it," Jessie said.

As Andy slowed down and brought the car to a stop, Jessie closed her eyes and did her best to give her body a brief reprieve before what came next. She would need every spare ounce of energy she had. After all, despite her meaningless promise to the mad woman who had kidnapped her from her own wedding, she had every intention of escaping the first chance she got.

CHAPTER SIX

6:46 a.m. Sunday morning

Jessie could tell they were at a travel center.

Even though Andy had parked well away from all the other vehicles, the sign for the Flying Y Travel Center was so massive and rose so high in the air that it was impossible to miss. Still Jessie pretended not to notice as she pliantly allowed her captor to gag her before re-checking her cuffs to make sure they hadn't loosened during the drive.

"I'll only be gone for a few minutes," Andy said soothingly. "Again, please don't try anything foolish. This is a test of our bond, Jessie. Let's see how strong it is."

She closed and locked the door and walked away. Jessie watched her blonde head recede into the distance and waited a good two minutes after that before moving at all. Only then did she twist her body, ignoring the discomfort it caused in her wrists and ankles. Now on her back, she could get a better sense of the terrain.

Unfortunately, it didn't reveal anything new. All she saw in every direction was the flat sprawl and occasional hills of endless desert, which only reinforced what she already suspected about her location. She craned her head around, hoping to catch sight of any sign that might mention a nearby town, road, or even a mile marker, but Andy had carefully parked in a spot where none of that was visible.

Jessie kicked at the cushioned seat in frustration. It had lost most of its loft over the years and offered little resistance. But she did notice that the action created a little friction, which had allowed her to shimmy slightly up the back of the seat. She immediately dug both feet into the cushion and pressed her right shoulder against the back of the seat. The move lifted her head up about six inches higher than it could otherwise get, just above where the bottom of the window met the door. She could barely see out.

She blinked several times, trying to process what was in front of her. Andy had parked a good fifty yards away from the next closest vehicle and more like seventy from the actual travel center building. The car wasn't even really in the parking lot but in a gravel annex for overflow traffic that wasn't needed at sunrise on Sunday morning.

Jessie counted less than ten total cars in the lot and only two people. One was pumping gas so far away that it was hard to identify their age or sex. The other was an older woman returning to her car with a big Styrofoam cup of coffee purchased from the travel center convenience store that Jessie assumed Andy was currently in.

She tried to look through the heavily tinted windows of the store to locate her when her attention was diverted by the running lights of a car pulling up unexpectedly close to her. Because of her angle, she couldn't see where it had parked but the sound of the door closing was awfully close, maybe within twenty feet.

Without stopping to think about it, she began grunting loudly, banging her free leg against the back of the front passenger seat, and clanging her handcuff against the metal of the seat she was attached to. That last act caused a spike of pain so intense that it ended the grunting with a sharp gasp.

She slunk back down in the seat, waiting for the feeling to subside. At some point she realized that her eyes were watering from the agony of the relentless, piercing tingling of her skin. The discomfort was just starting to subside when she was startled by a sudden rap on the window. She looked up to see a heavyset man in his thirties with light facial stubble wearing a San Diego Padres sweatshirt staring back at her. His eyes were as wide as saucers.

"Are you okay?" he asked loudly through the glass. "Who did this to you?"

For a second, Jessie wasn't sure he was real. But if this was a hallucination, she was glad to have it. She tried to think of how best to quickly convey her situation. Even if he smashed open the window, there was no way he'd be able to free her from the handcuffs.

They needed professional help. And it needed to come without Andy being aware it was on the way. That meant this guy had to be gone before she got back. But how to express all that with a gag in her mouth and limited time? In the end, she went the simplest route she could think of. She put her free hand to her ear as if holding a phone, then held up both hands, and displayed nine fingers, then one finger, followed by one again.

The guy nodded and pulled out his phone. Jessie shook her head vigorously to indicate that he shouldn't do it right then and there, but he seemed confused by her action.

"It's okay," he said loudly. "I understand. I'll call for help. And don't worry. I won't leave you alone."

Her heart sank at those words, then began to pound loudly at the ones she heard next.

"Can I help you?" the unmistakable voice of Andy Robinson asked from somewhere behind the man.

He spun around, blocking Jessie's view.

"Yeah," he said, with heartfelt outrage. "You can explain why there's a woman handcuffed and gagged in the backseat of this car."

There was a brief pause in which Jessie wondered if perhaps he'd stumped her, and she'd just try and run for it. But of course, that was wishful thinking.

"I'd be more than willing to," Andy said, her tone less defensive than offended. Jessie could sense that she was already playing the man. "But before I justify the medical precautions that I've taken to protect my sister from herself, could I at least put down the food I got for her?"

"Do it slowly," the man said.

Andy came into view. As she did, Jessie caught a glimpse of the dark gleam in her eye and felt sick to her stomach. Something was off. Andy was enjoying this. She had a tray with what looked like pastries and beverages, which she placed on the hood of the car. The she turned back to the man.

"My name is Jessie. That's my sister, Hannah. She has a severe form of epilepsy. She takes medication regularly to control it. But we're on a road trip and ran out last night. So, until a pharmacy opens later this morning, we're taking extra precautions. I could have brought her into the store with me, but there's always the chance that she could have a seizure on the walk over or while we're in the store. For her to come in would have required strapping her into the helmet we keep in the trunk, which can be embarrassing for a thirty-year-old woman. So, we decided to skip all that this time and just have her stay here in the car. The cuffs and gag are safety precautions. The cuffs are so she doesn't flail all over the car and break her limbs or neck. The gag is so she doesn't bite off her own tongue. We left off the helmet because we figured the cushions would offer protection for her head. I parked so far away from everyone else to avoid all the embarrassing questions we're getting from you now."

The man seemed like he wanted to believe her, and who could blame him? Andy spun a convincing tale. But then his brow furrowed. Jessie guessed why.

"But then why did she motion for me to call 911?"

Andy glanced over at her. Her penetrating blue eyes were ice cold. Up until now, this could have all been dismissed as a complication caused by an overly curious traveler. But now Andy knew that Jessie had "broken her word."

"I don't know," Andy said, her tone giving no indication of the fury lurking below the surface. "Maybe she was warning you that if you got closer, she'd call 911 on you. Why don't we end the suspense and just ask her? If you don't mind, I'm going to take out my keys to unlock the door. Then we can remove the gag and get the answers from Hannah herself. Would that be okay with you, sir?"

The man nodded and turned back toward Jessie as Andy reached into her pocket. Facing the car, he couldn't see what Jessie saw, which was that Andy didn't take out keys. Instead, she pulled out a switchblade. The man must have picked up on the look of horror in Jessie's eyes because he started to turn around, but he was too late.

As he spun back the other way, it was just in time to have the blade sink into his side, come out, and plunge in again. Jessie watched, in openmouthed but gagged shock as Andy jammed the blade into the man's kidney area somewhere between ten and fifteen times. Jessie tried to gulp or scream or do anything at all, but her mouth was dry from the gag.

The man slumped onto the windshield of the car, face first, and slowly slid down. His mouth was pressed up against the glass, fogging it up as he breathed on it. And then the fog stopped. The man's eyes turned glassy, and his body went still.

Thirty seconds earlier, he had been alive and trying to help her. Now he was dead. Andy wiped the blade on the guy's sweatshirt, glanced casually behind her, then unlocked the door, grabbed the tray of food and drinks, and put them on the front seat. Her right hand was drenched in blood. She looked back at Jessie and shook her head.

"It's hard to put into words how disappointed I am in you," she said quietly. "I have to take care of this situation, but once I do, we're going to have a little chat about meeting our responsibilities."

She closed the front door, moved into the back, and unlocked the cuff attaching Jessie's ankle to the back seat. As she did, the blood on her hand smeared all over one of Jessie's white sandals. Then she stepped back and held the passenger door open.

"Sit up," she instructed. After Jessie did, she asked, "can you see into that ditch over there?"

Jessie nodded that she could.

"Good," Andy said. "Watch what you made happen."

She moved over to the man, then bent down, and hooked her head under his torso and grabbed him by the waist with both arms so that she was able to drag him the ten feet from the car over to the ditch. Then she tossed him in. Jessie watched him tumble down about eight feet to rest at the bottom.

She heard a loud thump as his head hit the cement and, in that moment, a gaping hole seemed to open in her chest, comprised of horror, pity, and guilt. She tried to force it closed, aware that the stew of emotions would only compromise her judgement, but all she could do was shrink it slightly. It lingered, pulsing, gnawing at her.

Andy went to the trunk. When she returned, Jessie saw that she was wearing gloves and had two large, black trash bags. She proceeded to scurry down into the ditch and pull one of the bags over the man, starting at his head. It covered him down to his knees. Then she used the other bag to cover him from the feet up. That bag went up to his elbows.

Once that was done, she collected a series of large rocks and jammed them up against where the man's body met the ground, so that their collective weight prevented the bags from flying off in the wind. Then she clambered out of the ditch and looked down at her handiwork.

She seemed satisfied and Jessie understood why. To the average passerby, the black mass in the ditch looked like a big bag of trash that somehow didn't make it into a dumpster. With the wind blowing, and the rocks strewn about, it certainly didn't look like a dead body. The chances that someone would wander over to this isolated section of the travel center overflow parking lot, notice the trash bags in the ditch, and take any interest in it at all, was remote. The likelihood that someone would realize it was a crime scene, at least anytime soon, were virtually nil.

As she watched, Jessie realized that no matter what resources were brought to bear to find her, they were sure to fail. Andy was too smart. She had been planning this for too long. She had too much of a head start. The people looking for them would never find them in time. The only person who could rescue her was Jessie Hunt and she had to think of a way to do it before it was too late.

Andy walked over to the car and to Jessie's surprise, got in the backseat with her. She closed the door, muffling the wind that had been whistling up from the ditch.

"Here's the deal, Jessie," she said with sadness, "that man is dead because of you. You think I wasn't watching everything from inside the store? He was walking toward me when something made him turn around. You did something to get his attention. And the moment you did that—the moment you got him to walk over to this car, you signed his death warrant. You had to know that."

Of course, it wasn't true. Andy had killed this guy, not her. But it was hard to remember that in this moment.

Jessie lowered her head. She didn't want Andy to see the self-doubt she was feeling right now. She didn't want her to know she'd been thinking the same thing, that she'd gotten in her head. Andy continued anyway.

"You ought to know where I'm coming from here, Bestie. I'm not going to kill you if you do stuff like this. I would never do that. We're friends. But if I have to, I'll make it so you can't keep trying to escape. I don't want to do this but, if need be, I can incapacitate you. You ever hear of hobbling?"

Jessie almost laughed despite the living nightmare she was in. Andy seemed to sense that she wanted to say something. She glanced down at the gag preventing her captive from speaking and pulled it down. Jessie swallowed several times, trying to get some saliva back in her dry throat. When she thought she could finally speak, she began slowly.

"You *do* get that you're referencing a method used by a woman who was out of her gourd crazy, right? Is that really who you want to be compared to?"

"You say potato," Andy said with a too-sweet smile.

"Actually, I say bananas," Jessie shot back.

"You're missing the larger point, Jessie," Andy said, mildly annoyed now. "This isn't about what will happen to you. I told you before I went into the store that any attempt to escape would lead to others' bloodshed and your guilt and that's exactly what happened. You should have trusted me, Jessie."

"You're talking about trust?" Jessie demanded, incredulous.

"I am," Andy said sternly. "I'm the one who should have trust issues right now because *you* lied to *me*. You promised you wouldn't try anything and then as soon as I was gone, you did. This isn't the way to create the foundation for a strong friendship. You've got some real work to do to rebuild that bridge. And as long as we're on the topic, this is probably a good time to remind you of something I told you last night. Do you recall the warning I gave you?"

Jessie looked at her captor defiantly.

"You'll have to remind me," she whispered. "I might have forgotten something, what with being, you know, *drugged*!"

"So touchy," Andy said, as she grabbed a cup from the front seat and handed it to Jessie. "Here, it's an iced coffee, to keep your energy up. I gave you a very specific warning last night, which I will repeat now because I don't think it made the proper impression. But I suspect that you'll take it seriously after what just happened. Listen closely, Jessie. Are you listening?"

"I'm listening," Jessie assured her, making no move to drink the coffee. Her appetite was gone.

"I have a contingency plan," Andy said. "It's called Operation Z. And it's very simple. If anyone finds us, or if you escape, or try to contact anybody, or don't actively embrace living the life I'm creating for us, bad thing things will happen, things that will make what Livia Bucco and Eden Roth did back in L.A. look like child's play. Do you believe me?"

"Yes." Jessie said, because she did.

"And there's more," Andy said, unable to mask her glee, "if anything happens to me, this contingency plan will result in the painful deaths of the people you care most about. There won't be anything you can do about it, and you'll have to live with the knowledge that it could have been prevented, if only you had accepted your fate and joined me. So, it's pretty simple. Embrace a happy life with Andy and your loved ones miss you but survive and eventually move on. Take any other path and they die excruciating deaths that will haunt you forever. It's up to you. Also, I got muffins and scones for breakfast. Which do you prefer?"

CHAPTER SEVEN

Hannah saw Andy Robinson. The woman was just a few steps ahead of her and right now, she was looking the other way. It was now or never. Any delay could mean Jessie's death. Hannah didn't hesitate.

She stepped forward, fast and quiet, wrapped her left arm around Andy's chest, and with her right hand, grabbed at Andy's neck, got hold of the woman's trachea, and in one brutal motion, ripped it out of her throat.

Andy's body dropped heavily at her feet as she held the woman's bloody windpipe out in front of her. As adrenaline coursed through her system, she squeezed hard, crushing the rings of cartilage into mush. Then she dropped it onto the ground next to Andy's body. Every part of her prickled with a gurling stew of rage and pleasure.

A loud beep made Hannah twitch and her eyes opened suddenly. She realized she'd drifted off at some point during the night and that no one had woken her up. She was slumped on the couch in the police research office of LAPD's downtown Central Station, where Captain Decker had established the command center for Jessie's search. The beep had come from a nearby computer.

She glanced at the time on the digital clock on the wall above the bank of computer screens in the room. It read 9:29 a.m.

The last thing she remembered was from about 4:45 this morning, when she was looking at a screen with grainy security footage of cars in the Bevery Hills area Beverly Center Mall parking lot. Had she really been asleep for almost five hours? What had she missed in the interim?

Police researchers Jamil Winslow and Beth Ryerson were both at computer terminals, typing away on keyboards. Sitting next to them was Jim Nettles. He was the one member of Homicide Special Section detective squad, who had missed the wedding chaos last night. That was because he had volunteered to finish the last-minute paperwork on Jessie and Ryan's serial stabbing case. He was at the other terminal, typing more slowly, but concentrating just as hard.

Detective Karen Bray was standing in the corner of the room talking quietly to Brady Bowen, Ryan's former partner, who was supposed to be his best man. It was still hard for Hannah to accept that the guy was a detective. Squat, with a barrel chest, an ample gut, a mustache, sweat pouring off his brow, and his shirttails poking out of his seam-bursting slacks, he barely looked like he could walk across the room, much less investigate a crime. But he was deeply focused on what Karen was saying and taking copious notes on his small pad.

Ryan, Kat, Callum Reid, and Captain Decker were nowhere to be found, but that wasn't a shock. This was just one room. Homicide Special Section, or HSS, had a dedicated portion of Central Station's bullpen as well as access to Captain Decker's office. They'd need all that space to accommodate the various representatives of the FBI, Marshals Service, Sheriff's Department, and whatever other agencies had joined the search. Hannah sat up and stretched her arms.

"What did I miss?" she asked.

Everyone turned around, but it was Karen Bray that walked over and sat next to her. That made sense. Hannah knew that she was the only parent in the group, and she likely felt a natural sense of obligation to offer support to the minor whose guardian was missing.

"Where were things left when you drifted off?" she asked, without any parental saccharine, which Hannah appreciated. "I don't want to repeat stuff you already know."

"I was looking at footage from the Beverly Center from yesterday afternoon," she answered. "That was where Andy was supposedly watching a movie. We know that there were officers in the theater lobby and watching her car in the parking structure, so we were trying to find footage of her sneaking out into whatever vehicle ultimately got her to Peninsula. I must have crashed at some point during that process."

"That was probably the right move," Karen said. "The mall ended up being a dead end. There was just no way to determine how she left the theater or to track all those vehicles in a covered parking lot. But the good news is that we had more luck tracking vehicles leaving the Peninsula."

"Tell me," Hannah said excitedly.

"It was your find, Jamil," Karen said. "Do you want to explain?"

Jamil didn't respond as his fingers flew across his keyboard faster than Hannah could track.

"Don't take offense," Beth said from beside him, "he's in the zone. I'll catch you up. Jamil conferred with Peninsula's security team to review every vehicle that left the premises from the moment Jessie was last seen until they shut the resort down. That period was approximately twenty minutes and twenty-six vehicles exited during that stretch. I won't bore you with all the details but here's the short version: Andy used a laundry truck to get Jessie out."

"How do you know that?" Hannah asked.

"Because, after Jamil located most of the other vehicles but couldn't get a response on the truck, he put out a search for it. We were already suspicious that it might be the one because it seemed like the kind of vehicle that Jessie could be hidden in. The truck was found in the parking lot of an abandoned Norwalk strip mall this morning. The driver was dead, shot in the head, and buried under a pile of sheets in the back."

"Oh God," Hannah muttered under her breath. Her skin got suddenly clammy. If Andy was willing to kill a random laundry truck driver, what would she do to Jessie? "Were you able to track them from there?"

"We think so," Beth said. "There were no working cameras in the strip mall lot or at any business nearby. But we were able to use the GPS locator on the truck to determine when it stopped moving and when Andy likely changed vehicles, which we assume she stashed ahead of time in the strip mall parking lot. Jamil found a freeway camera video clip from a few minutes later showing a silver, four-door 1985 Buick Skyhawk driving east on Firestone Boulevard."

"Why focus on that car?"

"It's old, pre-GPS, which makes it hard to track. It would also be very cheap to buy for cash. No real paper trail required. She wouldn't have to worry about anyone trying to steal it because it's not worth it. Driving that thing is almost like being invisible. It's ideal for hiding someone you've abducted."

"So where is it now?" Hannah asked.

"That's why Jamil isn't being real chatty right at the moment," Beth said,' "He's trying to find out. He managed to get a few more street camera images of the vehicle which gave a partial license plate and showed the driver. She was wearing a wig, but facial recognition provided a 71% match for Andrea Robinson. So now we've got an APB out on the vehicle. We're hoping to get a hit soon."

"How long ago did Jamil put out the APB?"

"About an hour ago," Karen answered.

"And when did the laundry truck stop in that strip mall parking lot last night?" Hannah pressed.

"At 8:18 p.m." Beth said.

"That's over thirteen hours ago!" Hannah exclaimed. "They could be in Utah or Oregon or Colorado. Hell, they could be all the way to Texas by now. They could have crossed the U.S. border and be halfway down the coast of Baja Mexico at this point."

"We're checking every contingency," Karen told her in the calm voice that Hannah suspected she used when her son started in on a temper tantrum. That only irritated her more and she was about say so when someone else spoke up.

"She wouldn't have gone to Mexico," U.S. Marshal Patrick Murphy said, entering the room, followed by Ryan, Kat, and Captain Decker.

"Why not?" Hannah demanded.

"It's too risky," he replied with the certitude of a man who'd been dealing with fugitive apprehension situations like this all his life. His physical bearing reinforced that image. Short and trim, with tightly cropped light brown hair, he projected a no-nonsense sensibility. "That car might not attract attention on the open road but at a border patrol station, especially a huge one like the San Ysidro border crossing with Tijuana, which is by far the closest to us, it would generate a ton of interest. It looks exactly like the kind of vehicle that might be used to pack drugs. More importantly, there's no good place inside to hide a full-grown woman. After all the planning and effort that Robinson clearly put into this abduction, I don't believe for a second that she'd intentionally go anywhere near law enforcement if she could help it."

Hannah had to concede that he made a compelling case.

"Where then?" she asked.

"My guess," he said, "is that she already has a place set up and waiting—likely somewhere isolated and unpopulated, maybe the mountains or the desert. It might be worth seeing if she's got property in the Sierras or the Mojave or something similar in another state."

The mention of the mountains sent Hannah's mind spinning. It was just a few months ago that she had rushed to the small mountain town of Wildpines with Jessie and Ryan to hide from a serial killer known as the Night Hunter. In fact, it was Murphy who had helped arrange for them to be placed in a safe house there.

Unfortunately, the Night Hunter still discovered their location and nearly killed them before Jessie and Ryan apprehended him. But while he was on the ground in handcuffs, Hannah had shot him in cold blood. At the time, she claimed it was to end the nightmare he put them through.

But in truth, it was because she wanted to know what it felt like to kill a person, especially one who so richly deserved it. To her surprise, she discovered that it gave her a physical thrill, one that she found herself longing to recreate for weeks afterward. She imagined herself shooting or stabbing people who had had wronged her or other vulnerable people. Only when her lust for bloodletting became overwhelming and she didn't trust herself did she admit how she felt to Dr. Lemmon.

They eventually agreed, in conjunction with Jessie, that she would temporarily move into a treatment facility where she could work on controlling those urges and learn to channel her desire to punish wrongdoers into something more productive. After all, others had managed to do it. Jessie had a thirst for vengeance too. Hannah had seen it up close. Yet she somehow managed to direct her moral outrage into catching killers before they struck again.

If Hannah could pour her own rage into something similarly productive, she hoped it would keep the monster that still clawed at her insides under control. If not, she feared she might not only be ripping out tracheas in her dreams. The image of Andy limp at her feet snapped her out of her reverie.

Andy wasn't dead. She was alive and transporting Jessie somewhere isolated, where she might never be found, where she could be tortured or killed, and no one would ever know. There had to be something they could do to prevent that. But she had no idea what that was. She felt helpless.

"We've got a hit!" shouted Jamil.

"What is it?" Captain Decker asked.

"There's been a sighting of the vehicle we caught on camera last night in the last few minutes."

"Where?" Ryan asked, clearly trying to keep his voice level.

"Ehrenberg, Arizona," Jamil said.

"Where the hell is that?" Susannah Valentine wanted to know.

"I'm getting info on it now," Jamil told her.

"I know it," said Mitch Connor, Kat's Riverside County Sheriff's deputy boyfriend. "It's just on the other side of the California-Arizona border. You cross the Colorado River and you're in Ehrenberg. It's tiny. I only know it because there's a travel center there that I always stop at for gas when I'm headed to Phoenix, where my aunt's family lives."

"That's actually exactly where the car was seen," Jamil said, "at the Flying Y Travel Center on the southern side of the I-10 freeway."

Something in his tone was unsettling and Hannah wasn't the only one to notice.

"What else, Jamil?" Ryan demanded.

The head of research paused briefly before answering.

"The reason authorities noted the vehicle was because they were already investigating another crime. They found a body."

CHAPTER EIGHT

Hannah's body went limp at the words. She wanted to speak but couldn't form any words.

Jamil, still staring at his computer screen, didn't seem to realize that everyone was hanging on what he said next. He continued, reading slowly.

"A body was found in a ditch near the travel center parking lot and local law enforcement pulled camera footage from the area to identify potential suspects."

There was a long silence in the room.

"Have they ID'd the body?" Captain Decker finally asked, posing the question that everyone had but was afraid to broach.

"I'm trying to determine that now," Jamil said. "They were apparently working this case slowly and are a little overwhelmed with all the questions they're suddenly getting from another jurisdiction. All I have at this point is that another traveler's dog found something wrapped in a trash bag in the ditch and began tugging at it. The owner came down to investigate, saw that it was a body, and alerted authorities. There are no further details."

"Do you have the contact number for the senior officer on the scene?" Decker asked with preternatural calm. Hannah, who felt like simultaneously screaming and ripping her hair out, couldn't help but admire it.

"Getting it now, Captain," Jamil said. "Dialing. It's line one."

Decker picked up the phone and waited. After a few seconds a muffled voice could be heard on the other end of the line.

"Hello Sergeant," Decker said with firm politeness, "this is Captain Roy Decker of the Los Angeles Police Department. I run Central Station here, in addition to our Homicide Special Section unit. I understand that you have a body at the travel center there. Is that correct?"

The voice replied briefly.

"All right. We believe your body may be connected to a case we're pursuing back here in L.A. Can you please describe the victim to me?"

This time the response was longer.

"Got it," Decker said, relief flooding his face, "Male, thirties, heavyset, stabbed multiple times in the abdomen and lower back. That is very helpful. Listen, you should expect that we'll be sending a team of experts out there to assist in your investigation expeditiously. So, I'm going to ask you to avoid having your people do too much with the crime scene just now. I'm going to put you on the line with one of our detectives, Jim Nettles, who will explain the nature of the case we're pursuing and likely have several additional questions for you. Again, I want to personally extend my appreciation for your assistance and understanding. The LAPD, FBI, U.S. Marshals Service, Riverside County Sheriff's Department and several other agencies look forward to working with you to resolve this matter. Hold one moment for Detective Nettles."

He cupped the receiver to his chest and looked directly at Nettles.

"Tell him the truth about the situation. If they have them available, tell him to put drones in the air to look for that Buick. But no one is to try to make contact or apprehend if they see it. Make that crystal clear. Also, put the fear of God in him. I don't want any local investigator or coroner screwing up that crime scene. We've finally got a lead. Don't let them contaminate it. Got it?"

Got it," Nettles replied, picking up the phone.

Decker turned to face the others.

"I need everyone else to assemble in the conference room in two minutes," he said. "We've got to coordinate how we're moving forward on this, and we've got to do it fast. Kat and Hannah, I'd like the two of you to stick around here for a minute."

As Hannah watched everyone else except for Detective Nettles stream out of the room, she had a bad feeling about what was coming next. She noticed Kat's boyfriend, Mitch, linger in the hallway as everybody else hurried off. Decker, whose back was to him, was oblivious as he focused his attention on her and Kat.

"I'm sorry to say this," he said quietly. "But this is where you get off the train."

"What?" Kat asked, already fuming.

"Thank you both for your assistance," Decker said, "but at this point, we're dealing with what is exclusively a law enforcement operation. And despite your personal connection to the case—partly because of it—I can't have you hanging around the command center. It complicates things for my team to have civilians here. They need to be focused on evidence and leads, not worrying about you two."

"We're hardly typical civilians, Captain," Kat said, her voice tight. "Remember, we're the ones who found the white board in Corinne Bertans's apartment with all the details about the past acolyte attacks."

"That may prove invaluable," Decker conceded. "And I know that you're not like most civilians. I also know what you've both been through personally. But I have to set that aside right now. All I can focus on is the investigation. Every second is crucial at this point. And to be perfectly frank, having you both here is a distraction for my people. Remember, we all care deeply about Jessie and want to get her back. But we have to stay professional. It's hard enough to let her fiancé remain involved in the case. But having her little sister and best friend hanging around the station too? It's too much. Go home. Take Callum Reid with you. He's reiterated that he's willing to offer support to you both. I promise to make sure he's provided with updates, which he can pass along to you."

Hannah tried to control the anger rising in her chest. She noticed Mitch skulk off down the hall and wondered if he was hoping to avoid Decker's wrath, his girlfriend's, or hers.

"You can't just shut us out," she said to the captain through clenched teeth. "My sister is alive out there. And when she finds an opening, she's going to try to send us clues about where she is. Who do you think is more likely to pick up on them—Detective Valentine, who's worked one case with her? A U.S. Marshal? Or her sister and best friend? Come on, Captain, we'll stay out of the way, but at least let us be here to help. We could pick up on things that others might miss."

"If something like that comes up, I know how to reach you," he said unmoved, "but I'm sorry, this is the way it has to be. Even just talking to you now is costing me vital seconds that should be used to coordinate next steps among the agencies. I've got to go."

He turned and walked down the hall, which was now empty. Hannah watched him go, then turned to Kat, who looked as pissed off as she felt. But since Nettles was still on the phone with the Ehrenberg police sergeant, she motioned for Hannah to follow her down the hall to the break room. As she closed the door, her phone pinged. She held it up. It was a text from Mitch that read: *Will keep you looped in.*

"No offense, Kat, but your boyfriend's covering his ass," Hannah said. "He knows he wouldn't have a place to sleep tonight if he said anything else."

"Fair point," Kat agreed. "But I'm more focused on Decker. I don't know what he expects us to do. Does he think we're going to go back to the house and play Monopoly with Callum while we wait for text updates from him? That we're going to just sit around when we know that Jessie isn't even in this state anymore?"

Something about that statement caused a flicker in the back of Hannah's brain. She felt her anger harden into resolve as an idea formed in her head.

"I don't care what he thinks," she said. "That's not what we're going to do."

"It sounds like you have something in mind," Kat replied, intrigued.

"I do," she started to say, but stopped herself when Callum Reid came in.

He clearly sensed their discomfort.

"What?" he demanded defensively. "I thought I was supposed to be the body man for you two, at least according to Decker. But you're both looking at me like I'm wearing a sardine suit or something."

Hannah and Kat exchanged an uncomfortable look, neither sure how to respond.

"Listen," Callum continued, "I'd love to help. Jessie means a lot to me, and I was tasked with keeping her little sister safe. But if you don't want me around, that's fine too. I've got a wife and kids at home who are disappointed that I missed Sunday breakfast. I can still make it back for lunch. Just let me know so I can call Tanya to come pick me up, since if you'll recall, I left my car by your house when we dashed over to Corinne's apartment. Maybe when I get home I can wash off the sardine scent too."

Hannah looked at Kat, who shrugged as if to say it was up to her what to share with the man.

"You don't smell like sardines, Detective Reid—."

"Callum, please. I'm retired," he reminded her.

"Okay, Callum," Hannah continued, "we're happy to have your company, but we're not sure where your loyalties lie. You weren't in the research room just now, but Captain Decker has shut us out of the investigation from this point forward. Were you aware of that?"

"No," Callum said, "but I'm not surprised. That's standard procedure. The fact that you, or even I, have been allowed to participate up to this point is pretty unusual."

"Well, we don't intend to close up shop just yet," Hannah told him. "And I think a recently retired LAPD might come in handy as we pursue this, but not if you plan to report back to Decker about what we're doing. So, I guess I'm asking you point blank: do you want to stick with us and keep what we learn quiet until we choose to share it with the others, or would you rather beg off and go back to whatever it is that retired cops do at nine in the morning?"

Callum Reid smiled impishly and for a moment looked closer to his mid-thirties than mid-forties.

"I'm in," he said. "What's your lead?"

Hannah returned her attention to Kat.

"Before Andy Robinson was released, Jessie told me that you were helping her try to prevent it, right?"

"Yes," Kat answered. "I was poring through the Livia Bucco and Eden Roth records, trying to find any connection between them and Andy in order to prove that she helped plan their crimes ahead of time, exactly the kind of evidence we found in that medicine cabinet in Corinne Bertans's bathroom. If I had discovered anything like that in the official records, Andy would still be in jail, but there was nothing."

Hannah nodded, undeterred.

"I'm guessing that when you did that research," she continued, "you also did a deep dive into Andy Robinson's personal history too—her background, life story, etc., to determine if maybe she had connections to these women prior to their incarceration together?"

"I have detailed files," Kat confirmed. "They're in my office."

"That's where we need to go," Hannah said.

"Fine," Kat said. "We can be there in ten minutes. What are we looking for?"

"When you said earlier that they aren't even in this state anymore, it reminded me of something that Murph—that's U.S. Marshal Murphy—mentioned. He said that Andy has probably been planning this for a while and that she'd likely take Jessie somewhere isolated like the mountains or desert. He suggested we check to see if she owned property in the Sierras or the Mojave. Well, now we know that she's gone east of both of those. I think we should be checking to see if she owns property in Arizona, Nevada, Utah, New Mexico, Colorado, or maybe even west Texas. She knows she can't stay on the road for too much longer, especially after killing the guy at that travel center, so I doubt she'll go much beyond that. The dragnet will be closing in. She's got to go to ground soon, that is if she hasn't already."

"That's a good idea," Kat suggested, "but she has to know that we'll be checking her property records. Would she be so foolish as to go to a place she owns?"

"Maybe it's a place she used to own," Hannah countered, "or just somewhere she knows well. The more we learn about her, including her past and what shaped her, the better we can predict her future moves. That's what Jessie would do."

Kat smiled broadly at that last statement.

"Can I offer one suggestion?" Callum said, speaking for the first time since committing to the group.

"What's that?" Kat asked.

"Let's grab all your research and review it on the road," he said. "That way, when we make some brilliant discovery, we'll be in route, where can actually do something about it rather than be stuck in an L.A. office."

"Good tip," Kat said. "Let's go."

Hannah opened the door, happy to be leaving the break room and on her way to Arizona.

CHAPTER NINE

9:37 a.m., Sunday morning

Jamil tried not to fidget.

When Captain Decker had ordered everyone into the conference room, he'd gone immediately, taking nothing with him. Now he regretted not bringing his laptop as Decker rolled through the plans for everyone involved in the task force.

Beth had stepped up to the large whiteboard at the front of the room to take notes, leaving Jamil to sit helplessly in his chair. He wasn't used to not having anything to type on and pulled out his phone to at least mark some action items on that tiny screen.

After two minutes of that, he couldn't take it anymore and ran back to the research office to get his laptop. When he returned, agent Jack Dolan, whose weathered, suntanned face, longish, silvery hair, and surfer vibe seemed at odds with his FBI pedigree, was talking to the group.

"...and because this is no longer just a local matter, the situation has changed. As important as Jessie is to all of us, getting the unfettered resources I wanted for this case was proving challenging with my bosses. But now that we've got a previously convicted killer who has not just kidnapped a police profiler, but murdered two people across state lines, those limits are gone."

"What does that mean in practical terms, Agent Dolan?" Decker asked.

"It means that there will be a car here in five minutes to take whichever two-detective team you assign to the Hawthorne airport. A jet is there now, being fueled up for you. It will be wheels up in twenty-five minutes. Your team will be taken to Blythe, California. It's just west of the state border with Arizona and the closest town with an airport than can support landing the jet. From there a helicopter will take your team to the travel center. If all goes as planned, they should be on site in approximately seventy minutes. Obviously, you'll need to choose your team now and they'll have to be ready to go immediately."

Jamil looked over at Captain Decker, who didn't even glance up from his legal pad as he answered.

"Hernandez and Valentine, can you be ready to go in two minutes?"

"I'll get my heavy gear from the gun locker," Hernandez said, standing up. "I'll be in the lobby in sixty seconds."

"I'm ready now," Valentine said, standing up as well. Only then did Jamil notice that she was already wearing a bullet-proof vest. They both started for the door.

"Keep us updated regularly," Decker instructed as they left the room.

"I'll meet them at the car to provide final details," Agent Dolan said, standing up as well. "Those will include the fact that I've requested that an FBI crime scene unit and medical examiner based out of Phoenix meet your detectives at the scene. They'll fly in as well and can be there in forty-five minutes. By the time Hernandez and Valentine arrive, my people will already be conducting tests and potentially have some information to offer. I hope that helps."

Captain Decker nodded that that it did.

"One thing before you go, Agent," he said to Dolan, but clearly intending his remarks for all of the remaining people in the conference room, "I've been operating as the de facto leader of this joint operation without formal authorization from any of you, all of whom represent different agencies. If that's a problem for anyone, now would be a good time to raise your concerns."

"I've already cleared it with my higher ups," Dolan said "We're at your disposal, Captain. Until further notice, the FBI considers the LAPD the lead agency in this matter."

"Same here," Mitch Connor said," "I'm just a lowly Sheriff's Deputy but I meant to tell you earlier that the Riverside County Sheriff called me directly and authorized me to liaise with your department in this matter as long as you need me and to provide whatever help you require."

"Same for the Marshals Service," Marshal Patrick Murphy said. "I have full clearance to work with the department under your direction. I do have one concern however, Captain. Normally, I'd raise it in private, but considering our time constraints, I think I should broach it now."

"Please, go ahead Murph," Decker said.

"What happens if Chief Laird wants to take over control of the search directly?" he asked. "With all due respect, your chief of police isn't known for shying away from the media spotlight. The Marshals

Service is comfortable with you in the lead role on this case, but that might change if Laird took over, especially considering his involvement in Andy Robinson being released from prison in the first place."

"We have those concerns as well," Agent Dolan admitted.

There was a brief, uncomfortable silence in the room. Jamil tried not to visibly squirm.

"Let me be clear," Decker said, sitting up straight in his chair and removing his glasses. "I will *not* be handing over leadership of this case to Chief Laird under any circumstances. As you correctly note, we wouldn't be in this situation without his persistent efforts to free Ms. Robinson. The case stays with me. I will take whatever heat that decision brings. And frankly, if it leads to my dismissal, I recommend that your respective agencies begin your own investigations, because I wouldn't have confidence in ours anymore. Have I been clear enough?"

No one responded but no one needed to. Agent Dolan finally coughed, breaking the silence.

"I have to meet the car out front," he whispered and left the room.

"Detective Bray," Captain Decker said, putting his glasses back on and resuming as if he'd just finished placing a lunch order, "you and Nettles will work from here at the command center, in close consultation with Mr. Winslow and Ms. Ryerson from Research. Anything new you learn, feed it to Hernandez and Valentine in the field. When we're done in here, have Nettles brief you on what else the Sergeant in Ehrenberg gave him."

Bray nodded silently.

"What can I do?" Mitch Connor asked. The Bunyanesque, sandy-haired Sheriff's Deputy seemed anxious to help but a little embarrassed, as if he didn't belong in the same room with such law enforcement heavyweights.

"Blythe is part of Riverside County if I recall, correct?"

"That's right," Mitch assured him.

"It might be helpful if you could coordinate with your contacts there. Maybe the Sheriff's Department personnel in that area have some kind of relationship with Arizona law enforcement just over the border, one that can help grease the communication wheels. Any kind of informal information-sharing that can break down any natural reluctance to trust the big city guys swooping into their territory would be much appreciated."

"I'll see what I can do," Mitch said, hopping out of his chair and darting down the hall.

Decker looked at the people in the room he hadn't directly assigned tasks, including Marshal Murphy, Dr. Lemmon, and Ryan's old partner, Brady Bowen. He focused his attention on Janice Lemmon.

"Dr. Lemmon," he said, "I know it's not fair to ask this of you, but I'd appreciate a preliminary profiling assessment of Andrea Robinson. Anything you can share could be helpful."

Dr. Lemmon shrugged.

"I wish I had some brilliant insight, Captain," she said, "but nothing I say will shock you. She's clearly willing to kill anyone who gets in her way. And she's obviously obsessed with Jessie. What's not obvious is her ultimate goal. Does she plan to kill Jessie at the end of all this? Punish her in some other way? Whatever she intends, I can say one thing for certain. You shouldn't underestimate her. She's outsmarted everyone so far. As your team proceeds, if something seems too easy, it probably is. She loves to misdirect, to confound. Don't let her play you."

"Maybe you can help us with that, and I don't just mean the doctor," Decker replied, waving his hand at Murphy and Bowen, who were seated next to her. "If you three have the time, I'd love it if you could pool your collective knowledge."

"What did you have in mind?" Lemmon asked.

"We've got enough people running around gathering minutiae," he explained. "But maybe you all could take a step back. Dr. Lemmon, you're an expert in human behavior and a former criminal profiler. Murph, as a U.S. Marshal, you've tracked countless fugitives in your day. And Detective Bowen, my understanding is that you have a reputation in West L.A. Division for locating perps who don't want to be found. Maybe if you all put your heads together, you can figure out where Andrea Robinson is taking Jessie, or at least why she took her? I'll settle for that at this point. You can use my office. It's more private and definitely quieter. I have to run an errand anyway."

He stood up and looked at the whiteboard where Beth was scribbling furiously, then over at Jamil, who was waiting for more direct instructions and had stopped typing. Feeling the Captain's eyes on him sent an anxious tingle through him, like he was back in class, about to be called on by a professor.

"Winslow," he said. "I need to know where that car went after it left the travel center. All we have is that it was identified near the murder scene, close to the entrance for Interstate 10 East. But that sighting was three hours ago. I realize that there aren't as many cameras out there in the desert as in the city, but you have to find some footage for me, okay? Robinson could be headed to Phoenix, Yuma, Las Vegas, or anywhere between or beyond. No drone is going to help if we don't have somewhere to start from."

"Yes, Captain," Jamil said, deciding that now wasn't the time to tell his boss that he was already doing everything he possibly could. "Where will you be if I uncover something?"

"I'll be in a meeting," he answered cryptically. "It's important, but if you find that car, call anyway."

As he walked out of the room, Jamil thought he picked up on something that he'd never seen in Captain Decker before: nervousness.

CHAPTER TEN

10:49 a.m., Sunday morning

Kat finally pulled the beacon strobe light siren off the roof of the car.

For most of the hour-long drive from downtown L.A., they'd had to battle traffic. The beacon, along with the siren she'd had installed, had been essential to clear a path. But it was well past morning rush hour now, and they were outside the heart of the city, currently passing the town of Redlands. She could go ninety without worrying about changing lanes, much less hitting slowdowns.

She looked over at Callum Reid in the passenger seat, who was rifling through some of documents they'd taken from her office. Hannah was doing the same in the backseat. She glanced at the GPS on her phone. Even if they continued at this speed, it would take almost two more hours to get to Arizona. If what Mitch had texted her earlier was accurate, Ryan and Susannah Valentine would be landing at the travel center any minute.

"How are we doing, Scooby gang?" she asked, as much to break the silence as to get an answer.

"Not great," Callum conceded. "I've gone through all of Robinson's property records. Since she's so rich, there are quite a few. In addition to the Hancock Park mansion, she's got a condo in Malibu and a beach house up the coast in Morro Bay. According to Beth in HSS research, even though we know Andy went east, both those places have been searched and there are units sitting on them in case she tries to go back to one of them."

"Any others?" Kat asked as she pushed a little harder on the gas, sending her Subaru Crosstrek speeding past a Porsche in the fast lane.

"Yep," he answered. "She's also got an apartment in New York on the Upper West Side and a place on Nantucket. I figured we could skip those for now. The one other option is a cabin she has in Aspen. The route we think that she's on isn't the most direct way to Colorado, but she could still theoretically get there with a few twists and turns, which may be what she wants to do anyway."

"I still have doubts that she'd go anywhere that she knows we have a record of," Kat muttered.

"Me too," Callum agreed, "But I was going to reach out to a buddy of mine in the Denver Police Department. He used to work for LAPD but moved a decade ago. It's about a four-hour drive from there to Aspen and I could probably convince him to make the trip and stake her place out just in case. That way we wouldn't have to reach out to the Aspen Police, which might tip Decker off to what we're doing. What do you think?"

"I say that if he's willing, it's worth a shot," Kat told him. "Better safe than sorry. Just have him keep a low profile and warn him not to directly engage if they do show up. As the poor guy at that travel center learned the hard way, people who underestimate Andy Robinson put their lives in danger."

Callum nodded and pulled out his phone to call his friend. Kat glanced in the rearview mirror at Hannah, who seemed transfixed by what she was reading.

'You look like you discovered the Dead Sea Scrolls or something," she noted. "Care to let me in on what's so compelling?"

"I'm just going through the personal history you compiled on Andy," Hannah said, not looking up. "Did you review it closely?"

"Only to the extent of trying to find connections with Livia Bucco and Eden Roth," Kat answered. "I was searching for overlaps—times or places where their lives might have intersected. Other than that, I didn't study it that deeply. Why?"

Hannah looked up from the papers and locked eyes with Kat through the rear-view mirror.

"I figure we're flying blind here," she said. "We know that Andrea Robinson is a killer. We know that she's had a fixation on Jessie for a while, one that ultimately led to what happened last night. And we know that she is both unstable enough to be thrown in the mental ward of a prison and brilliant enough to trick people into letting her out. But what we don't know is what made her do any of these things, what turned her into the person who is capable of all this. I'm hoping that if I can understand what led her down this path, it might tell us where she's planning to go next."

"You don't think that Jessie would have already told us that?" Kat asked, "After all, she's the one who makes a living reading people like this and predicting what they'll do."

"But she wouldn't have had any reason to profile Andy until now," Hannah pointed out. "Remember, once Andy realized that Jessie had figured out that she'd murdered Victoria Missinger, she poisoned and almost killed her too. She was caught and convicted for both those crimes right away, so there was no need to do any profiling. And ever since then, at least until last week, Andy's been behind bars. Yes, she was plotting and planning, but there was no reason that Jessie would have had cause to delve into her formative life experiences. It wouldn't have seemed relevant at the time. But it is now."

"You think something from her past will tell us where she's headed?"

"I'm hoping," Hannah said, "If not the actual location, then at least her emotional destination. Think about it. Didn't your experiences, some probably traumatic, as an Army Ranger in Afghanistan and Iraq lead you to take that position as head of security at that state hospital prison where you first met Jessie?"

"Eventually, yes," Kat conceded.

"Right," Hannah said. "Just like Jessie seeing her mother tortured and killed by her serial killer father—our shared father—when she was six years old, was central to her becoming a profiler who hunts down serial killers; just like watching that same man slaughter my adoptive parents forever changed me. Knowing that his blood is my blood and that his darkness is part of me keeps me up at night. It's a big part of the reason I asked you to let me work with you, to be your private investigative apprentice. I want to channel that darkness into something constructive, to use the rage that gurgles up inside of me to stop bad people in ways that won't get me arrested. We all have our formative moments, when we experienced something so momentous that it changed the course of our lives. Maybe it was seeing a loved one die and being helpless to stop it. Maybe it was watching an atrocity during wartime. But I guarantee you—Andy Robinson had one too, something big enough to send her down the dark path she's on now."

Kat was impressed by the insight of this young woman, who was not yet even old enough to vote. But maybe she shouldn't have been. Hannah Dorsey had seen more ugliness in her seventeen years than most people face in a lifetime. The fact that she wasn't a budding serial killer herself was some kind of miracle on its own.

She still remembered a conversation she's had with Jessie less than a month ago, when Hannah was first voluntarily hospitalized at that Malibu rehab center, trying to get control over her seemingly unquenchable desire to snuff out another life. They'd been at the downtown coffee shop where they so often met.

"I'm not sure she's going to pull through this thing," Jessie had said, stirring the coffee she'd added a half dozen sugars to but had yet to sip from after sitting at the table for ten minutes. Her green eyes were damp.

"Didn't Dr. Lemmon say she was making progress?" Kat had asked, trying to sound optimistic.

"Sure," Jessie told her, her hand trembling as she picked up her coffee cup, then put it back down. "But progress is relative. She acknowledged that the idea of seeing the light in a person's eyes flicker out gives her an adrenaline rush. That's a long way from *not* having that fantasy."

"It might take a while," Kat had reminded her softly. "She's been through a ton. You can't expect her to be a fully functional human being in a matter of weeks."

And yet, here it was, barely a month later, and Hannah was out of rehab, back in school, asking to be a private investigator trainee, *and* doing an informal, on-the-fly psychological profile of the woman who kidnapped her sister. She seemed to be holding up pretty well.

"Kat?" Hannah asked.

"What?" she said, realizing, she'd drifted for a second.

"We were talking about the formative moments that can send people down a dark path and how uncovering Amy Robinson's might help us determine where she took Jessie."

"Right," Kat said, embarrassed that she'd briefly lost the thread. "What about it?"

"I found something."

CHAPTER ELEVEN

"You discovered her formative moment?" Kat asked excitedly.

"Well, I didn't find a specific event," Hannah replied, "but I think I may have found the general timeframe when it might have happened."

"Go ahead, tell me," Kat said, lifting her foot off the accelerator slightly as she realized she was approaching 100. It was one thing to go fast but getting pulled over would cost them valuable time. She resolved to keep the speed to ninety.

"I'm going through her school transcripts and juvenile records," Hannah said, before adding. "I thought those were supposed to stay sealed, by the way."

"That depends on who you know," Kat replied, glancing furtively over at Callum Reid, who was speaking quietly to his Denver cop buddy on the phone and didn't seem to be paying attention. "You were saying?"

"Right," Hannah continued. "Up until the age of fourteen, everything seems hunky-dory. Andy got good grades, all 'A's' actually. No disciplinary problems. Won the science fair twice, the spelling bee three times. Was a mathlete. Played on her middle school tennis team. But then something happened."

"You don't know what it was?" Kat pressed, though she knew that if Hannah had the answer, she would have given it already.

"No, but whatever it was, it happened some time when she was fourteen, between the end of eighth grade and the start of high school. During her freshman year, her grades dropped off a cliff, she quit every club and team she was on within a few months, and she started getting into trouble."

"At school?" Kat asked.

"Yes," Hannah said, "but not just there. There were fights with fellow students and she got busted for smoking and drinking on campus. But she was also arrested multiple times."

"I saw that," Kat said, "but it wasn't for anything violent, so I dismissed it."

"That's true," Hannah acknowledged, "But you have to look at it in context. We shouldn't be comparing her crimes as a teenager to the killer she became as an adult. We should be comparing them to the good kid she was just a few months earlier. From the age of fourteen to sixteen, she was arrested six times, including three times for drug possession, twice for shoplifting and once for stealing a car. She spent a total of five months in juvie during her freshman and sophomore years."

"You said that all happened up through sixteen," Kat observed. "What happened then?"

"It looks like her father got sick of it and shipped her off, first to a boarding school in Europe for a year, then to a military academy in Virginia."

"And that worked?" Kat asked, surprised.

"Well, we know it obviously didn't work in the long run," Hannah said, "but it might have put a bandage on the situation. There's no record of how she did at the boarding school, but it looks like she straightened up at the military academy. Her grades turned around. She took on some leadership positions."

Kat glanced in the rearview mirror and saw that Hannah was biting her lip.

"You don't sound entirely convinced of her transformation," she said.

"I don't know," Hannah said. "It's just that she would have been about the same age as I am now and I'm putting myself in her shoes. I can picture her putting on a good show for her rich daddy, making him think she's turned over a new leaf, so she doesn't lose access to his millions. So, she goes overboard to prove she's a goody-two-shoes now. She gets into a good college—Stanford for undergrad and Caltech for graduate school. She follows the proper path from that point forward."

"But you don't buy it," Kat pushed.

"Look," Hannah said with a shrug, "either she really did have a change of heart that lasted from the age of seventeen until about thirty, when she killed her lover's wife and tried to poison the profiler who found out, or that extended period was all an act and the Andy Robinson we know now was always lurking underneath, clawing to get out. Hell, maybe she was committing all kinds of crimes in the interim and never got caught until Jessie showed up. Which seems more likely to you?"

Kat was about to answer when she saw a silver car pass by on the westbound side of the freeway. She was going so fast that she couldn't be positive, but it sure looked like a Buick Skyhawk and the person at the wheel appeared to be a female with blonde hair.

Without a word, she pumped the brakes as she veered into the carpool lane. She scanned the median, looking for a spot where she could cross over to the westbound lanes without ruining the undercarriage of her car, but there was debris-laden gravel as far as the eye could see. She decided she couldn't wait any longer. She moved over to the shoulder and slowed down even more.

"What are you doing?" Callum asked, stopping in the middle of his phone conversation.

"I just saw a car that looked a lot like the one we're after," she explained as she suddenly swerved, cutting across the median, just missing a television that had failed to make it to its final destination.

"What the hell, Kat?" Hannah screamed from the backseat. "You're going to get us killed."

"Very unlikely," Kat said, hitting the gas as she drove back in the opposite direction on the westbound shoulder, waiting for a moment to pop into the carpool lane. When it came, she veered in quickly, ignoring the honking horns of multiple vehicles. She moved over two lanes and picked up speed.

"What makes you think that could possibly be them, knowing everything we know about their route so far?" Callum asked, clearly to keep his cool.

"Think about it," Kat said as she zipped through traffic, making sure to keep multiple cars between her and the old Buick so that their approach would be hidden. "Wouldn't it be just like Andy to pull a reversal like this? Make everyone think she's headed east while she returns west? And the timing fits too. That old clunker probably tops out at about forty-five to fifty miles per hour. From Ehrenberg to here is about 170 miles, which would take her about three and a half hours, maybe more, and that's assuming they never stopped. What was the timestamp on the video clip of the Buick near the travel center?"

"That was at 6:56," Hannah recalled. "It's 10:55 now. That's four hours."

Both she and Callum fell silent as Kat got closer to the sedan. She wasn't about to call them out for their skepticism. Nothing had been proven yet. It could just be a fluke that another thirty-seven-year-old

Buick Skyhawk with the same coloring was on the same stretch of road at the same time. But it would be quite a coincidence.

They were only three car lengths back now and it was apparent that the driver was indeed blonde. At this angle it was too difficult to get a good look at her face, but Kat was reluctant to get too much closer. She didn't want to draw any attention, especially when Andy was surely on edge.

"Maybe move all the way to the right," Callum suggested, "then get well ahead of her, cut across into the carpool lane and slow down. She won't be as suspicious of a car slowing down in front of her as one speeding up next to her. Plus, that way, I'll be closer to her and can get a good look. You could put your hair up and throw on some sunglasses now, before we get anywhere near her. Hannah—when we get closer, get down on the floor back there. When she glances over, she won't recognize me. If it's her, we'll just drop back, call it in, and tail her from a distance. Sound good?"

Kat had already moved two lanes over before he'd finished talking. Within three minutes, they were in position. Hannah got on the floor even before they entered the carpool lane just to be safe. Kat was having troubling putting her hair up while driving and dealing with her suddenly fraying nerves, so she just borrowed Callum's baseball cap.

She dropped her speed slowly, so as not to be obvious and hoped the old Buick didn't suddenly change lanes. Callum glanced to his right well before they were parallel with the car so it would appear that he was just staring out the window, daydreaming, and not specifically looking in that direction. Kat stared straight ahead.

"Okay, we're almost there," Callum narrated, as the car caught up to them on the right. "There's hair in the driver's face so it's kind hard to—."

Callum stopped talking suddenly. It took all of Kat's self-control not to look over right then.

"What is it?" she hissed through her teeth.

"It's not her," he said, deflated. "Look for yourself."

Kat glanced over and saw that the driver had moved the long hair out of the way. A clear view of their face was visible. The person at the wheel was male, likely in his fifties, with several days' worth of stubble. He looked over at Kat with watery, gray eyes, clearly unaware that he'd briefly been the focus of a potential multi-jurisdictional search. He nodded at her absently and she did the same.

At the earliest possible spot, Kat got out of the carpool lane, moved all the way to the right, exited the freeway, took the underpass turn-around, and got back on the I-10 again, headed east. She glanced at the clock.

It was 11:01 a.m. Her mistake had probably cost them fifteen minutes, precious time that might be the difference between Jessie living and dying. No one in the car said anything, but Kat knew they were thinking it. And she knew it was her fault.

CHAPTER TWELVE

11:31 a.m., Sunday morning

Susannah Valentine could feel the hope slipping away.
She glanced at her phone. She and Ryan Hernandez had been at the Ehrenberg Flying Y travel center for close to forty-five minutes and didn't have much to show for it.
First, they met with the senior officer on the scene, Sergeant Otis Campos of the La Paz County Sheriff's Department, who, despite looking overwhelmed, had managed to restrict the local crime scene technicians from doing anything other than the most basic tasks until the Phoenix-based FBI team had arrived.
"The dead man's name is Robert Mosby," Campos told them. "He went by Bob, according to his wife, who I spoke to a few minutes ago. Apparently, he was headed home to San Diego after spending the last few days in Phoenix for spring training. He was a big Padres fan. She said that he left extra early this morning so he could get back in time for church at ten."
By the time he led them to the body a few minutes later, the FBI medical examiner out of Phoenix, an extremely tall woman who went by Sedgewick, was ready with a preliminary briefing.
"We had been trying to officially lock down time of death," she said, "which I suspect will match the video footage from the travel center cameras. I can tell you that he was stabbed with a knife approximately four inches long. I'm guessing a switchblade or something similar. There was a total of eleven punctures, all to the left abdomen and kidney, tightly packed. The attack was impressive as far as these things go—lots of precision, all the wounds near the same depth, very clean. No hesitation. Nothing amateurish about it. Your suspect knew what she was doing."
Susannah noted that Andy also knew what she was doing when she first pulled up to the travel center. She couldn't help but appreciate how cleverly Andy Robinson had planned everything. She had parked so far away from the actual travel center building complex that, had it not

been for the unfortunate Bob Mosby incident and the overly curious dog that found his body, the old Buick Skyhawk likely never would have been noticed on the Flying Y travel center cameras. If not for that horrible stroke of luck, Jamil might still be searching for the brief video clip that showed the car about to get back on the freeway and head east toward Phoenix.

They looked at the video footage from the security office inside the store again but weren't able to glean any stunning new insights from it. The images reinforced what the M.E. said. Andy moved fast and without indecision. Bob Mosby was half-dead before he even knew what was happening.

The Buick was too far away from the building and the video was too grainy to see inside the car, so there was no way to tell what Jessie's status was or even if she was in the vehicle. But it was clear enough to tell that Andy had been carrying something out and put it on the hood of the car before attacking Mosby. That led to their one sliver of good news.

"She ordered a blueberry scone, a banana nut muffin, a medium latte and a medium iced coffee," the young woman at the register had told them after being shown the footage of the customer in question along with the timestamp of her purchase.

"At least that suggests Jessie is still alive," Susannah said to Ryan. "It's hard to imagine Andy would order all that just for herself."

"Agreed," Ryan had said. "Plus, it makes sense that she'd get an iced coffee. She wouldn't want to give Jessie a hot beverage for fear she'd toss it at her."

Susannah was glad to see that Ryan was both staying positive and picking up on details. She had been worried that he'd be too consumed by despondency to do his job properly. But he seemed to be even more focused than usual. She turned her attention back to the employee.

"Did the woman say anything when she ordered?" she asked. "Any comment at all that you can remember?"

"I don't think so," the girl, who couldn't have been more than sixteen, answered. "She just ordered her items, paid for them, and left. I wouldn't have thought about her twice if not for all this business."

After that, Ryan had gone back to the security office to review the video of the killing again. He said he hoped he might pick up on something he'd missed before. Susannah was pretty sure she'd gotten all she could out of it and stepped back outside.

It was almost midday, and the Arizona heat was starting to assert itself. As she stared out at the harsh beauty of the desert, she was tempted to take off her bullet-proof vest, but shook away the thought. Though it was unlikely, there was always the chance that Robinson was somewhere out there with a long-range rifle, patiently waiting for the chance to pick off other people in Jessie's orbit.

Susannah sighed in frustration. 11:31. Three quarters of an hour of investigation and the only thing they knew for certain was that Andy Robinson was an efficient killer. Actually, that wasn't entirely true. Because of some pastries and an iced coffee, they also felt somewhat confident that at 6:50 a.m., Jessie had likely been alive.

Susannah had hoped for more when she had stepped onto the jet at the Hawthorne airport. She felt sure that she'd be the one to make the crucial break in the case, and that she'd do it fast. Though she'd never say it out loud, she didn't just want to crack this case, she *needed* to.

She and Jessie Hunt hadn't left things on the best of terms. The idea of that being how their relationship ended, forever trapped in the amber of unspoken antagonism, was unacceptable to her. She had to get Jessie back, if only out of her own admittedly selfish need to clear the air and wipe away any lingering guilt.

They had gotten off on the wrong foot from almost the very start. When Susannah had joined HSS two months ago, Jessie had been on leave, working as an instructor at UCLA. During her absence, Susannah had worked hard to prove herself to the other members of the unit, with moderate success.

Deep down, she resented that she had to prove anything. After five years as a beat cop on the streets of Los Angeles and two more as a detective in Santa Barbara, she'd returned to L.A., in part to care for her ailing mother, but also because she won a slot with the coveted Homicide Special Section squad. She'd earned her place here through blood, sweat, and dozens of closed cases.

Even so, she tried to keep her head down and accept her role as the newbie, doing her best to ignore the leers of others at the station. She was used to it by now. Everywhere she'd gone, Susannah had gotten stares and catcalls from cops who thought they were complimenting her by telling her that, with her curvy figure, long, dark hair, and olive skin, she should be modeling swimsuits instead of wearing a police uniform. In retrospect, she'd been naïve to think that simply joining HSS would make it end. No one in the unit was like that, but that didn't stop others at the station.

Regardless she had pressed ahead in her own hard-charging way, which won over some of her colleagues, but others not so much. Maybe she was a little aggressive in her investigative style. Maybe she took more risks than most. But sometimes she just couldn't help herself.

And maybe she flirted with Ryan Hernandez more than she should have. She wasn't entirely sure why she'd done it. She suspected part of it was because she'd heard he was already romantically involved—engaged actually—and sensed that he was a gentleman who would never reciprocate, so it felt safe. With so many jerks coming on to her all day, it was nice to be playful with someone she knew wouldn't make a move, which he never did. In fact, he was clearly uncomfortable with her flirtations, but too polite to call her on it.

And if she was truly honest, she also did it because Hernandez was damn hot, and his fiancée wasn't around. Without her there, it was easy for Susannah to forget that she was teetering on a line of inappropriateness. And then Jessie came back.

Within minutes of her return to the office, two unexpected realities became clear to Susannah. First, she learned that Ryan Hernandez's fiancée' was Jessie Hunt, the returning criminal profiler. Susannah considered Jessie a personal hero and had specifically applied to HSS to work with her. The couple had apparently kept their relationship quiet, so that only other members of the unit knew, and none of them had loose lips. Susannah was appalled to realize that she'd been hitting on her own hero's guy.

Second, it was obvious that Jessie sensed something was off almost right away. Susannah didn't know if she gave off a guilty vibe or if Ryan seemed especially embarrassed around her, but Jessie was studying her through narrowed eyes almost from the moment they met, and little had changed since.

When they were assigned to work a case together investigating the death of a record executive who was murdered while partying on a private jet coming back from San Francisco, there was constant tension. Susannah had done everything she could to impress Jessie and prove her investigative mettle, but it only seemed to deepen the rift. Even after they solved the case, and Susannah saved Jessie from becoming the killer's next victim, the best they could muster was an uneasy détente.

It didn't help that when Jessie stopped taking Andy Robinson's calls from prison, the manipulative killer had turned to Susannah, offering up Eden Roth on a platter. Susannah had been so ambitious to crack that case and get ahead that she didn't think of the consequences of her actions or how she was being played.

Ultimately, she was just as important in securing Andy's release as Chief Laird or the governor. If she had stopped to ask why Andy was helping her, why she chose her specifically, maybe they wouldn't be in this situation right now.

But they were here now, and this couldn't be how they left things. Jessie couldn't die at the hands of this psycho, leaving Susannah saddled with the weight of responsibility she felt for her role in it all, forced to sift through the remnants of a relationship defined by mistrust and resentment, one she had originally hoped might bloom into a friendship.

She had to save Jessie. It might be the only way to save herself.

"Susannah!" Ryan called out urgently from the other side of the travel center, snapping her out of her pity party.

She turned in his direction and could tell right away that something big had happened.

"We just got a hit on a matching vehicle," he shouted. "It's headed north on US-95. And in thirty seconds, so are we. We're taking the helicopter. Let's get moving!"

CHAPTER THIRTEEN

Ryan slammed the chopper door shut.

"So, what's the situation?" Susannah Valentine asked once they were seated with their headsets on.

Ryan was about to answer when the helicopter suddenly rose into the air, making his stomach do a small flip. He'd been in them on more than one occasion, but this pilot, a heavily bearded, bored-looking Army veteran named Rusty who used to fly Black Hawks before becoming a contractor for local law enforcement, knew that time was a priority and had apparently decided that prepping his passengers before liftoff wasn't necessary. They were already several hundred feet in the air and veering to the north before he got a word out.

"A California Highway Patrol squad car headed south on Route 95 spotted a vehicle that looks like a match driving north about halfway between Vidal Junction and Needles."

"I don't know where that is," Valentine admitted.

"It's about seventy-five miles north of here," Ryan explained as the copter tore across the desert, making the cacti below look like blurry green sticks. "The highway will go all the way to Canada eventually, but the next major city it hits is Las Vegas."

"So, what did the CHP officer do?" she asked.

"Luckily, he didn't engage," Ryan said. "He called it in right away. There's another squad car that will be passing by them in about ten miles and should be able to confirm they're still on the highway. And the Sheriff's office in Needles has a drone. It'll be on top of the car in ten minutes to give us real time status updates."

"But I don't get it," Valentine said. "I know that clunker is slow but even plodding along, it shouldn't have taken them more than an hour and a half to go seventy-five miles. Based on the video snippet Jamil found, they left the travel center before 7 a.m. That was almost five hours ago. Shouldn't they be much farther north than that by now?"

"That's a great question," Ryan agreed. The same thought had occurred to him when he'd first been informed about the sighting, but he'd been so excited that he hadn't considered the issue until now. "Maybe they broke down at some point."

He could tell from her expression that Valentine wasn't any more convinced by that explanation than he was. But there had to be a reason. Andy wouldn't have lingered around this area for any longer than necessary. That is, unless she didn't have a choice.

"It's possible that Jessie did something to mess up her plan and slow her down," he suggested. "Based on that breakfast order, we're assuming that Andy is keeping her alive and has plans for her. So Jessie might have figured she could throw a few obstacles in her kidnapper's path without fear of being killed. Maybe she found a way to stall her, hoping that we'd be able to use that time to catch up."

"That seems more credible," Valentine said. "But if that's what happened, I hope Jessie knows where to draw the line. Andy Robinson may want to keep her alive for whatever reason, but at some point, she may decide her captive is more trouble than she's worth."

Ryan knew that Valentine was just thinking out loud and didn't mean any harm, but her words hit him like a punch to the gut. The only thing keeping him going right now was his belief that his fiancée could use her savvy and experience to outsmart Andy long enough for him to find her. If he lost that hope, then this chopper might as well aim straight for the desert floor because he didn't feel much like going on without Jessie Hunt.

"Sorry," Valentine said, apparently realizing her insensitivity a little late.

"Don't worry about," he said with a dismissive wave. "Decker didn't assign you to come with me because of your empathy and warmth. You're here to find clues and hunt down a murdering kidnapper. Stay focused on that."

She nodded, apparently convinced. He was relieved. What she said had stung and he did wish she had just a dab of sensitivity, but he couldn't say that out loud. If he did, she'd start doubting herself and maybe hesitate. He couldn't have that. Valentine's biggest strength as a detective—and sometime her biggest weakness—was her fearlessness. She was a bull in a china shop, willing to charge in and knock everything over if she thought it would result in an arrest. He might end up needing that recklessness before this was over. He didn't want to temper it.

"How long before we catch up to them?" she asked.

Ryan repeated the question to Rusty the pilot.

"Depending on how fast the car is going," Rusty answered, "we should be on them in twenty-five to thirty minutes."

"I thought you used to fly Black Hawks," Valentine challenged. "I figured you could do better than that."

Ryan saw the pilot's jaw tighten and knew they'd be there on the shorter end of that estimate. Having Valentine as his partner was already paying dividends.

*

Twenty-three minutes later, the car came into view.

Ryan had instructed Rusty to stay well overhead to avoid tipping Andy off to their presence. Two CHP vehicles were about a quarter-mile behind her, ready to catch up fast on his orders. Another half dozen cars from the San Bernardino Sheriff's Department were waiting a few miles up, hidden behind an overpass bridge. Everyone was listening for approval to go from Ryan. Back at Central Station, the task force at the command center was patched in too.

Ryan had to either give that approval soon or instruct everyone to let her keep going without incident. The silver Buick Skyhawk had just passed Parker Junction and was now only about five miles south of Needles, a town of 5,000 people. There was no way he was going allow any kind of confrontation in a populated area.

But once they passed through Needles, they'd hit the Colorado River, which was the dividing point between California and Arizona in the north, just as it was further south. If they crossed the state border, the chase would be complicated by all kinds of additional jurisdictional issues. Down in Ehrenberg, they'd gotten the La Paz County Sheriff's Department to defer to LAPD, but up here, they'd be dealing with the Mohave County Sheriff. He had no idea if they'd be as amenable and wasn't inclined to find out.

"She's three miles from the outskirts of town, Detective Hernandez," the deputy operating the drone said, giving the warning that Ryan had asked her for. "At that point we start to enter the business district—strip malls, fast food spots, that sort of thing."

"Okay," Ryan said. "Let's get those CHP cars behind her to catch up now but keep your lightbars and sirens off and stay out of her line of sight as long as possible. When I say so, I want four of the San Bernardino vehicles to pull out onto the highway well ahead of her. Once she goes under the bridge, CHP vehicles are to come up on either side of her with lights flashing. Order her to pull over. The remaining two SBSD cars pull out at that point too and run a rolling roadblock to block all the traffic behind her. SBSD cars up ahead, when you see those sirens behind you, slow down to get behind all the other traffic, put your sirens on, and form a roadblock across all lanes. We'll land the chopper on the highway somewhere near that roadblock. Hopefully she stops without incident but be prepared for anything. Everyone got it?"

There was a chorus of assents. The Buick was now less than a half-mile from the overpass. If he waited any longer to put things in motion, Andy was sure to spot the cars pulling out up ahead.

"It's time," he instructed. "Let's have those four SBSD vehicles pull out and ease into traffic now. Keep your speed low. She's about forty-five seconds behind you."

He saw them pull out just as he'd requested.

"Rusty, let's start to head down," he said to the pilot. "I want to target an area about a quarter-mile past the overpass for our landing site."

Rusty nodded in understanding and began a steep descent.

"CHP," Ryan said, his voice rising in anticipation, "you're going to reach that overpass in about twenty seconds. I want you right next to her with lights flashing the moment you're on the other side of it. That's everyone else's cue to do as instructed. Cars still at the underpass—prepare for a traffic break. Cars up ahead—start to slow down now and prepare your roadblock maneuver. She hits the bridge in three, two, one, go!"

Ryan watched it all happen as they swooped down, dropping from over 4,000 feet to under two hundred in the space of a long exhale. As they sliced through the air, both CHP cars pulled up next to the Buick and turned on their lightbars and sirens.

The SBSD cars pulled out from behind the overpass with lights on and began snaking back and forth on the freeway, causing the cars behind them to slow, and come to a stop. Up ahead, the other four SBSD vehicles, now behind all the civilian cars, had turned on their lightbars and sirens as well. They lined up in a row across the highway, creating a wall of metal and tires. Ryan could hear one of the CHP officers in a squad car alongside the Buick barking orders over his vehicle's loudspeaker.

"Slow down and come to a controlled stop," he demanded.

It seemed to be working. The Buick, now about five hundred yards away from the roadblock, had reduced its speed considerably.

"Can you describe the driver?" Ryan asked.

"Yes," the CHP officer said. "It's a female with blonde hair. She's—."

Before he could finish, the Buick suddenly sped forward again and veered sharply left, clipping the hood of the CHP vehicle on that side. The collision sent the Buick skidding sideways onto the left shoulder, and then down toward a deep ravine. It was going too fast and when it hit the bank of the ravine, it flipped into the air, landed on the steep embankment, and flipped twice more on the way down before coming to a stop, upside down, at the bottom.

"Land this thing now," Ryan ordered, surprised at how calm his voice was, considering that every part of his body was inflamed with dread.

The helicopter was already close to the ground and touched down less than ten seconds later, just beyond the spot on the highway where the Buick had slid off the road onto the shoulder.

"Wait for the rotor to stop," Ryan heard Rusty shout as he tore off his headset, yanked open the door, and jumped out.

Despite having still been in the air before the accident happened, Ryan got to the edge of the ravine before any of the officers on the ground. To his enormous relief, the vehicle didn't appear to be on fire. But that could change at any minute. He pulled out his weapon, got to his knees, and slid down, backside first, to the bottom of the ravine. He stood up and was about to approach the vehicle when he heard something behind him. He spun around. It was Valentine, sliding down the ravine wall, also with her gun drawn.

"Go ahead," she said when she reached the bottom, "I've got your back."

He returned his attention to the vehicle, moving slowly toward the driver's door. Unexpectedly, it opened, and someone tumbled out. He couldn't see a face, but the person had blonde hair and appeared to be female.

"Freeze!" he shouted.

The person, who was groaning softly, stopped moving.

"Keep your hands where I can see them and lift your head so I can see your face," he instructed.

"I'll try," the person mumbled, "but my neck kind of hurts."

The voice sounded scratchy. More troubling, it wasn't familiar. When the person lifted her head, Ryan's concern was validated. It wasn't Andy Robinson.

CHAPTER FOURTEEN

Ryan wasn't sure whether to be relieved or despondent.

If Andy wasn't the driver, then Jessie almost certainly wasn't in the car either, which meant she wasn't hurt or worse. But if she wasn't in the car, where was she? Was she in a different ditch? Speeding down another highway? Was she tied up? Was she in a trunk? Was she even still alive?

Suddenly, he remembered Valentine's inadvertently callous line from before, about Andy potentially deciding that Jessie might be more trouble than she was worth. What if he was kidding himself about the situation?

What if all the pastries Andy bought this morning were just because she was extra hungry? What if the two coffees were just to make sure she stayed awake? It had been over sixteen hours since Jessie was taken. What reason did he have to believe that Andy hadn't already tortured her and dumped her on the side of a desert road?

The very thought filled him with horror, and almost immediately after that, with self-loathing. Not only was that kind of mentality counter-productive, but it was also insulting to the woman he loved. It had to stop now.

Focus on what you know. Evaluate the evidence.

He stared hard at the driver. She appeared to be in her thirties, just like Andy, but she had a haggard, worn-out look, entirely unrelated to the car accident. Her face had deep creases and her teeth were yellowed and nubby. Her eyes were bloodshot. Her hair was ragged. Ryan strongly suspected she was an addict.

"Is there anyone in the car with you?" he demanded.

"No, man," she said lazily.

Ryan checked anyway. The woman wasn't lying.

"We should move her," Valentine said. "I know we need answers, but I see gas leaking over there. We don't want to be anywhere near here if this thing blows."

More officers were sliding down to the ravine floor now. Ryan pointed at two of the SBSD deputies.

"Can some of your team escort the driver down the ravine to a safe distance so my partner and I can question her? I assume someone is calling fire and EMT? Everyone else should stay clear of the area until they arrive. Detective Valentine noticed that gasoline is leaking from the vehicle. We should probably block off a couple hundred-foot safe zone ASAP."

"Yes, Detective," the taller of the two extremely young-looking deputies said as two more of his compatriots slid down into the ravine.

As the deputy turned to them and began to pass along the instructions, Ryan and Valentine walked along the ravine floor, away from the car.

"How likely is it that this is just a coincidence?" Valentine asked, broaching another question that Ryan had been considering ever since he saw the driver. "Do we really think some random blonde woman just happened to be driving the same kind of car as Andy Robinson in the same area that we might expect to find her? Am I overreading this?"

"We're about to find out," Ryan said, stopping at a log at the edge of the ravine. It was big enough to sit on, and at 150 feet from the car, it seemed far enough away should it suddenly ignite.

They both sat down and waited as two SBSD officers brought over the woman, who was limping, but not as badly as one might expect, considering the severity of the accident. She was bleeding slightly from her forehead but didn't seem aware of it. Nor did she appear to notice that one of the deputies had handcuffed her. She wore blue jeans and a long-sleeved, red, and white striped shirt that reminded Ryan of *Where's Waldo*, if Waldo hadn't washed his shirt in several days.

"Have a seat," he said, motioning for her to sit next to him as he pulled out his phone and called the HSS main line at the command center.

"Hernandez?" Decker asked anxiously.

"Hi, Captain," Ryan said. "I know you want an update after what you saw on the helicopter's video feed. Neither Jessie nor Andy Robinson was in the car. Valentine and I are with the driver now. We're about to question her and thought you might like to listen in."

"Very much so," Decker said.

"Can you read the lady her rights, Valentine?" he requested.

As she did, Ryan considered how best to go about this interrogation. Based on what he already suspected about this woman, he had a feeling how she might fit into the big picture. If he was right, and handled this properly, there was a chance he might still be able to salvage something out of this wild goose chase.

"...with those rights in mind, are you willing to talk to us?" Valentine concluded.

"Whatever," the woman said with a shrug.

"Is that a 'yes'?" Ryan asked

"If it gets me out of this sun quicker, then sure," she said.

"Great," Ryan replied. "We'll see what we can do about that sun. I know we've got an ambulance coming to check you out. What's your name?"

"Rosalind Wallace," the woman said, "Roz."

"You were pretty lucky Roz, I have to say," he noted. "After a crash like that, rolling over three times, and landing in the bottom of a ravine, most people would be pretty messed up. But you seem to have come out of it with just a bit of a limp and a bump on the head. Why do you think that is?"

"I don't know," she said petulantly.

"I'm thinking it could be because of all the drugs in your system," he suggested. "Maybe they had your body so relaxed that it didn't tense up when you rolled over and you just sort of rode the wave of the crash."

"I don't know," Roz repeated, not denying the possibility.

"Here's the thing, Roz," Ryan said, leaning over to her conspiratorially. "When you get to the hospital, they're going to draw blood and find out if I'm right, so we'll get the answer to that eventually. You also tried to evade the police just now, which is a crime. And you hit one of their cars—also a crime. So, you're in a tough spot. But I'm guessing this isn't the first time you've had a run-in with the law. Am I right?"

"Don't be a jerk, man," Roz muttered.

Valentine, normally the one to go for it, gave him an apprehensive frown, apparently concerned that Roz might shut down and leave them with nothing. Ryan knew he was at risk of alienating his only current lead, but something told him to keep going. He might not have Jessie's preternatural profiling talent, but after more than a decade on the job, he knew how to read an addict. And he aimed to use that knowledge to find the woman he still intended to marry.

"I'm actually your best friend right now, Roz. You know why? Because I think you might have information that could be helpful to a case that I'm investigating. If it turns out I'm right, I might be able to get the authorities in these parts to overlook the accident you caused, evading the police, and even the very chemicals coursing through your veins right now. But if you make things tough for me, you'll probably be spending the next two to four years in a prison in the California desert, which sounds like a pretty miserable time, if you ask me. So, what do you say? Are you willing to answer my questions directly and without an attitude?"

Roz squinted at him in the midday sun, deliberating. After a few seconds, she replied.

"You promise you can get me off?" she wanted to know.

"I can't promise," Ryan said. "But if you're honest and your information is helpful, I can probably make your situation a lot better."

"Okay," she said. "What do you want to know?"

"That's not your car, is it?"

"No," she said.

"How did you get it?"

"Some woman came to me a few days ago in L.A.—that's where I'm from—and offered me a deal. She said I could have the car and $2000 if I drove it to the Best Restin' Desert Dream hotel near the travel center in Ehrenberg."

"Who was the woman?" Valentine asked, speaking for the first time since reading Roz her rights.

"She didn't give her name, but she was tall with brown hair, and she had terrible breath."

Ryan and Valentine exchanged a look. They could both guess who that was.

"She didn't explain why she chose you?" Valentine wondered.

"No, other than checking that I had a valid driver's license, she didn't ask many questions," Roz said. "She came to this shelter where I was staying at. I saw her talk to some other woman before me, but I guess she didn't like her."

"Was the other woman blonde too?" Valentine asked.

"I think so."

"So, when were you supposed to go to Ehrenberg?" Ryan asked.

"She said to drive out here yesterday afternoon, check in at the hotel, and stay there overnight. She also gave me a car cover and told me to put it over the Buick."

"Why didn't you just bail with the car and the money?" he pressed.

Roz smiled at the question.

"That would have been dumb," she explained. "She told me there was more money coming. She said that I should wake up by 4 a.m. this morning, that I should set a bunch of alarms. Then I should go over to the travel center, sit in the coffee shop, get some breakfast and coffee, and wait."

"For what?" Ryan asked, trying not to sound too excited.

"She said that sometime this morning a woman would show up. It might be at 4:30 or 8:30. I would know her because she'd be blonde and driving the exact same car as me. She'd come into the coffee shop and sit down across from me. And if I did as I was told, then that other woman would give double the money with a promise of more to come."

"And did she?" Ryan pressed.

"She sure did," Roz told him. "I had to wait a couple of hours. I even fell asleep a few times. But I was awake when she walked in. Blonde, kind of pretty, super intense blue eyes. She handed me an envelope with $4000, told me to count it if I wanted. I didn't want to seem rude, so I didn't do that. She also gave me a map and instructions."

Ryan thought Roz would continue but her eyes got hazy, and she seemed to lose her train of thought, so he prompted her.

"What were her instructions?"

"Oh right," she said, snapping back, "she said to go north on Route 95 to Laughlin, Nevada. She gave me an address, which she said was a casino, and a locker number with a combination. She told me that the locker would have $8000 in it. She also said I could keep the car. But she gave me very specific instructions. She said I couldn't go faster than fifty-five miles per hour. She also said I couldn't leave until 10 a.m. this morning. I was to go back to the hotel right after our talk, stay there until ten, check out, then go to the car, remove the cover, and leave without making any stops. She said she'd know if I left early or exceeded the speed limit. So, I did everything she said, exactly as she said. And somehow, that got me here."

"She didn't say anything else to you?" Ryan demanded.

"No."

"Did she look strange to you? Did you notice any blood on her? Anything like that?"

Roz shook her head.

"Did you see anyone else in her car?"

"I could barely see it at all, it was parked so far away."

Ryan looked over at Valentine, who shook her head. She didn't have any other questions either. It was just as well. They could hear the sound of the ambulance approaching in the distance.

"Can we leave Roz with you guys?" he asked the deputies, who nodded.

He and Valentine scaled the ravine wall and emerged out onto the shoulder of the highway again, both sweating profusely. The helicopter was still on the road about two hundred feet away, waiting for them.

"Can you hear us, Captain?" he asked as they began walking briskly back to the chopper.

"I can," Decker said. "We're all here. Any thoughts?"

"I'll set aside my first thought," Ryan said, "which is that we still have no idea where Jessie is, and move on to my second, which is that Andy Robinson knew she'd be going to that travel center days in advance."

There was a brief silence, which Captain Decker broke.

"Go ahead, Detective Bowen," he said. Apparently, Ryan's old partner Brady Bowen, who was back at the command center, had something to say.

"Yeah, thanks Captain," Brady said. "This makes me wonder about the killing of Bob Mosby this morning. Was he just at the wrong place at the wrong time or was killing him actually an intentional act all along? If he hadn't come over to the Buick in that parking lot, would Andy Robinson have killed another traveler? She must have had some plan in mind to draw our attention to such a random location as the Ehrenberg Flying Y travel center. She wanted us there. And she didn't do all this stuff with Roz Wallace just for the fun of it. She wanted us to find her too."

"Agreed," said someone Ryan identified immediately as Karen Bray, "but as far as diversions go, it's an odd one. Why would Andy have Roz Wallace wait so long after killing Bob Mosby before leaving the hotel? Roz could have been to Laughlin and moved on if she had left right after they met up. I wouldn't be surprised if she kept heading north to Vegas from there. Why not have her start earlier so that we'd be searching a bigger stretch of territory?"

"I have a guess on that last question at least," Dr. Lemmon said. "Based on what I've gleaned about Andy Robinson, I doubt there's any money in that locker in the Laughlin casino. I wouldn't even be confident that there *is* a locker. If I'm right, Robinson might have figured that once Roz Wallace discovered that, she could become a loose cannon. So better to keep her under her thumb as long as possible."

"That makes sense," Decker said, "but we'll still have the local police check out the casino just to make sure."

"But none of that addresses the question that's eating at me," Valentine said, stopping at the door to the helicopter.

"What's that?" Decker asked.

"What made Andy Robinson so confident that the entirety of southern California law enforcement would go after the Buick that Roz was driving? Why wasn't she worried that we'd be following her car too?"

Ryan thought about it for a second and the answer suddenly became clear.

"What time is it?" he asked.

"12:09 p.m.," Jamil said immediately.

"And when was that freeway image taken of Andy's car about to get on the I-10 East after killing Bob Mosby?" Ryan pressed, knowing the researcher would have the answer at his fingertips.

"6:56 a.m.," Jamil replied without hesitation.

"And in the five plus hours since then, other than Roz's vehicle, we haven't run across any other images of a 1985 silver Buick Skyhawk in the area—not on freeway cameras or from drones or highway patrol vehicles?"

"Not yet, Detective," Jamil said.

"And," Beth added, "we've expanded our search field extending 300 miles in every direction away from the travel center, including back here toward Los Angeles."

"Then I think we have the answer to Detective Valentine's question," Ryan said as he climbed back into the chopper. "The reason Andy's not worried about us finding her in that old Buick is because she's not driving it anymore. She's ditched it for something else. But she must have still been worried that we'd find her. So, she sent us all chasing after Roz. And when our backs were turned, she snuck out the back door without anyone noticing."

"So where does that leave us?" asked Kat's boyfriend, Mitch Connor, sounding defeated.

Ryan understood the man's frustration, but he refused to give in to the same feeling. He'd already let despair nearly consume him once. He wouldn't let it happen again.

"It leaves us back in the last place we know they were—the Flying Y travel center. We must have missed something before. If we can find out what it is, that's how we'll pick up their trail. That's how we'll find Jessie."

CHAPTER FIFTEEN

FOUR HOURS EARLIER
7:58 a.m., Sunday morning

Andy considered that prison was good for one thing at least.
That's where she had learned to meditate.
She'd pretended to do it back in her pre-incarceration, country-club, cocktail-party life but had never really committed to it. Once she was locked up in a cell for sixteen hours a day, she gave it another shot, and found that it was a huge help. The walls didn't feel like they were closing in on her as much. The middle of the night banshee screams of other inmates weren't as unsettling. And the desire to smash her head against the bars of her cell wasn't as strong. It was one of the things she credited with keeping her sane in that place, which was ironic, considering it was a facility that housed the insane.
Whatever eventually brought her to it, meditation was helping her now. If not for the breathing techniques she'd learned inside, it would have been much harder to deal with her current situation. And that situation was daunting.
She still had another two minutes to wait until Isaac's Auto Body opened at 8 a.m., which was frustrating. She'd already been waiting for fifteen minutes, parked deep in a ditch on the side of a road, listening to Jessie's annoying, gagged grunts coming from the backseat.
Apparently, Ms. Goody-Two-Shoes was still upset about having to watch her gut Tubby McPadre back at the Flying Y. What her travel companion didn't know was that if it hadn't been him that she turned into a human colander, it would have been someone else, probably that old biddy that she'd noticed hobbling back to the shower rooms at the travel center.
Would that have been better—to break a creaky hag's neck, carve *AR &JH were here* into her back with the switchblade, and lock her in a sleep pod to be discovered a few hours later? After all, her plan required someone to stumble across a dead body this morning one way or another. It just so happened that Jessie had to witness the dying part.

To add to Andy's frustration, on top of all the sitting around and the grunting from the backseat, she'd just spent the forty-five minutes before pulling up to Isaac's Auto Body navigating some tricky terrain. In order to make it the twenty miles from Ehrenberg to Quartzsite, Arizona, without triggering any freeway cameras or attracting the notice of Arizona Highway Patrol, she had to take a circuitous path along Dome Rock Road West. It was not fun, especially in this car, which she feared might conk out at several points along the way.

But it was necessary. If they were spotted before she could make her next big move, everything she'd done up to this point would be for naught. So, she'd taken the winding road that snaked back and forth across the freeway, periodically following it along barren, dusty, unmarked stretches of dirt track that made her wonder if she'd taken a wrong turn at some point.

But she hadn't. And they hadn't passed any law enforcement vehicles either. Her constant scanning of the sky hadn't revealed any helicopters or drones, although it would have been tough to spot the latter. Once they arrived in Quartzsite, she'd settled so deep into the ditch that, while they couldn't be easily seen from the road, they also likely couldn't get out, which meant she was fully committed now.

She heard a rattling sound and looked across the road. A large man in gray coveralls, maybe Isaac himself, was unlocking the chain-link fence and pulling back the gate. The clock showed 8:01 a.m. They were officially open. She glanced back at Jessie.

"How are you doing back there?" she asked, not really expecting any kind of enthusiasm just yet.

Jessie didn't even acknowledge her, instead looking past her out the window.

"I get it. You're upset. I wish you didn't have to see that unpleasantness back there at the travel center. But like I said, it wouldn't have happened if you'd kept your word to me. Still, I'm willing to let bygones be bygones if you are too."

Jessie continued to stare blankly out the window. This wasn't what Andy wanted but she wasn't hugely surprised. Until their surroundings changed, their dynamic couldn't either.

"Listen, I have to run a little errand," she explained, "but it won't take too long. Even so, I'm going to leave the windows open a little for you because it's starting to get warm out here. If I wouldn't leave a dog locked in a car with closed windows, I certainly won't do that to you.

See how I'm meeting you halfway? It would be nice if you did the same."

Still nothing from Jessie. Andy refused to take offense.

"You just hang out here and try to stay comfortable," she instructed. "I know that's hard with the cuffs and everything. But my hope is that you'll be out of those pretty soon. What I'd like is for you to use your alone time to think about how you want this experience to work, going forward. You can continue to act like a petulant child if you like. But I've told you the consequences to your friends and family of not embracing our grand experiment together."

Jessie's eyes darted toward her. Now she had the woman's attention. Smiling, she continued.

"Or you can decide to stop fighting me all the time, relax a little, and give this shared adventure a chance. You might discover it's not as bad as you think. I'll let you sit with that while I take care of my business. Back in a jiff."

She got out, locked the car, and scrambled up the ditch to the road. There was no traffic at all. She scurried across Acacia Road, then resumed walking casually as she passed through the gate.

As she made her way to the auto body shop entrance, she prepared herself, getting in the right headspace for this encounter. She needed to win this guy over, but not be so memorable that he'd have a lot to say about her later. She smirked to herself at the thought. If there was one word that she'd never heard anyone use to describe her, it was unmemorable.

She opened the door and the metal bell above it dinged. The same man who had unlocked the outer gate before came out from a back room. She hadn't fully appreciated it from her vantage point in the ditch earlier, but the guy was huge. Easily six and half feet tall, she guessed that he was pushing three hundred pounds as well. He had a couple days of stubble and blondish hair that was halfway to bald. She guessed that he was in his early thirties, just like her.

"How can I help you?" he asked in a gentle voice at odds with his physical bearing.

She flashed him a big grin.

"Are you Isaac from the sign out there?" she asked.

"Yes ma'am, I am," he said, "Isaac Grimes."

"Well, Isaac Grimes, here's how I hope you can help me," she said. "I noticed quite a few cars on your lot, and I was wondering: do you just do auto body work, or do you possibly sell vehicles as well?"

Of course, she already knew the answer to that question. She wouldn't be at Isaac's Auto Body in the random town of Quartzsite, Arizona—population 2,200--if she hadn't done her research. She'd checked online at Isaac's surprisingly robust website and knew that he liked to repair older cars in his spare time. He kept them on the shop's lot for sale and, as of yesterday morning, had an inventory of nine vehicles.

"I do have a few cars for sale," he said, his expression of mild befuddlement giving way to a shy grin. "But I have to tell you, I mostly fix them up to keep myself entertained. They're all pretty old. If you're looking for something to last you for a long stretch, these might not fit the bill. But if you're in the market for something cheap, you've come to the right place."

"Should we go out and take a look?" Andy asked, her tone balancing somewhere between impressed and mildly flirtatious.

"Sure thing," he replied and came around the counter.

He held the door open for her and she stepped back outside. It seemed that in just the two minutes that she'd been inside the temperature had gone up ten degrees.

"What are you looking for?" he asked. "They're all clunkers, but if I know what you're looking to get out of the vehicle, I might be able to guide you in the right direction. Are we talking about a daily commute, a cross-country-trip, doing some off-roading?"

"Here's what I need, Isaac," Andy explained, set to describe the very car she'd already picked out. "It should be something that can handle the bumps and bruises of desert driving, even on some beat up, gnarly roads. Definitely all-wheel drive—I don't want it getting stuck. It should have a trunk. I don't need anything fancy, but it can't conk out on me out there in the desert, Isaac. I'm putting my faith in you. This doesn't need to last me a year, but I'd like it to survive a month. Now I'm willing to pay cash, right here, today, but I won't go a penny over $2000. And I don't like fancy colors. I know you probably don't have a ton of inventory but if there's something in the gray universe, I'd be just fine. Do you have anything that fits that description?"

She watched his shy grin give way to a wide smile as her every word matched a car that she knew he'd been trying to sell for three months now.

"I have one that I think is right up your alley…I'm sorry, I never got your name."

"Katherine Gentry," Andy said. "But you can call me Kat."

"Okay Kat," Isaac continued, "there's a gray 1992 Mitsubishi Galant VR-4 out back with 160,000 miles on it. It's weathered and the interior is worn beyond salvaging, but I've cleaned up all the dents, dings, and scratches. It's all-wheel drive, runs clean, with solid suspension for desert driving. I don't know that I'd count on it in cold weather anymore, but around here, you wouldn't have to worry about that until late fall, so I think your one-month window should be fine. And the best part is that I'm listing it for $1,899, so you'd come out a little ahead, pricewise. Wanna see it?"

"Sure, Isaac."

"All right," he said. "Give me a minute to get the keys and bring it around front. I'll be right back."

He hurried back to the office, walking as fast as he could without actually running. Andy took the opportunity to look over at the ditch across the street. She could see the very top of her car if she squinted just right. Out of habit, she glanced both ways down the road, just to make sure Jessie hadn't broken free somehow and was currently trying to flag down a driver. But the road remained silent and empty.

She leaned against the hood of an old pickup truck while she waited, wondering when she'd be able to stop worrying about Jessie trying to escape. The initial glee at the success of her abduction plan had carried her through most of last night and this morning. None of her guest's attempts to argue or cajole her way out of the situation had ruined the good vibes.

But now, in the harsh light of the day, with the morning sun beating down on her, and only her thoughts to contend with, she couldn't help but have doubts. Pretty soon, she and Jessie would be together, safely hidden away from the dragnet that was currently in hot pursuit. What would happen then?

How would things go once she finally had the woman that she'd spent two years thinking about where she wanted her, with no one to interfere in their future together? What exactly did she anticipate happening next. Did she see herself replacing Kat Gentry as Jessie's best friend, as she always claimed she wanted? Was that enough? Did she want to be closer, a sister like Hannah Dorsey? Something more than that? How could she expect Jessie to be what she wanted when she wasn't certain what that was?

And would Jessie be willing to be *anything* to her? Until this moment, Andy had never had any doubt that their future together was already written, a thing of destiny. But these last few hours had been more trying than she'd anticipated. Jessie was fighting that shared destiny more stubbornly than she'd expected.

Andy knew to her very bones that their paths were aligned, that they were meant spend the rest of their lives together. But once they got to their final destination, their future wouldn't be up to her alone anymore. At some point after their arrival, she would have to loosen the reins. She would have to give Jessie a chance to prove herself, to show that she was genuinely on board with this new life. Otherwise, she'd never be anything more than a glorified pet. And that's not what Andy wanted.

Maybe knowing that her loved ones' very lives depended on her getting with the program would cause a real change in how Jessie behaved once they got to their new home. Because that was the truth: their lives did depend on it.

CHAPTER SIXTEEN

"And the best part is that I'm listing it for $1,899, so you'd come out a little ahead, pricewise," Isaac offered. "Wanna see it?"

Jessie listened intently as she lay in the backseat of the car across the street.

"Sure, Isaac," she heard Andy reply.

"All right," Isaac said. "Give me a minute to get the keys and bring it around front. I'll be right back."

As exhausted as she was, as much as her wrists and ankles thrummed with a mix of numbness and pain, Jessie still managed to find a new layer of anxiety.

If Andy switched cars, the already slim chances that they'd be found went to near zero. Somewhere deep down, Jessie had been holding out hope that maybe one small bit of good could be salvaged from the death of the good Samaritan at the travel center. Eventually, someone would notice that he was missing or see that his car hadn't moved. Maybe a dust storm would blow the trash bags off his body. Something would happen that would lead to his discovery. People would check the security footage from the center, see his murder, and note the car the killer drove off in.

But if Andy wasn't driving that car anymore, the lead was useless. And based on the route she'd taken to get to this town, pointedly avoiding the freeway completely, it was clear that Jamil and the gang back at HSS weren't going to be able to use cameras to track them either. They'd have no way of even knowing the car was here unless someone happened to glance down in this ditch in this tiny town in the middle of the desert.

But it was worse than that. By the time this old car was finally discovered in the ditch, they'd be long gone in the one that Isaac was getting right now. And Jessie doubted that would be the last vehicle they'd use either. Andy was too smart to leave such an obvious trail. So, even if someone put the pieces together and decided to question the guy from the auto body shop across the street, whatever Isaac told the police would be another diversionary tactic.

Jessie could feel despair starting to creep into the cracks in her flagging spirit. How was she was supposed to win this deadly game? Andy had been preparing for this day for weeks, months, maybe years. Every move had been planned meticulously well in advance. She was so far out front that she seemed to be toying with her pursuers, taunting them, giving them tiny clues that would offer brief, false hope.

Jessie imagined the crew of HSS, after discovering her disappearance and guessing the culprit, leaping into action. They were all right there in one place at Peninsula. They had representatives from the FBI, the U.S. Marshals Service, the Sheriff's Department, and more. She envisioned Captain Decker setting up a command center, utilizing the resources of every agency. She pictured Jamil Winslow and Beth Ryerson hunched over computer screens, scouring databases, and squinting at fuzzy surveillance footage for any morsel of useful information.

But it wouldn't be enough. They'd always be playing catch-up. Andy kidnapped her from Peninsula in a laundry truck. She left Los Angeles in a nearly-forty-year-old, hard-to-trace clunker. She was about to switch to another vehicle that was almost as old, somewhere in an isolated desert town.

There was no way they could realistically keep up with the speed and complexity of her moves. Then Jessie had another thought that allowed the despair to slither even deeper inside her: did she even want them to catch up?

Andy had warned her that if she tried to escape or if she was rescued, innocent Angelenos would be in danger. With many people, that might be an idle threat, but not with Andy Robinson. She'd just spent two years in a psychiatric prison for poisoning her lover's wife and framing the couple's maid for it. She'd tried to kill Jessie when she found out. She'd orchestrated the murders of six people from behind bars, and just over an hour ago, she'd brutally stabbed a man to death with a switchblade and dumped him in a ditch. There was no doubt she'd take out anyone else who got in her way.

Andy had also promised that if she died, Operation Z would be activated, leading to the death of not just countless residents of Los Angeles, but Jessie's loved ones as well. She didn't know what this Operation Z was, but she had to take it seriously. Andy was the vengeful type, who would take great pleasure in knowing that even in death, she could make others suffer. And the people who would suffer would be Ryan, Kat, and Hannah. She couldn't let that happen under any circumstances.

Andy had already proven that she had the ability to make terrible things happen without doing them herself. Three of her fellow prisoners, Livia Bucco, Eden Roth and most recently, the imposter bride, Corinne, had wreaked havoc at her behest. It would be foolish to doubt that she had at least one more acolyte out there, willing to do her bidding, even after her death. In fact, her death might well be the call to action. Maybe this disciple was a sleeper agent, instructed not to "wake" unless her mentor was killed. Was that what "Z" referenced—"z's," as in sleeping?

Jessie shook her head, as if physically forcing the question out of her brain. That was the sort of issue she could ponder for hours if she was in her office, in profiler mode. Right now, she had more pressing concerns, like regaining her freedom.

And in that moment, she realized that she'd been buying into a false choice. Her own personal autonomy wasn't negotiable. No one, not even Andy Robinson, could force her to live under their dominion, locked down, her body and soul constrained by their concept of how the rest of her life should be defined.

Besides, what other choice besides fighting for herself could she make and still look in the mirror, assuming there even was one where she was going? She wasn't going to simply consent to living with an unhinged person for the rest of her life and be her…what exactly? What did Andy even want from her? But that too was a question for another time.

She had to try to escape. She'd deal with the fallout later. She had to have confidence that she'd figure something out. That's what she did. That's who she was. She would outwit Andy and find a way to save herself, those closest to her, and the people of L.A.

But for that to happen, the folks looking for her had to have some shot at finding her. She needed to leave them some kind of breadcrumb, a signal that she had been here, was alive and still fighting. But short of biting off one of her fingers and spitting it out of the half open window, she couldn't think of anything. Hell, even that wouldn't work because of the gag in her mouth.

But as her eyes darted desperately around the car, they landed on another item that might work just as well. The white sandals she'd picked out for the wedding were still on her feet. But the heel strap on the left one had started to fray after the endless hours of rubbing against the edge of the cuffs on her ankle. That was the same sandal that Andy had smeared her bloody hand on when she briefly removed the cuff on her ankle after stabbing the good Samaritan to death.

Jessie started to plot out a potential scenario. It wouldn't take much effort to snap off what remained of the heel strap. If she could somehow scratch a message in the still-drying blood and get the sandal out of the car without Andy noticing it, *and* if it was discovered by the HSS team, they'd have a piece of evidence tying the location and the car to her and to the murder at the travel center. It would let them know that she had been here, approximately when, and that she was still fighting. Admittedly, it was a long shot, but at this point, that was all she had left.

Just then, she heard the sound of tires on gravel. Despite the discomfort, she pushed herself up off the seat and saw that Isaac was pulling the car around. Andy was engaged in conversation with him as she checked it out. There would never be a better time to do this.

Anchoring her left foot against the back of the seat, she hooked her right toes around the heel strap of the left sandal and tugged. It gave a little but didn't break. She tried a second time, ignoring the sting of the cuffs digging into her skin, and actually heard the thing creak. Finally, on the third try, it snapped.

She slid her foot out and kicked the sandal up to her shackled hands. Grabbing the heel in her left hand, she found the top sandal strap with the most blood and was about to use her fingernail to scratch in the words "Jessie alive." Then she reconsidered. If they actually found the sandal and the note, that fact would be obvious.

She needed to convey something more useful. She thought about "see Isaac" but worried that if Andy found the shoe, she'd use the words as an excuse to kill another innocent civilian. But time was running short. She could hear from Andy's tone that she was almost done checking out the car. Any second now, she'd hand over the money, sign the paperwork, and start back over.

Ultimately, she chose two other words, ones she hoped wouldn't put Isaac at risk. They were more cryptic, but hopefully one of her colleagues would be able to make the connection. If not, at least she wouldn't have blood on her hands. She chuckled darkly through her gag at that thought, since she did literally have blood on her hands now.

"I think we can skip the title documents, don't you, Isaac?" she heard Andy say with a lilt. "Let's just keep this between you and me, shall we?"

Jessie didn't think she could generate another jolt of adrenaline but somehow one came. Without paperwork, Andy could simply put the car in drive and be over here in thirty seconds. There was no time to waste.

It would be easier to toss the sandal out the window closer to her head and hands, but that one also faced the road, which meant there was a better chance Andy would see it when she came to collect her. She'd have to try to fling it out the other window, down near her feet. It was a longer, much harder toss. Just as bad, the sandal would be on the wrong side of the car. No one would notice it unless they first noticed the car. By that point, it might be too late. But she didn't have much choice.

Clutching the heel of the sandal with both thumbs and forefingers, she flung it back across her body toward the window. It hit just above the open pane, before falling straight down, teetering briefly on the edge of the window, and toppling back onto the seat.

"Thanks again, Isaac!" Andy called out as the engine of the car revved across the street and the gravel crunched under the tires.

Jessie was too exhausted to panic. She stared at the sandal near her feet through narrowed eyes, as if it was her nemesis, personally out to get her. She refused to be defeated by a damned piece of footwear. Fully aware that she had mere moments left, she grabbed the thing with her toes and flicked it back up toward her hands. It landed well short of them, getting snagged in the space between where the back of the seat met the waistband of the sweatpants Andy had dressed her in.

Jessie would have laughed if she hadn't been concerned that Andy was close enough to hear the strangled grunting sound. In fact, Andy should have been pulling up by now. Why wasn't she?

Jessie pushed herself up just high enough to see the road. Strangely, Andy was driving the Mitsubishi away from Isaac's, back in the direction they'd come from as they entered the town. For a second, she was confused. But only until she saw Isaac waving to her from the outer gate of his lot. Andy *had* to drive away to avoid piquing his curiosity. Once she turned left onto a side street, he ambled back inside. Thirty seconds later, the Mitsubishi reappeared, slowly making its way back.

Jessie slumped back down, no longer able to support her weigh while battling the vicious bite of the cuffs. But as she did, a startling, amazing thing happened. While she was pushing upward to look outside, the sandal had been pinned between the back of the seat and her stomach. But as she dropped back to the seat, the sandal partially slid under the waistband of her sweatpants.

As Andy's new car came to a stop on the road just above where the Buick rested, Jessie decided that maybe the sandal wasn't her nemesis after all. She lifted up again, this time only slightly, then slid down again just enough for the shoe to lodge securely under the waistband. She wriggled slightly so that the oversized "Manilow's Mob" shirt covered any potential bulge that might be visible when Andy moved her. Only then, confident that if she stood up, the sandal wouldn't fall out of her waistband, did she allow herself to relax.

"Sorry I took so long," Andy said, her head suddenly appearing in the open window. "But we've got a new ride. You ready to go?"

Jessie nodded.

"Great," Andy said, seemingly heartened that her captive was being responsive. "Now I've got good news and bad for you. The bad news is that I have to put you in the trunk, at least for the next little while. And you will still have to stay cuffed. But here's the good news. If you promise me that you won't make a fuss when we move over to the other car, I won't tie your cuffs to anything. You'll be able to move your hands and feet around. Even better, once you're in the trunk, I'll remove the gag. Best of all, I'll give you a bottled water. I know you must be parched. Are those terms you can agree to, lady?"

Jessie nodded.

"Excellent. I think we may have finally turned a corner."

*

Jessie was glad to have the water, but it was brutal tradeoff.

The trunk wasn't roomy and whatever road they were on was incredibly bumpy. Every few seconds a new part of her body slammed into a section of metal or plastic. Still, it was nice to be able to breathe through her mouth. She wasn't sure how long she'd been back there when the car finally stopped but she guessed it was at least a half-hour.

Suddenly the trunk popped open, and a figure silhouetted against the blistering sun stared down at her with both hands full. After her eyes adjusted, Jessie saw that Andy was holding a water bottle in one hand and the switchblade in the other.

"What did I do to deserve that?" Jessie asked, nodding at the knife. "I've been stuck in the trunk this whole time."

"I just had to be cautious," Andy said sweetly. "I didn't know if you had tried to fashion your water bottle into a weapon or something. One can never be too careful. But you didn't. See how we're building that trust? It's good choices like that that will allow me to let you spend the rest of the ride in the backseat."

"Thanks," Jessie said, calling on all her willpower not to let sarcasm sneak into her voice as she started to lift herself upright.

"Hold on," Andy barked, holding her hand out like a stop sign. She was looking at Jessie's feet. "Where's your left sandal?"

Jessie looked down, trying to act surprised. She could hear her preferred response in her head: *Oh that? I tossed it under this car while you popped the trunk back near the auto body shop. It's lying on the shoulder of the road less than fifteen feet from the vehicle you caged me in for half a day, just waiting for someone to notice it, you psycho bitch.* But she didn't think that would go over so well. So, she went a different way.

"I'm not sure," she said, doing her best to appear genuinely perplexed. "I haven't had it in a while. Maybe it fell off at the travel center when you opened the door and undid that cuff for a while. It's all kind of hazy to me."

She hoped that by referencing the travel center, Andy would let it go. There was no way she would go back there at this point. Though unlikely, there was always the chance that the good Samaritan's body had already been discovered. It wasn't worth the risk. But from Andy's skeptical expression, she didn't appear to be buying it.

"What did you do with it?" she demanded, with none of the charm from earlier.

"I honestly have no idea what happened to it," Jessie lied. "Does it matter?"

Andy stared at her with silent fury. Jessie watched her force it down as she calculated just how much it did matter. It was just a shoe after all. Was that any more significant than if the Buick was found?

Jessie sensed that Andy was more upset that her captive had gotten one by her than by the ultimate import of the item itself. She also suspected that her kidnapper knew that it was too late to go back anyway. Based on Jessie's limited vantage point, it looked like they were deep in the desert now, with heavy brush, hills, and a dirt road as their only companions.

"You know what this means, don't you?" Andy asked.

"That we're not going to Disneyland after all?"

"It means that you'll have to stay in the trunk the rest of the way," Andy said, unamused, "and I'm afraid that we still have a long trip ahead of us. But I can offer you this."

She pulled a protein bar out of her pocket and tossed it into the trunk, along with the other bottle of water. Jessie was a little surprised she was even getting that.

Thanks," she said, leaning over to grab them.

As she did, she felt a prick in her left arm. She glanced back over her shoulder to see a syringe being removed.

"It's the same drug from just before your wedding," Andy said nonchalantly. "You remember how fast acting that was?"

Jessie did. She could already feel the edges of her brain getting fuzzy and her eyes and tongue growing heavy.

"I was just going to let you drift off by eating the protein bar. It's laced too. You could have slept in the backseat the whole way. But you clearly don't deserve that. Maybe a few extra bone bruises and a concussion or two will teach you a lesson."

Jessie could hear the words, but they sounded very far away, like they were being spoken on an old-timey telephone. She noticed that neither her wrists nor her ankles hurt anymore. She felt her body fall back and she knew that she had slumped into the trunk again, but she didn't actually feel it.

Andy said something else, but Jessie couldn't hear it anymore. She saw the trunk door start to close but she was out before it slammed shut.

CHAPTER SEVENTEEN

12:28 p.m., Sunday afternoon

Captain Roy Decker wasn't used to being nervous.

Sometimes he could go weeks without anything ruffling his feathers. But this was the second time in just a few hours that he'd found himself shifting uncomfortably in a chair outside the office of someone much more powerful than him.

This time he was outside the door of Richard Laird, the Los Angeles Police Department Chief of Police. He'd had to rush over here after listening in to the compelling, but ultimately fruitless helicopter chase along US-95 just minutes ago. His whole morning had been like that, pinballing back and forth between supervising the search for Jessie Hunt, and navigating a series of political landmines that threatened not just his career and the future of HSS, but potentially the credibility of the entire LAPD. The first such meeting had been tough. He anticipated this one being even worse.

"He'll see you now," the chief's assistant said.

Roy hadn't been expecting this. The meeting was scheduled for 12:30. Laird usually kept people waiting. Starting early would require him to state his case without all the firepower he'd been hoping to have at his disposal. He could try to stall, but that would look weak. And it wasn't really his style anyway.

"Thank you," he said, standing up slowly.

He felt all of his sixty-one years as he rose to his feet. His back ached, a remnant of the time he was pushed off the second-floor balcony of a bar while trying to break up a fight as a patrol officer in his early twenties. His knees cracked loudly, reminding him of the time in his late twenties when he allowed his squad car to be T-boned by the drunk driver of a pickup truck in order to prevent the guy from speeding through any more stop signs in a family-filled neighborhood on a Friday afternoon. As he stepped into the office, his left foot still had a dull burning sensation every time he put pressure on it, a gift from the drug dealer who shot him there during his first year as a narcotics detective.

"Thanks for stopping by, Roy," Laird said, even though he wasn't the one who'd requested the meeting. The chief, a diminutive man with too-white teeth and perfectly coiffed hair that was dyed aggressively blonde, didn't bother to get up from behind his desk to shake hands.

Roy wasn't surprised by any of it. While that was his first name, he had long ago noticed that the chief mostly used first names rather than titles as a way of undermining people who worked for him. It was as if he felt too threatened to give them their proper due.

It matched the rest of his persona perfectly. Around those he viewed to be more important than himself, like politicians and celebrities, there weren't enough honorifics to go around. But in the office, with people who reported to him, it didn't matter how many years they had on the job.

He was also an unrepentant self-promoter who never met a camera he didn't like. If he could do a press conference instead of releasing a statement, he would. If he could claim credit for someone else's bust, it would happen. If he could parlay good press into an invite to a red-carpet movie premiere, he was in heaven.

The downside of that to the rest of the department was that his thirst for media attention often led to poor management decisions, jeopardized cases, and now, finally, putting one of the department's own in mortal danger. Roy had enough of it.

"Thanks for making the time, Chief Laird," he said, betraying none of his true feelings.

"Quite a situation we have here with Robinson," Laird said, making no mention of the fact that there would be no "situation" if the chief himself hadn't pressed for Andrea Robinson to be released in the first place.

"Yes, sir."

"Well, let's have an update," Laird said, scooping up a spoonful of what looked like a yogurt parfait and shoving it in his mouth. It was important to stay trim when he was in the public eye so much.

"The suspect is still at large and Jessie's whereabouts are unknown, although we continue to believe she remains a captive," Roy detailed. "I just came from monitoring a chase along the California-Arizona border that turned out to be a misdirection on Robinson's part. We think that the women are still together and somewhere within a two-hundred-mile radius of the travel center where the body was found this morning."

Laird sighed heavily, and to Roy's mind, over-dramatically.

"Well, that's not what I was hoping to hear, Roy," he said with a sad shake of the head. "I think we may have reached an inflection point here."

"What do you mean?"

"Now that it's become a multi-state manhunt, or woman hunt," Laird corrected himself with a self-satisfied chuckle, "I think it's time we let the feds take over as primary on the case. We're well outside our jurisdiction at this point. And frankly, we can't afford to use up city resources at this clip. It's simply irresponsible."

Roy nodded in understanding, doing his best to keep his interior seething from bubbling to the surface.

"I see," he replied. "Did you plan to schedule a press conference to make that announcement?"

"Oh, I don't think that's necessary," Laird said, offering a dismissive hand wave. "A press release should suffice in this situation: just a line or two indicating that we're ceding authority to the FBI and expressing our deep hope that Ms. Hunt returns safely."

Roy glanced at his watch. The time was 12:32 but he couldn't wait any longer. He had reached his breaking point.

"No, sir," he said matter-of-factly. "We won't be handing over the case. We're keeping it in-house."

"What was that?" Laird asked, his mouth full of another scoop of parfait. He seemed unsure that he'd heard correctly.

"We're keeping the case," Roy repeated, keeping his voice level, refusing to betray the disdain he felt for the man in front of him. "Jessie Hunt is one of ours and we have a responsibility to get her back. I'm leading a joint operation task force from a command center based out of Central Station. Our HSS detectives and research unit are running point. All the relevant agencies are cooperating. I have two detectives on the scene, but travel is being provided by the FBI at no cost to us, so there's no concern about resource allocation. At this late time, it would be too disruptive to switch operational control. But you already know all this."

"I appreciate your concern for your team member, Roy," Laird said, wiping yogurt from his face with a linen napkin, "but it's not in the department's interest to take a leading role in this investigation."

"You mean it's not in *your* interest."

"Excuse me, Captain?" Laird said, using Roy's proper title for the first time as he stood up.

There was a knock on the door, followed immediately by someone swinging it wide open.

"Gentlemen, sorry I'm late."

Walking into the room was a tall, dark-haired Latino man in his early forties. He had the confident bearing of someone who didn't need permission from assistants before entering offices. That made sense, considering that he was the mayor of Los Angeles, Esteban Alvarez.

"Mr. Mayor," Laird said, clearly taken aback, "I didn't realize we had a meeting on the schedule."

"Actually, this is an impromptu gathering," Alvarez said enthusiastically. "I thought we should talk, Chief. And I asked Captain Decker to join us. Why don't we all come over to your dining table so it's not as stuffy?"

Laird came around from behind his desk and joined the other two men at the mahogany table with seating for four.

"What's this all about, Mr. Mayor?" Laird asked, sensing that something was off.

Alvarez put his hands on the table and clasped them together. Roy noticed that his jovial demeanor from just moments ago was gone, replaced by a more somber energy.

"Partly, it's about the unfortunate events of the last seventeen hours," Alvarez said," but in truth, I think we need to acknowledge that it's about something much deeper than that. I spoke with Captain Decker a few hours ago and, after our meeting, I had to face a reality that I'd been allowing myself to ignore for far too long now."

Laird looked over at Roy with suspicious eyes, then returned his attention to the mayor.

"I'm not sure I understand," he said with unconvincing naiveté.

"Of course you do," Alvarez told him. "In the last year alone, the following incidents have occurred. You covered up a situation involving former Commander Mike Butters, who was sleeping with an underage porn actress that was later murdered. You may recall that Sergeant Hank Costabile, who worked for the Commander, tried to have Jessie Hunt killed when she uncovered their affair. He's currently serving ten to fifteen at Lompoc."

"Sir, I—," Laird started to say.

"I'm far from done," Alvarez said, not stopping. "You also took multiple, large donations on behalf of the department from a dubious organization called the Eleventh Realm without properly vetting them. If you recall, the group turned out to be a cult that was sexually enslaving some of their members, something that Jessie Hunt also uncovered. That was a bit of a black eye, especially when the department had to return hundreds of thousands of dollars."

Laird looked like he wanted to respond but managed to restrain himself, which was good because Alvarez was on a roll now.

"And then I learned just this morning about a poor fellow named Jeff Sullivan, a plastic surgeon whose wife was murdered just three days ago. Even though he was cleared as a suspect by guess who—Jessie Hunt—you insisted he be kept behind bars. And why? Because we still had a serial killer going around stabbing people and you preferred the public think we had the murderer in custody, even if a newly grieving widower was being wrongly held."

"That's not an accurate—."

"And finally," the mayor plowed ahead as if Laird hadn't said a word, "you were Andrea Robinson's knight in shining armor. Despite repeated, clearly expressed concerns from Jessie Hunt that Robinson wasn't actually helping you solve crimes but rather might be manipulating the situation, you chose to disregard her warning. Let me reiterate that this was the very woman who caught Robinson for murder in the first place and who was almost killed by her in the process. And yet, even though she asserted that Robinson might be masterminding the attacks of her former, fellow inmates, you pressed ahead, championing Robinson's parole, fully aware that she had a fixation on Hunt."

He stopped talking, almost daring Laird to defend himself. The chief did not.

"It's almost as if, after all the bad press you suffered at Hunt's expense, you held a grudge against her. If I didn't know better, I'd think you were glad that Robinson was released, free to pursue her obsession with the woman who put her in prison for two years."

"Mr. Mayor," Laird said, putting on his best affronted tone. "Let me assure you that I would never—."

Alvarez stood up. Laird stopped talking.

"In light of this series of…missteps, I've decided it's time to make a change, Richard," the mayor said. "As of this moment you are no longer the police chief for the LAPD. Harry?"

Upon hearing his name called, a stocky officer with a giant neck stepped into the office.

"Yes, Mr. Mayor?"

"Richard, this is Officer Harold Downey," Alvarez said calmly. "He's the head of my security detail, as I believe you know. Officer Downey has coordinated with other officers to escort you from the building. You'll be taken to your home. As a courtesy, you will be allowed to remain in your uniform until you get there, when you can change into civvies and turn in what you're wearing, as well as any other department-issued attire that you may have in the house. You can hand over your phone now. Your personal effects will be boxed up and delivered to you before the end of business today. Do you understand?"

Laird most definitely did not look like he understood. Roy watched as his now-former boss sat at the table, open-mouthed, his eyes wide in disbelief. Finally, after several forced blinks, he seemed to comprehend the situation.

"Mr. Mayor—Esteban, don't you think this is a bit of an overreaction?' he pleaded. "I acknowledge that there was some poor judgment in the past, but at least give me the opportunity to rectify my mistakes."

"Frankly," Alvarez said, clearly unmoved, "you're lucky I don't recommend your arrest to the district attorney, although that's not off the table. There's an argument to be made that you aided and abetted in the abduction of Jessie Hunt. Your best move right now is to go home, and as hard as this will be for you, keep your mouth shut. No press conferences. No tweets. No one-on-one interviews with friendly media. Definitely *don't* trust your instincts. Officer Downey will assist you now."

Downey guided the still-stunned Laird out of the room, leaving Roy alone with the mayor. For several seconds neither man spoke. Roy tried to hide his shock at the sudden, dramatic turn of events when Alvarez stood up and extended his hand.

"Captain Decker, I'm appointing you as interim chief of police."

Now it was Roy's turn to have his jaw drop. When he'd gone to meet with Alvarez this morning, it was a desperate move to ensure that the search for Jessie wouldn't be short-circuited. Alvarez had promised it wouldn't. That was what this joint meeting was supposed to be about. But he had no idea that the mayor intended to fire Laird, much less that this mind-bending development was coming. He stood up too.

"Sir—Mr. Mayor, I'm flattered," he said, standing up as well, "but there's a chain of command. The next logical choice for interim chief would be Deputy Chief Molto."

"I'll well aware of that," Alvarez said. "But Molto is part of Laird's team. He brought him over when he came over from Cleveland. Same with most of the higher-ranking deputies and captains. They were either Ohio transplants or people Laird put in place once he got here. They're all indebted to him. I need someone more dedicated to this city than to Laird. How long have you been on the job here in L.A., Decker?"

"Next year will be my fortieth, sir."

"All right then," Alvarez said with a smile. "I think that qualifies you to handle the gig for a little while until we can start the search for a permanent hire. What do you say, Chief Decker?"

Roy found the logic hard to argue with. More importantly, he realized there was no point. The mayor of the city of Los Angeles had the authority to make this decision and he apparently already had. Roy's only options were to accept or retire. And he had no intention of retiring. A bubble of pride began to swell in his chest, but he forced it down. That was something he could indulge another time. Right now, there were bigger priorities.

"Yes, sir, thank you. I accept," he said, shaking the mayor's hand. "I appreciate your confidence in me. But I have to ask, what about the search for Robinson and Jessie Hunt? If I'm pulled off command of that, it'll be just as disruptive as if Laird took over."

"I get that," Alvarez said. "Don't worry. While this is your office now, I want you to go back to Central Station. Resolve this case. I'll contact you there regarding any administrative issues. But this is your top priority. Get Jessie Hunt back."

"That's the plan, Mr. Mayor," Roy said. "It always has been."

"I know it is," Alvarez said. "And I know that's why you came to see me in the first place. This situation is personal to you. But I need to be clear with you. What happened up to this point is a stain on Richard Laird. Anything that goes wrong going forward is on all of us—this department, this entire city. That's how the media will see it. That's how the public will see it. They won't care who's in charge. If Jessie Hunt dies, they'll just know that the profiler who caught some of the worst murderers this city has ever known was killed on our watch."

Roy shook his head.

"Believe me, Mr. Mayor," he said. "If she dies, it will be on me. And I don't intend to let that happen."

CHAPTER EIGHTEEN

6:31 p.m., Sunday evening

Hannah had a headache.

Part of it was from Kat's siren, which she had blasted at full volume on the entire drive from Redlands to the Ehrenberg Flying Y Travel Center, where they were now. She'd left it on to make up time after misidentifying a Buick heading the other way on the freeway. But considering that they'd been here for six hours, Hannah couldn't blame her headache exclusively on that.

Maybe it was because of the painfully uncomfortable argument a while back between Kat and Ryan. Even remembering that made her wince. She closed her eyes tight then opened them wide, hoping that might reset her throbbing head.

Nothing about the ache or her situation had changed. She was still in the travel center coffee shop, sitting with Kat and Callum at the very same table where Andy Robinson gave Roz Wallace her driving instructions almost exactly twelve hours earlier. She stood up and went outside to get some air.

As she leaned against the wall, trying to clear her head, she wondered where it had all gone so wrong, although she had a pretty good guess. She, Kat, and Callum had arrived at the travel center around 12:30 that afternoon, just after getting a text from Mitch Connor informing them of what had happened moments earlier.

It had read: *Robinson set us up. Had a drug addict drive same car north on US-95 starting at 10 a.m. Ryan thinks it was diversion so she could slip away unnoticed. Thinks she's driving a different car and didn't leave Ehrenberg area until after cops did. Will update when I know more. Love you.*

Soon after that, the helicopter with Ryan and Susannah Valentine returned to the travel center. Hannah had joined Kat and Callum as they rushed over, hoping to get more details from the detectives about the situation. But Ryan wouldn't tell them anything. He didn't even mention that there had been a chase. Kat went off on him, right there in the middle of the parking lot.

"I expect this from Decker," she chided as he brushed past her. "He's got to stick to department regulations and avoid stepping on toes, but I can't believe you're holding out on us, Ryan. You're just going to pretend like nothing happened out there? Why?"

"Kat," he implored, not slowing down as he marched toward the building. "I'm not deliberately holding out on you. I'm just being pulled in a million different directions."

"I get it," Kat said, keeping pace with him every step of the way while the rest of them trailed behind, "but we know Jessie better than anyone. We can help. And you're going to shut us out?"

Ryan stopped walking and spun around to face her.

"I just thought I saw my fiancée die less than a half hour ago," he snapped. "Forgive me if I'm not in a super chatty, information-sharing place right now."

"I'll bet you're sharing info with her!" Kat shot back, nodding at Susannah Valentine.

"What the hell is that supposed to mean?" Valentine demanded.

"Like you don't know," Kat hissed.

"I don't know where you think you get off—" Valentine growled, taking a step forward.

"Okay," Callum interjected calmly, sliding in between them, "Susannah, why don't you and I head over to the Cinnabon inside and get a little snack?"

He didn't wait for a response as he grabbed her forearm and pulled her away. Ryan stared at Kat.

"Setting aside the implication you just made," he said, his voice low and cold, "I'm trying to coordinate with multiple agencies across two states. Looping you in hasn't exactly been my top priority. I'm sorry if that hurts your feelings but I can't worry about that at the moment. Now if you'll excuse me, I'm going to go do my job."

That was six hours ago. The two of them hadn't spoken since. And whether it was coincidence or not, neither the law enforcement group nor the little trio of Hannah, Kat, and Callum had made any progress in the search for Jessie since.

Ryan, Valentine, and their team had taken over a suite at the Best Restin' Desert Dream hotel next door, the same place where Roz Wallace had spent last night. The B Team, as Hannah had taken to calling their group, sat at the coffee shop, making use of the travel center's Wi-Fi to do their research.

Hannah looked through the window at Kat and Callum, hunched over the table, studying the documents that Kat had collected on Andy Robinson when trying to prevent her release from prison. Suddenly she felt guilty for being out here in the fresh air, headache or not. Besides it was getting chilly. The sun would be setting in the next half-hour. She went back inside.

She sat down at the table and looked for a new pile of documents to review. She picked up one labeled "prison correspondence" and opened it up.

"That's a dead end," Kat said. "Most of the letters are to powerful former friends, asking them to exert influence. Not a single one responded."

Hannah sighed in frustration. She was about to toss the file when something she couldn't explain stopped her.

"You said most of the letters were to former friends," she noted. "Not all?"

"Yeah," Kat said. "There was one in there that I couldn't identify. It was a postcard to someone back east. Ginny maybe? Something like that. There was no last name and with the crush of documents, I didn't have time to look into it. But it was returned to sender too."

Hannah flipped through the letters until she found it. It was a basic postcard with a "Hollywood" sign backdrop. It read simply: *Rinny, Miss the good times. Andy*

It seemed innocuous enough, although Hannah had learned that nothing Andy Robinson did was ever as innocent as it seemed. Then she noticed the address.

"Did you see where it was sent?' she asked holding it out.

Kat looked up absently.

"Yeah," she said. "That's right. Rinny, not Ginny. I checked the address. There was no one with anything close to the name Rinny at that location."

"But the address is Nantucket," Hannah said. "Doesn't Andy own a place there too?"

"Yeah," Kat replied. "I assumed that's how she knew Rinny—that he or she was another powerful friend from back in the "good times."

"But Andy never asks Rinny for help in the postcard," Hannah pointed out.

Kat looked up again, less dismissive this time.

"That's a good point."

"That's a really good point," Callum agreed.

Hannah had an idea.

"Callum, do you think Jamil would be willing to help us out again?"

The retired detective shifted uncomfortably.

"I'm hesitant to go back to that well."

"Would you be willing to call him and then put him on the phone with me?" she asked sweetly.

Callum smiled.

"You seem like a nice young, lady but you're actually a killer, aren't you?"

The words sent a shiver down Hannah's back. Callum Reid was just joking around but he didn't realize that his words were literally true. Not only was she a killer with a taste for the thrill that it provided, but she had also gone to rehab so she didn't have a relapse. Of course he didn't know any of that.

"You have no idea," she told him.

Callum pulled out his phone and called Jamil.

"Hey buddy," he said warmly.

Hannah couldn't hear Jamil's response, but it was brief and apparently terse.

"Don't give me that," Callum said. "I know you guys haven't had a quality hit in hours. You can surely spare a minute for an old, broken-down veteran cop who has given his body and soul in the service of our fair city."

As Jamil replied, Callum winked at Hannah. Despite his worn features and lack of sleep, he had a buoyant energy and an impish smile. She could tell that he was rejuvenated by actually being involved in a case that mattered.

"Listen, my young genius friend, I'm not trying to make you feel guilty," he said. "I'll leave that to others more sophisticated than myself. But rather than talk your ear off, I have someone else here who would like a word. Hold on a second."

As he handed over the phone to her, he whispered, "Make it good, Ms. Sophisticated."

Hannah gave him a wink of her own as she took the phone

"Hi Jamil, this is Hannah Dorsey. Do you remember me?"

There was a several second pause.

"Of course, you were on my office couch this morning," he finally said awkwardly. "How are you?"

"I've been better," she answered. "As you know, my sister was kidnapped by a psycho, and I'm worried she might kill her. But after hours of fruitless hunting, I think I might have a lead that could just possibly go somewhere. Unfortunately, I don't have the technical skill to pursue it on my own. But I know you do. I also know that your big command center team has hit a dead end too. So, I was hoping that, even though I'm not a part of that team, you could do me a solid and help me out."

"Um, I'm not suppose to liaise with people outside the department—"

"Jamil," she interrupted, trying to sound as charming as she'd heard Jessie be in these situations. "I know the official line on this. But I also know that it wouldn't take a fraction of your skill to help me out. And this could be the break that brings Jessie back. We're talking about my big sister, the only family I have left. I promise I won't tell anyone outside of our little circle. Will you please help me out, Jamil?"

The line was quiet for a few seconds.

"Let's make it quick," he finally whispered.

"Great," she replied. "I'm putting you on speaker with Callum and Kat Gentry too. The first thing I need is everything you have on the property ownership records for an address in Nantucket."

She gave it to him, and they all waited quietly, listening to him type over the phone.

"I have it belonging to an Arnaud Renault of Paris," Jamil said. "It's his family's summer residence. He bought it last spring."

"That's what I had too," Kat noted.

"What about before that?" Hannah pressed.

"Prior to that, it was operated by a holding company," he said, before adding, "hold on."

"What?" Hannah asked.

"This is interesting," Jamil. "The name of the holding company that operated payments and upkeep of the house has changed multiple times over the last forty years, but they were all subsidiaries of the same foundation, TDR."

"Do we know what that is?" Callum asked.

"We will in a minute," Jamil replied, but it only took ten seconds. "It looks like that's a foundation started by brothers Thoreau and Daniel Robinson. Thoreau was Andrea Robinson's father, who died when she was in graduate school. Daniel was her uncle. It seems they wanted to claim that home, along with another just up the beach, as a charitable deduction rather than as a vacation property. Andrea used the other house as a vacation residence. The one you asked about was most often inhabited by someone named Erin Reed, who sold it outright last April."

Hannah looked up at Hannah and Callum.

"Rinny," she said quietly, "Could be a nickname for Erin."

"And since Andy was in prison," Kat added, "she wouldn't necessarily have known that Erin had moved."

"Who is Erin Reed, Jamil?" Callum asked.

"I'm glad you asked, Detective," Jamil said, forgetting that Callum was retired as he started to get into the spirit of the endeavor. "Reed is formerly Erin Robinson, daughter of Daniel Robinson and first cousin of Andrea Robinson."

"Do we know if Erin and Andy are close?" Kat wondered.

"A good question," Jamil replied, "which is why I've already pulled up all her social media. It seems that she makes no mention of her cousin anywhere, which isn't a shocker considering Andy Robinson's reputation, but let's pull up some of her deleted posts from before Andy was arrested."

"You can do that?" Hannah asked, aghast.

"I can do a lot of things," Jamil said. "Remember, the internet is forever."

Hannah looked across the table at Kat and Callum. Neither of them seemed anywhere near as troubled as she was that old, deleted posts, could be sucked out of the ether, and used by anyone with the technical skill to take advantage of them. It only took another second for her to feel silly that she'd ever been so naïve as to assume that wasn't the case.

"So, we've got some stuff here," Jamil said. "I don't know how meaningful it is, but I can pass it along."

"What kind of stuff?" Kat asked.

"Nothing overtly suspicious," Jamil replied. "Mostly photos of them together when they were younger. It looks like Reed just wanted to scrub any connection to Andy to avoid the embarrassment of having a killer for a cousin."

"How much younger are we talking in those photos?" Callum wanted to know.

"I'm not great at gauging ages," Jamil admitted, "but they look pretty little in some of them. I'd guess that they were as young as seven or eight. The collection goes on for quite a few years. It looks like they used to spend summers together. There are lots of picture of them on horses and swimming in a stream, that sort of thing."

As Jamil spoke, Hannah's brain started to do that thing where it began to hum, warning her that she should be paying attention, even if she wasn't always quite sure why. But this time she knew the reason.

"What's the oldest you'd say they are in those pictures?" she asked.

"Early teens, maybe?"

"Fourteen?" Hannah asked leadingly.

Kat and Callum both waited on the answer, sensing where she was going.

"Hard to say for sure," he replied. "Why?"

"Never mind," she said. "You mentioned that there were horses and a stream. Did this look like a summer camp?"

"No," he answered. "It's only ever just the two of them in the photos. I'd say it looks more like a ranch."

Based on the sudden gasp they collectively shared, all three people at the table clearly had the same idea at once. Kat pointed at Hannah.

"Go ahead," she said. "This is your rodeo."

Hannah didn't need to be told twice.

"Jamil," she asked hesitantly, almost afraid of what his answer might be, "Can you check Erin Reed's other property records to see if she owns a ranch?"

"One sec," he said, typing furiously, before suddenly stopping. The long pause told her they'd hit paydirt. "As a matter of fact, she owns a large ranch property in Bouse, Arizona, which is approximately forty miles from where you're sitting right now. It's called Rintoo Ranch. She inherited it from her father when he passed away five years ago."

Nobody said a word for a good ten seconds.

"You know, I'm obligated to share this information with Detective Hernandez," Jamil finally said.

Hannah could hear the reluctance in his voice and knew where it came from. It wasn't that he didn't want Ryan to know. It was that he'd be asked how he figured it out and that would inevitably lead to the revelation that he'd been talking to the B team.

"No," Hannah said, "we'll tell him. Kat had access to a lot of these records from when she was doing a deep dive into Andy Robinson's background. If you don't mind missing out on the credit for finding the ranch, you can avoid any consequence for working with us too. Send us the address and I promise we'll give it to Ryan soon as we hang up with you."

"I feel like I'm violating protocol here," Jamil said under his breath.

"You are," Kat acknowledged. "But none of us is going to tell. And if it gets Jessie back, who gives a damn, right?"

Jamil was quiet for a second before replying.

"Texting you the address now."

"Got it," Hannah said once it arrived.

"Go get her," Jamil whispered, then hung up.

Kat smiled across the table at her.

"Okay," she said. "Looks like you're headed to the Best Restin' across the street."

"Uh-uh," Hannah replied, shaking her head. "No way I'm giving him this. You're the one who's going to walk into that suite and hand him that address."

"I think that would be a bad idea," Kat objected.

"You're mistaken," Hannah said, standing up. "You were upset earlier. Then he got upset. It's understandable. This is a pretty tense situation. But no good is going to come from you two giving each other the cold shoulder. We all need to be working together. That's how we get Jessie back. So go over there, give him this lead as a peace offering, and smooth things over."

Kat nodded.

"You're right," she said. "I've been letting my bruised ego get in the way. I can't believe a seventeen-year-old kid is being more mature than the supposed adults around here."

"Hey, I've been pretty mature about the whole thing too," Callum noted, raising his hand. "Don't I get any credit?"

Hannah gave him a playful smirk before turning back to Kat.

"But remember, after you've made nice, make sure to extract your pound of flesh."

"What do you mean?" Kat asked.

"Take him away from where the others can hear you and remind him who came up with this lead," Hannah said. "Insist that from now on, he make us equal partners. Even if he has to do it on the down-low, he needs to keep us looped in. I know the guy. There's no way he'll say no after that."

"Wow," Kat said, impressed. "Aren't you the onion? Every few minutes, we pull back another layer."

"Here's one more for you," Hannah said, starting to get the hang of this thing. "Once you pass that address along, get back here quick."

"Why?"

"Because we're paying a visit to that ranch too."

CHAPTER NINETEEN

Jessie tried not to freak out.

It wasn't easy, considering that after she opened her eyes, she remained in darkness.

She was still groggy, so it took a few seconds to remember why she couldn't see. She knew she was in the trunk, where she'd been dumped just after Andy had dosed her again with whatever drug she'd used to knock her out at her wedding.

But the darkness was especially unsettling for another reason. When she'd been in the trunk earlier, after they'd left Isaac's Auto Body, small streaks of sunlight had snuck in through tiny slits. There was none of that now. That could only mean one of two things. Either she was indoors or it was nighttime.

The sudden jolt that made her back slam against the top of the roof told her that it wasn't the former. The car must have been temporarily stopped to traverse some obstruction, but now it was moving again, bouncing mercilessly along the pockmarked surface that passed for a road.

A few times she thought they were stuck, but Andy managed to gun the accelerator or turn the wheels at just the right angle to get out of trouble. After another five minutes the vehicle finally came to another stop and Jessie heard the engine turn off.

The trunk popped open to reveal that she'd been wrong. It wasn't quite nighttime yet. In the distance, she could see the sun setting behind some nearby hills. In another fifteen minutes, she figured that it would be completely gone.

Jessie estimated that it was about 7 p.m., though she couldn't be sure. Since she didn't know how far they'd traveled since she'd been drugged, she couldn't accurately gauge the time. Other than being in the desert, she had no idea where they were. The sun set at different times, depending on their location, and they easily could have gone as far east as Utah or New Mexico by now.

"Nice to see you up, sleepyhead," Andy said as she stepped into view, blotting out the light. She wore a headlamp and had on a small backpack. "You need to get out. We're not done traveling yet and it's getting dark. You don't want to step on a rattlesnake out here at night. It doesn't usually go well."

Jessie didn't respond as she carefully extricated herself from the trunk. Her whole body felt like one giant bruise. Andy pointed her toward a nearby tree and she limped over slowly, appalled at how unresponsive her limbs were to her brain's instructions.

"Give me a second," Andy said, as she attached the handcuffs to a high, thick, tree branch.

Then she returned to the Mitsubishi, put it in neutral, and slowly pushed it down a slight slope into a nearby culvert. After that, she covered the top of the car with some brush. It was virtually invisible. Jessie doubted that it would be much easier to see in daylight, even if someone knew what to look for and was standing just yards away.

Andy returned, unhooked her from the branch, and pointed off to the right.

"Follow that game trail. I'll be right behind you."

"What trail?" Jessie asked sincerely. She didn't see one.

"The opening in the brush over there," Andy said. "The grass beyond it is flattened out, where animals have passed through. Go that way."

Jessie did her best to follow what she thought was the flatter grass. With just one sandal and traversing such uneven ground, each step was treacherous. Every now and then, Andy redirected her, prodding her in the back with a thick stick she'd found along the way. Jessie considered trying to grab it, beat her kidnapper to a pulp, and walk back out. But that seemed risky for a number of reasons.

First, it was almost completely dark now, other than Andy's headlamp. Plus, it was getting cold, and Jessie only had the sweatpants and Barry Manilow shirt. She was weak and sore, and her hands and ankles were cuffed together. Finally, she had no idea where she was. There might be a phone in that backpack but then again, there might not. The safer bet seemed to be to wait until the odds were a little more even.

"We're here," Andy said a couple of minutes later.

Jessie stopped. She guessed that they'd walked about a mile but didn't see anything that signified "here." All that surrounded them was more brush, along with cactus and some big bushes. Andy stepped over to one large bush and grabbed at it, giving a hard tug. To Jessie's surprise, the top slid off.

Her exhausted brain needed a moment to process that the top was actually a tarp and that the bush was a very old crew cab pickup truck. The cargo bed was piled high with duffel bags and coolers. Jessie's heart sank. There looked to be enough supplies to last weeks. If there was ever an any doubt, it was gone now. Andy was clearly in this for the long haul.

"Get in," she ordered.

Once Jessie was strapped into the passenger seat—an upgrade—with her hand cuffed to the center console, Andy got in the driver's seat, and turned on the ignition. The engine wheezily coughed to life.

"Ready for our final journey?" she asked excitedly. "Next stop, our new home."

She didn't wait for an answer, instead putting the truck in drive and moving ahead slowly but steadily. There was no road that Jessie could discern, only a path that appeared to exist in Andy's head. They went over some tough territory, including an impressively deep creek and an incline that threatened to make everything in the back topple out. But after a while, (still fighting off the after-effects of the drugging, she couldn't be sure how long) they rounded a series of rocks, and the truck came to a stop.

"We're here," Andy said giddily.

Jessie followed the woman's gaze, tracking the line of the headlights. At first, she wasn't sure that she understood what she was looking at. But as Andy inched the truck closer, it became clear to Jessie exactly where she'd been taken and why.

The realization filled her with dread as one thought clawed its way above all the others in her brain.

They'll never find me here.

CHAPTER TWENTY

7:17 p.m., Sunday night

Ryan watched the cattle scatter.

As the helicopter began to descend toward an open patch of grass on the Rintoo Ranch, a woman he guessed to be in her early thirties stormed out of the main house. She had a shotgun in one hand and a flashlight in the other. He didn't blame her, considering that they hadn't called ahead.

In the distance, he could see two lines of law enforcement vehicles approaching from different directions on one-lane dirt roads, their lights bright in the nearly dark sky as they approached the ranch. They were coming from multiple agencies across two states, and some would arrive in less than two minutes.

This time he waited for the rotor blades to come to a stop before getting out and walked slowly toward the woman, whose flashlight was shining in his face. He kept his arms out wide at his side. One hand was empty. The other held his LAPD badge and ID.

"You've got some nerve landing that thing on my property like this," she shouted. "I'd be well within my rights to lay you out first and ask questions later."

"I'm not sure that's entirely true, ma'am," he said, making sure his tone was firm but relaxed. "You might not get the benefit of the doubt from a jury later on, considering that I'm properly displaying my identification. I also don't think my partner, who has her weapon trained on you as I speak, would appreciate you—how did you describe it—laying me out. Nor would the nearly two dozen officers driving this way right now. So, what do you say we lower the temperature a little bit? You put away that shotgun and I'll explain why we showed up in your backyard via helicopter without calling first?"

The woman didn't lower the shotgun, but she did move the flashlight over from Ryan's face to his ID.

"Does that say LAPD?"

"It does," Ryan assured her. "I'm Detective Ryan Hernandez. You're Erin Reed. And I'm pretty sure that you can guess why I'm here. Have you seen the news lately?"

Erin Reed lowered the shotgun.

"Andy?" she asked.

"That's right," he said. "We need to talk about your cousin."

"You better come inside."

*

Ryan watched Erin closely, making allowances for her situation.

It was clearly hard for her to concentrate with over twenty officers moving in and out of her living room, shouting at each other in person and over radios, all while he tried to question her.

He noticed that while she was the same age as her cousin—thirty-three—she looked older, more worn down somehow. Her hair was also blonde, but unlike Andy's, it was brittle. Her eyes were blue, but not blazingly so. She looked like a washed-out version of her more vibrant L.A. relative.

"We can do this somewhere else if they're too distracting," he offered for a second time, nodding at the officers as he, Reed, and Valentine sat in chairs in a corner of the room.

"No," Erin said. "I feel more comfortable knowing what's going on. But how much longer is this going to take?"

"They need to finish searching every building on the property and the surrounding area," Valentine explained. "Vehicles are also examining the boundaries of the property all the way to the fence lines in every direction. They're also talking to everyone currently on the ranch. How many did you say that was again?'

"Other than me, there are just four ranch hands here right now," Erin explained. "They live in the back house."

"Besides them, you live here alone?" Valentine pressed.

"Usually my son is here too, but he's with his dad for a few weeks."

"You're divorced?" Valentine asked, even though she knew the answer. Ryan understood that she was probing, testing to see how the woman would react to sensitive questions, but his area of interest lay elsewhere.

"Yes," Erin said without malice. "It was finalized last spring. I had been living back east but I wanted a simpler life. A lot of the best memories of my youth are from here so I decided to come back; to give

Danny a chance to live in a less structured environment. You know, the ranch is partly named for me. My name is Erin and my mom's name was Marin. When I was little, I used to say that I was a 'Rin too,' like her. So Dad named it Rintoo Ranch."

Her eyes clouded over, and it was clear that she was focused on a memory from long ago. Ryan almost felt bad about pulling her back from it, but not enough that he didn't do it.

"Erin, has Andy contacted you at any point in the last few days?"

"No," she said adamantly, snapping back into the present.

"What about any time prior to that—earlier this week or during her time in prison?"

She shook her head vigorously.

"I haven't heard from her at all," she insisted, "not for years."

"What was the nature of your relationship?" he asked.

"We had none," Erin told him, "I mean, not anymore. We were really close as kids. We'd visit each other all the time, every year. I would go stay with her in Los Angeles, usually over the holidays. She would come out here for a few weeks in the summer. We had such a great time. Then she just stopped coming."

"Why?" Valentine asked.

"I have no idea. She always had an excuse as to why she couldn't make it. We still saw each other from time to time when I would come to L.A. But then she started finding ways to conveniently be gone when I'd come into town. She cut off contact completely a few years ago, even before all this killing stuff happened. I felt like there had to be a specific reason, but I didn't know what it was."

"You never got any kind of explanation for the break in communication?" Ryan wanted to know.

"No," she said. "I tried to reach out many times, but she wasn't interested. Eventually I gave up. We lost touch completely. But I still kept tabs on her. I mean, I was aware that she had problems as a teenager, got into some trouble, even went to juvie for a while. She got sent off to a boarding school and a military academy. But she seemed to set herself straight after that, went to college, was even working on her master's in chemical engineering until her dad died and she dropped out. You know that's how our family got rich, right? Her dad invented some polymer when we were toddlers. This ranch and everything else came from that invention. Anyway, to answer your question, we weren't in touch when I heard the news."

"About the murder," Ryan confirmed.

"About all of it," Erin replied. "I thought she was leading the life of a boring, country club lady of leisure. Then I find out that she was having an affair with a married guy, killed his wife, framed the maid, and tried to kill the profiler who figured it out. When I heard the news, despite having lost contact with her, it was still a shock. I had no idea she was capable of any of that."

Just then, one of the officers came into the room and walked over. Ryan recognized him as the Deputy Sheriff from La Paz County, which had jurisdiction in this part of Arizona.

"Sorry to interrupt, Detective Hernandez," he said.

"What have you got?" Ryan asked.

"We still have units searching the perimeter of the property along the fence line, but it's not looking promising. We haven't found anyone unexpected in the buildings or any sign of vehicles other than ones we can account for. We'll keep looking, but I don't think they're here."

Ryan tried to hide his disappointment. How was that possible? When Kat had brought him the information, it had seemed like a home run. The ranch was in the immediate area of the travel center. It was clearly well known to Andy but not obviously traceable through records searches. It was well off the beaten path.

And yet, they had come up empty again. Was this another diversion? Did Andy know they would come here? Was she off somewhere, laughing at them? That seemed unlikely. Finding this ranch had been challenging. As far as false leads went, it felt like an elaborate one without much payoff. Despite what the deputy was telling him, he wasn't ready to give up yet.

"Check it again, please," he said. "Robinson might have set up some kind of hiding spot here, even without her cousin's knowledge. Look at any structure, be it a hunting blind or a well. It might be masking something underground."

He looked over at Valentine, who said nothing, though her skeptical expression spoke volumes. He ignored it and focused on Erin Reed.

"I'm afraid we're going to need your phone, ma'am," he said. "I can get a warrant if I have to, but it would save a lot of time, and potentially someone's life, if you just handed it over."

"Why?"

"We need to confirm that you haven't been in communication with Andy."

"You don't believe me," she said, apparently hurt, "after everything I told you?"

"It's not a matter of believe, Ms. Reed," he said without emotion. "My job is to get Jessie Hunt back safely and I will use every tool at my disposal to accomplish that task. Nothing else matters to me right now, certainly not your bruised feelings. So, are you going to make this easy or hard?"

She handed over the phone.

CHAPTER TWENTY ONE

8:02 p.m., Sunday night

Ross felt like an idiot.

He should have gone to the bathroom back at the travel center in Ehrenberg. Janet had even warned him that he'd regret it if he didn't. But he just hadn't needed to go at the time. Of course, now he did—badly.

In fact, he wasn't even sure he could make it to the gas station at the next exit in the tiny town of Quartzsite. Desperate, he pulled off the freeway one exit earlier, got off the access road, and rolled to a stop on the shoulder, along the first dark stretch of road that he could find.

"What are you doing?" Janet hissed. "There's nothing here."

"I can't wait. I really have to pee," he insisted as he hopped out. "I'll just use the car to block the view and go on the side of the road. It's no big deal."

"But what if someone comes by?" she pleaded. "What if a cop comes by? You could get arrested!"

But it was too late. He was already taking care of his business. As he finished up, he noticed an old, abandoned, beat up car in the ditch just below the shoulder.

"Podunk town," he muttered to himself.

When he was done, he walked back around the front of the car, pulling some hand sanitizer out of his pocket as he walked. He wasn't looking where he was going and tripped over something on the shoulder. He landed hard, slamming his knee into the gravel.

"Damn!" he grunted, grabbing his leg in pain.

"Are you okay?" Janet asked from the passenger seat.

"Yeah," he said, "I just tripped over this stupid—."

He stopped, staring at the thing that had led to his discomfort. It was a shoe, a sandal actually. But that wasn't what had made him stop mid-sentence. The white sandal, illuminated in the car's headlights, seemed to be caked in what looked very much like blood. And etched into the blood were two words: *car corpse*.

"What is it?" Janet asked.

"I…it's just…. there's this sandal on the shoulder of the road and it's kind of weird."

"Weird, how?"

"It looks like there might be blood on it," Ross said, "and also writing."

Janet was quiet for a moment, before asking the inevitable question.

"What does it say?"

"Car corpse," Ross told her. "And it looks like it was scratched into the blood."

"Huh?" Janet said, apparently not sure if he was messing with him. "What the hell does that mean?"

"I don't know," he admitted.

"I think someone in this town is bored and figured this was a way to freak people out," she told him.

"Yeah," Ross said, "except there's a car in the ditch right there. You don't think—?"

Neither of them spoke for a while. The only sound was the zoom of cars speeding by on the freeway a few hundred yards north.

"We have to call the police," Janet finally said.

"But it could be nothing, like you said," Ross protested. "A prank."

"Maybe, but what if it's not?"

"I could just go down there and…look."

"No way," Janet told him. "Who knows what's down there? Besides, if there really is a body in that car, then this is a crime scene. You shouldn't touch anything, shouldn't go near it. Bumping that shoe might have disturbed evidence. Let's just call the cops and let them figure it out. If it turns out it was a prank, then they got us, and we're the butt of some local joke. But if it's real, we can't just do nothing."

"We're supposed to be in Phoenix tonight," Ross complained. "Our reservation will be canceled if we arrive after midnight."

"Ross Rydell," Janet said in the tone he most hated to hear from her. "How are you going to feel if we drive off and do nothing and someone's daughter is dead in that car? We might have a daughter someday. Now get out your phone and call 911 before I turn *you* into a corpse."

*

"Thanks, Jamil," Ryan said. "It was worth a shot."

He hung up and gave Erin Reed back her phone. Valentine raised her eyebrows from across the room where she was conferring with the deputies who'd interviewed the ranch hands. Ryan shook his head.

Erin Reed's phone was clean. There was no sign that she'd had any contact with Andy Robinson recently. In fact, their last communication was a text she sent four years ago, saying she was coming to L.A., would be taking her son to Disneyland, and did Andy want to come too. There was no reply.

He walked over to listen in to the deputies' updates with Valentine when his phone rang. It was a FaceTime call from one of the Phoenix-based FBI agents who'd been part of the team.

"What's up, Dean?" he asked once the agent came on the screen.

"Hey Ryan, I'm in Quartzsite, about eighteen miles east of the travel center and twenty-six miles southwest of your current location. I need you to look at something."

"Okay."

Agent Dean Bland held out his phone, showing what looked to be the shoulder of a road. It was brightly lit. As Dean moved forward, he focused the camera on something out of focus on the ground. Even before the image cleared up, Ryan knew what it was.

"That's one of Jessie's sandals from the wedding," he said.

All conversation in Erin Reed's living room stopped.

"That's what I wanted to confirm with you," Dean said. "There's writing on it, Ryan."

He held the phone close enough for Ryan to read the words. He could feel panic start to clutch at his chest.

"Listen," Dean said quickly. "There is a vehicle in a ditch near the shoulder, but as far as we can tell, there's no body in it. But the car looks to be the Buick we've been searching for all this time."

"Have you got a CSU team en route?" Ryan asked.

"They'll be here in ten minutes," Dean said.

"Good," Ryan said. "Text me the exact location. With any luck, I'll be there around the same time."

It occurred to him that he needed to let Kat, Hannah, and Callum know what was going on too. He'd been so caught up in searching the ranch that he hadn't time to give them any updates. But they deserved to know that it had been a bust.

At least now he could soften that with news of another potential lead. And since they were only twenty miles away from Quartzsite, he could even give them the address. After all, he needed them there.

It was clear to him that Jessie had written that message on the sandal and left it for them, hoping they would find it and decipher it. But if there was no one dead in the vehicle in the ditch, then he had no idea what "car corpse" meant. Maybe one of them could figure it out.

"One more thing," Dean said, making Ryan realize he'd forgotten to hang up.

"What?"

"The sandal is covered in dried blood. It looks like the words were scratched out of it."

"I'm sorry, out of what?" Ryan asked, confused.

"Out of the blood."

CHAPTER TWENTY TWO

Jessie would have panicked if she could have.

The only reason she hadn't was that she was too tired and sore. Otherwise, the moment that Andy started driving the pickup toward an abandoned mine entrance nestled at the base of a large hill surrounded by overgrown brush, she would have tried to rip free of the cuff attaching her to the truck's center console, even if it meant breaking her wrist.

But she hadn't. Instead, she'd sat quietly as Andy pulled up to the mine opening. As her captor got out and undid the padlock on the rusty, sand-covered, metal gate, Jessie read the signs posted out front.

One read "Danger! Abandoned Mine. Stay Out!" Another read "This mine has a history of cave-ins. It is unstable and may collapse at any time. Stay clear!" A third read "Dangerous area. Toxic gasses. Poorly Ventilated. Rotten Timber. Falling Rocks." And if that wasn't enough, one last sign read "Entry not permitted by order of La Paz County. Violators may be fined or imprisoned."

The chances that anyone would ever come across this place, in the middle of nowhere, were infinitesimal. Other than the signs, which were tattered, rusted, and partially covered by brush, the mine blended into the landscape.

Even if someone did stumble across it, they'd have no reason to think any human would voluntarily go inside, much less set up camp here. The only way they'd ever find her here was if a recovery crew inadvertently uncovered her crushed carcass after the inevitable implosion.

"What do you think?" Andy asked once she got back in the truck.

"Looks homey," Jessie replied, unable to hide her disdain.

"I know the exterior can be intimidating but give it a chance."

Jessie didn't respond as Andy drove inside, re-fastened the padlock, and inched the truck ahead through the mine shaft. It was a tight fit, and the roof scraped the rocks periodically. After about thirty yards, they rounded a bend and continued another fifty yards until coming to a spot where the space opened up slightly. Andy steered the vehicle into a darkened corner that Jessie hadn't noticed was there, turned off the ignition, and unlocked the cuff.

"We're here," she said as if they'd just arrived at a summer beach house.

Jessie got out and trudged along beside Andy until they arrived at two heavy, soundproof, metal curtains attached to poles drilled into the rock walls. Andy pulled them back dramatically. Jessie needed a second to process what she saw.

Beyond the curtains was a cavernous space, easily the size of the sanctuary for a moderately-sized church. The giant room was modestly furnished. It had a small wooden table with two wooden chairs, a couple of cots and even a few pieces of patio furniture. There was also a long flat slab of rock on a raised platform in the middle of the room.

At the far end of the cavern were a series of large plastic cabinets, the kind that could be purchased from a big warehouse store and assembled at home. In front of them was a high-topped table, almost like a small kitchen island.

As if all that wasn't enough, behind that was a freezer, a small refrigerator, and what looked to be an electric stove. Each of them was hooked up to a generator in the corner, as were a series of lights embedded into the rocks at various places.

"Come on in," Andy said, leading her to a patio chair with a cushioned back.

Once Jessie sat down, Andy took the handcuff and quickly connected it to a metal ring that had been nestled unobtrusively behind the chair. The ring was attached to a square metal plate that had been screwed into the rock slab in the middle of the cavern. As a result, Jessie could only move that arm about twelve inches in any direction. She couldn't go anywhere.

"That's not very welcoming," she said.

"Sorry," Andy said. "But after the incident with our travel center friend and the missing sandal, you're going to have to earn back my trust. Still, you should be happy. You might be tied up, but at least you get to take a load off. I'm the one who has to bring in all those supplies."

Jessie desperately wanted to make a crack about how, yes, it was really Andy who had it rough in this situation, but she stopped herself. That wouldn't help her get out of this place. She wondered if this new environment might be the ideal opportunity to change the dynamic.

After all, she had chosen not to make a move in the darkened desert in the hopes of finding a better time for one.

Here, with the stress of avoiding capture gone, and the possibility of their "new life" in sight for Andy, it seemed like the perfect time and place. If Jessie could reduce the tension between them, maybe Andy would lower her guard. Nothing else had worked so she might as well try.

"Before you start unloading stuff," she said, "could I make a request?"

Andy looked at her skeptically.

"Please don't ask for a cell phone, Jessie," she said darkly. "It's been a long day and I'm not in the mood."

"No, I was just hoping that you might have some ointment for my wrists and ankles where the cuffs have been digging into the skin. I think they might be starting to get infected. And if you've got any, I'd love some ibuprofen, like maybe ten of them. The cuts really sting and the bruises from riding in the trunk make it hard to move and you know, breathe. I also wouldn't mind a piece of bread and bottle of water if you have it."

Andy stared at her, the expression on her face unchanged. Then it softened.

"Of course," she said. "You'll have to forgive me. I've been out of practice as a hostess. I can get you all that and more. How about a drink? I have some vodka in the freezer. I can mix up something for you to take the edge off. I promise not to slip in any peanut oil this time."

She chuckled gently at the memory of the time she'd tried to kill Jessie by pouring the liquid into her cocktail, fully aware that her guest was deathly allergic to all things peanut. It was right after she realized that Jessie had discovered that she'd murdered her lover's wife. Jessie wasn't as amused by the memory.

"Water will be fine, thanks."

"Okay, okay," Andy said, holding up her hands. "I guess on that front, I'm the one who needs to earn back a little trust."

She walked over and put the key to the handcuff on the high-top kitchen table, almost like she was teasing Jessie by leaving it out in the open. As she collected the various requested items, Jessie let the passive-aggressive move go, deciding instead to use the window of goodwill to create the impression that she might be willing to open her own door to some kind of conciliation.

"How did you find this place?" she called out as Andy searched through one of the plastic cabinets in the makeshift kitchen. "I'm assuming that it's not on the Airbnb website."

"It is a little out of the way," Andy conceded. "But it holds a special place in my heart."

"An abandoned mine does?" Jessie asked, sensing that the woman wanted to tell her more but needed to be drawn out.

Andy walked over with a three Advil, a bottled water, along with Neosporin and gauze bandages.

"I can only give you so many pills," she said. "Can't have you overdosing. And you'll have to apply these bandages yourself. With just the one wrist cuffed, I can't risk helping you and having you grab me and try to choke me out."

"Okay," Jessie said, taking the materials. She couldn't blame Andy for her paranoia, but tried to play it off. "Is that your way of saying you don't want to talk about why the mine is important to you?"

"No, I'll tell you. But first, you tell me. Do you want a turkey or roast beef sandwich? Until I pull those coolers in from the truck, meals are going to be pretty basic."

"Turkey's fine, thanks," Jessie said as she popped the pills and chugged the water.

"So, to answer your question, I used to come here a kid," Andy said, her voice suddenly less theatrical than usual. "Obviously, not to this mine, but to the area. My family has a ranch not too terribly far from here, much too far for you to walk to if you were to ever get out of this place, by the way. But within driving distance if you had a truck like Old Betsy back there."

"Good to know," Jessie said as she dabbed the ointment on her wrists.

"Anyway," Andy continued, as she went to the fridge and pulled out the cold cuts, "I would spend summers at the ranch with my cousin. We would ride horses, swim, go hunting and fishing, and we'd always wrap up the visit with a big hiking and camping trip with her dad. Do you want sourdough bread or whole wheat?"

"Wheat please," Jessie answered, hoping not to do anything to distract Andy from her story. She could feel something major coming.

"Wheat it is," Andy announced. "So this one year, when my cousin and I were both fourteen, we were on the camping trip, but Erin—that's my cousin's name—wasn't feeling well. I think she had her period, but she was embarrassed to say it because we were with her dad. So, she stayed in the tent that day while me and Uncle Dan went on the hike alone. Do you like mustard or mayo?"

"That's okay," Jessie said, slowly wrapping the gauze on her wrist, though her attention was fixed on Andy's words. "Maybe just a slice of cheese?"

"Let me see if I have any," Andy said, rifling through the fridge. "So, we came across this mine. He convinced me to go in, said it would be a cool adventure. But once we were inside, in this very room actually, he threw me down on the ground and raped me repeatedly. When he was done, he said that if I ever told anyone, he'd kill me, my dad, and even my cousin, Erin—his own daughter. I'm sure that if my mom wasn't already dead, he would have threatened her too. I have cheddar or American."

"What?" Jessie asked, stunned. Her brain, already at its tipping point due to shock, fear, pain, and drugs, seemed to have temporarily frozen at the words she just heard.

"I have cheddar or American cheese," Andy said with the same casual ambivalence her in her voice as when she had described being assaulted. "Which do you prefer?"

Jessie stared at Andy, whose back was to her, and tried to process this news. Was this where the woman's life had had gone off the rails? How could it not have been? For the briefest of moments, she could feel sympathy threatening to cloud her judgment before immediately beating it back.

Compassion could come later. Right now, Jessie needed clarity. She focused on what Andy's words revealed about her. No wonder the woman was so desperate to get back here. If she was telling the truth, this mine, and what happened here, might be the Rosetta Stone that helped explained how Andrea Robinson turned out this way. Andy turned around with an expectant look, holding up a package of cheese in in each hand.

"Which cheese?" she repeated.

"Cheddar, I guess?" Jessie replied, trying to mask the jumble of pity and horror that was filling her gut despite her best efforts.

"One slice of cheddar coming up," Andy said, almost to her herself, before resuming. "So, at some point, probably about a decade ago, I started to build this facility up. The mine was owned by the family, but it had been abandoned and essentially forgotten years earlier, so I could come and go as I pleased. My plan was to bring Uncle Dan back here, torture him within an inch of his life on that stone slab over there, then blow the mine up so that he'd die in the explosion. His body would never be found."

She placed the cheese on the bread, followed by two slices of turkey, then added the second piece of bread and brought the sandwich over.

"I'm sorry but I haven't unpacked the plates yet, so you'll have to just hold it."

"That's okay," Jessie said quietly, taking the sandwich as she looked at Andy. The woman's voice was calm, but those intense blue eyes were stormy. "I'm guessing that the plan didn't work out?"

"Nope," Andy said, sitting down on the patio chair opposite her. "Five years ago, he dropped dead of a heart attack. I was about four months away from my 'torture target date.' There were some...hard-to-get items I had on back order, ones that I planned to use on Uncle Dan, which would have helped him understand how I felt when he attacked me. But there were supply chain issues and the chance slipped through my fingers."

"That must have been infuriating for you," Jessie said without judgment.

Andy looked at her quizzically, then seeming to accept that she was being sincere, nodded.

"Things haven't been the same since," she acknowledged. "After that, I figured I'd just let go, enjoy myself, and let the chips fall where they may. So, I partied hard, but kept it hidden from the Hancock Park elite. I had my way with an endless series of boy toys and girl toys alike. Eventually it escalated. You know how that turned out."

"You're talking about murdering Victoria Missinger," Jessie said quietly.

Andy nodded.

"Yes," she said, "but all that's in the past. We're here now. And I guess part of me was hoping that bringing you here would be a cathartic experience for me, that maybe together we could turn this into a place that has positive memories. After all, you've been through some stuff too, right? I mean, I realize that's a massive understatement, considering your family history, but you came out the other end. I'm hoping that you can help me do the same thing. I'm doing something that's really hard for me here—I'm asking for your help. What do you say?"

Jessie took a big bite of her sandwich to give herself extra time to stall. Her brain was swimming with overlapping, cascading thoughts, and it was difficult to keep them organized, but one thing was clear: Andy was even more damaged than she'd thought.

She talked about achieving catharsis but didn't seem to comprehend that kidnapping someone and bringing her to the place where she was raped would only exacerbate the trauma she experienced there, not help abate it. She seemed to understand intellectually that the horror she suffered here nineteen years ago had shaped who she was, but had no concept of how to deal with it.

She seemed to think she could blot out her pain, first by punishing the perpetrator in the same location, and then by forcing someone else to live here with her, replacing her excruciating memories with newer, better ones. She either couldn't see, or simply refused to, that the seeds which made murdering Victoria Missinger possible were planted when she was brutalized here, and then flowered when her uncle died before she could kill him.

Everything she'd done since, whether she admitted it or not, stemmed in part from her failed attempt to punish Uncle Dan for his crimes. Jessie suspected that even the fixation that Andy had on her was just some kind of twisted replacement for the obsession she had with her uncle, only painted in rosier terms.

But maybe Jessie could use that. Maybe her best way out of this wasn't to free herself from her cuffs or find a gun as part of some rash escape attempt. After all, even if she was successful, even if she killed Andy, that would still leave Operation Z in place. It would still leave her loved ones in danger.

But if she could convince Andy that she was on her side, that she was willing to help her, both out of professional interest and personal sympathy, perhaps her kidnapper would open up, reveal something, get soft or sloppy. If she got soft and thought Jessie was here to stay, maybe she could be persuaded to cancel Operation Z. If she got sloppy, maybe she'd let slip what the operation was or who was supposed to carry it out. Either way, once Jessie got that information, she had a chance.

There was no point in outsmarting Andy if the goal was merely to escape, not with this other, larger threat looming out there. She needed to convince Andy that she had no intention of leaving, that she was so moved by her personal story of trauma that she was now committed to staying here and making this strange arrangement work.

If she could do that, then she was back in the game. And if she was in the game, she had a chance to win it.

CHAPTER TWENTY THREE

8:41 p.m., Sunday night

Zoe Bradway pushed down hard and listened to the satisfying spurt of butter-flavored popcorn oil topping as it sprayed out onto the extra-large tub ordered by the couple.

"Here you go," she said. "Enjoy the show."

She watched as they scurried toward the theater. They were already fifteen minutes late, so she didn't see what the big rush was at this point. She turned to help the next customer and realized there was no one else in line. One register over, Byron gave her a happy smirk.

"Everybody's got their feedbag on," he said happily, "Time to chillax."

Byron was an idiot, always trying to sound cool by using lame phrases he thought were clever. It had taken Zoe several months to figure that he was so constantly annoying because he had a crush on her and was trying to impress her.

Everything inside her was repulsed by the idea of this scrawny, pimply, curly-haired community college nerd getting near her, but she had forced the revulsion down for weeks now, realizing that she could use it to her advantage.

She didn't know exactly how or when, but at some point, probably very soon, Andy would call on her, and if she could deploy a useful idiot like Byron in the service of The Principal, then all the better.

"I'm going to check the restrooms," she told him, reminding herself to offer a playful smile before leaving. It was important to throw him a bone every now and then.

As she walked off, her mind drifted to Andy, wondering when she'd finally be called into service. She knew she had to be patient. She'd been warned that she would be the final shoe to drop, but it was still hard to see Livia, Eden, and now Corinne all get their moments in the sun, while she still hid in the shadows.

She entered the restroom, pulled the broom and and dustpan out of the utility closet, and stared at herself in the mirror. She didn't look like the last warrior standing in Andy's Army. Barely a shade over five feet tall and tipping a hundred pounds on a good day, she seemed innocent enough. That was partly why Andy had said she was her secret weapon. With her short, dark hair, her soft brown eyes, and her bird-like frame, she seemed too delicate to do damage to anyone but herself. And sometimes she wondered if that was true.

But as she turned to focus on the first bathroom stall, she reminded herself that she was last because Andy trusted her the most. That's what she'd said on that last night before Zoe was released from Twin Towers five months ago, when she'd slipped into her cell and into her bed. Even as she slid her hands under the blanket and did things to make Zoe gulp and perspire, she'd whispered urgently in her ear.

"You're the smartest. That's why you have the hardest job. That's why I've assigned you Operation Z. No one else has a mission named after them. You might have to wait months or even years to set it in motion, but you will get your chance. Do you remember the activation code phrase?"

"Uh-huh," Zoe had said, trying not to moan and draw the attention of one of the guards.

"Tell me," Andy had instructed, her breath hot and prickly on Zoe's neck.

"It's a new day and I plan to step into the light."

"That's right," Andy had whispered as she nibbled on her earlobe. Between that and what was going on below the sheets, Zoe thought her head might explode.

"What is the other cue to activate?" Andy had asked.

Zoe remembered how that question had pulled her out of the ecstatic moment. She'd turned to Andy and shook her head.

"No," she pleaded.

"Tell me," Andy insisted, her face still and focused even as her fingers kept moving diligently.

"If the news reports say that you died," Zoe said quietly.

"That's right," Andy murmured approvingly, picking up the pace down below. "If you hear that, then Operation Z is a go. You promise you'll finish the job for me, Zoe, just like I'm finishing the job for you right now?"

"Mmm hmm," Zoe had sighed.

"Everything good in here?"

Zoe looked up to see her manager, Destry, staring at her, from across the women's restroom, with a curious expression. She realized that she'd been standing, unmoving, in front of a stall, with the broom and dustpan in her hand, for quite a while.

"Yeah, sorry," she said. "I guess I'm just tired. I must have faded out there for a second."

"Okay, well try to save the fadeouts for after the shift's over, Zoe," Destry said. "You're not getting paid to daydream in front of toilets."

Destry was gone before she could reply, not that she would have had a good comeback anyway. That was okay. Her comeback would come in another form. It was all set. She just needed to make a few small adjustments to an instrument here and there and Destry, along with everyone else in the immediate vicinity, would keep their smart-aleck mouths shut for good.

But that was just part one of Operation Z. After that, she had the list of names to punish, people close to Jessie Hunt. Andy had explained that she wasn't to kill Jessie herself, although she could certainly harm her. But the whole point was to leave her alive, so that she would suffer, would have to forever live with the knowledge that her loved ones were dead, and that it was her fault.

That was the part Zoe was most excited about. She fervently hoped that she got to carry out Operation Z because Andy activated her with her words, not with her death. But either way, she'd complete the mission.

CHAPTER TWENTY FOUR

9:04 p.m., Sunday night

By the time Kat pulled up to the scene, it was a madhouse.

She'd gotten the call from Ryan telling them about the sandal when they were about ten minutes away from the ranch. She'd promptly turned the car around and headed back toward the town of Quartzsite, which they'd passed through just twenty minutes earlier.

By the time they retraced their route back to the town, not only had the helicopter carrying Ryan and Susannah arrived, but so had the La Paz County Sheriff's Department, the FBI, and several interested onlookers. She got out of the car, accompanied by Hannah and Callum, and headed toward the crowd.

"Remember," she muttered to them under her breath, "if anyone asks, we're here because we heard about the discovery on the radio, not from the primary detective on the case."

"That's all well and good," Hannah said. "But it won't get us past the police tape."

"We'll cross that bridge when we come to it," Kat told her.

Ten seconds later they had arrived at the tape and a sheriff's deputy holding up his hand for them to stop.

"Authorized personnel only," he said.

"It appears that we've reached that bridge," Callum noted drily.

Hannah turned to Kat.

"How hard do I need to push here?" she asked quietly, though her eyes were fiery. "Should I bust out the 'sister of the missing victim' card or hold off? Because I'm ready and willing."

"Let's hold off a minute," Kat said. "Maybe we can get in without going that route. But keep it in reserve just in case."

"Ma'am, I need you and your friends to step back please," the deputy said, more tersely this time. "You can't just wander up to a crime scene."

"Even if I have information relevant to the investigation?" Kat asked.

The deputy's eyes widened.

"What information?"

"I'll only share it with Detective Hernandez," she said. "If you have him come over, I'm confident he'll be interested in what I have to say."

The deputy looked at her hesitantly, but ultimately his desire not to ignore a potential lead overwhelmed his apprehension that he might be getting played.

"Hold on," he said.

He walked over to where Ryan was conferring with a guy in a lab coat who Kat assumed was part of the crime scene unit and tapped him on the shoulder. They spoke briefly. When Ryan looked over and saw them, he waved them through. Kat gave Hannah a squeeze on the shoulder.

"Maybe you can use your sneaky skills next time," she said as they ducked under the tape and walked over.

They were just arriving when Susanna Valentine walked over too.

"What are you doing here?" she demanded. "I thought it was made pretty clear that you're not supposed to be involved in—."

"It's okay, Valentine," Ryan interrupted, "as long as they're here, I think they might be able to help."

"We can try," Kat said, doing her best not to let Susannah Valentine get under her skin. "What's the situation?"

"Come with me," he said, leading them over to the shoulder of the road and pointing to the ditch below, "a young couple found this vehicle when the husband stopped to go to the bathroom. We've confirmed that it was the Buick Andy Robinson used for her getaway after killing the laundry truck driver."

Kat and the others nodded as if it was the first time that they'd heard this information. Ryan continued as if it was the first time that he'd shared it with them.

"As he was leaving, the young man tripped over what we've determined to be Jessie's sandal from the wedding. It had blood on it. They've typed and it's a match for Bob Mosby, the guy Andy killed at the Ehrenberg travel center."

That was actual new information. Ryan must not have known it when he briefed them earlier.

"So, we know that Andy dumped the car here and that Jessie was still with her at that point," Callum said.

"Right," Ryan said.

"And we're thinking she switched cars here?" Kat wanted to know.

"Well, we don't think they hitchhiked from this point on," Valentine said.

Kat felt the urge to throw a punch, but Hannah spoke before she could act on it.

"But why change cars here?" she asked. "Why not just do it at the travel center, where she was stopping anyway? Why this random place?"

"It's possible that she was worried about cameras catching a glimpse of the new car at the travel center," Ryan said. "That's much less likely around here."

"So, we have no way of knowing what kind of vehicle they used or where they went?" Hannah asked, getting increasingly upset. "How do we know that one of Andy's acolytes wasn't just waiting here for them, ready to serve as chauffeur? The two of them could have shoved Jessie in the new car and they'd be gone. We wouldn't have a clue how to find them."

"Actually, we do have one clue," Ryan said, "which is why I let you all past the police tape. I'm hoping you might be able to help decipher it."

He went over to the CSU van and grabbed an evidence bag. When he came back, Kat saw that it had the bloody sandal he'd mentioned earlier.

"This is the sandal that came off when they switched cars?" Callum confirmed.

"I don't actually think it just 'came off'" Ryan said. "I think Jessie took it off and left it, hoping we'd find it."

"What makes you say that?" Kat asked.

"For one thing, it was left on the shoulder right in front of where the car was parked in the ditch. If not for that guy who had to pee, who knows when we might have found the car. I think Jessie had that same concern and left the sandal as a breadcrumb for us to find the car."

"You don't think it was just an accident?" Callum pressed, sounding dubious.

"No, for two reasons," Ryan replied. "First, if Andy had seen the sandal, she wouldn't have left it behind for the very reason that it would have drawn attention. I'm sure it was left there surreptitiously. The other reason I'm sure is this: there's writing on the sandal."

They all peered at the spot on one of the straps that Ryan was pointing to. He was right. Someone had clearly scratched into the blood, likely with a fingernail.

"Does that say, 'car corpse'?" Callum asked.

"Yes," Ryan said, "but don't worry. We've checked. There's no body in the car. We think it was just a clever way for Jessie to get someone's attention, so they'd call the police and have the car searched."

"Well, apparently it worked," Callum said as Hannah rested on the hood of the nearest squad car and breathed a sigh of relief.

"My question is whether that's all it means," Ryan added.

"You think it means more than that?" Valentine asked skeptically. "I think that's pretty impressive all on its own, don't you, considering the stress she must have been under in that moment?"

"No, he's right," Hannah said suddenly. "Jessie had to know that this might be her last chance to communicate with us. She was about to be transferred to another vehicle, one that she feared we'd never be able to trace. Why only give us information about a car she's no longer in. That doesn't help us find her. There has to be more to it than that."

Kat tended to agree. In her experience, Jessie wouldn't want to waste an opportunity like this. She would have wanted to pass along a message that could help investigators. But it was also tricky because it would need to be vague enough that if Andy found it, she couldn't shut down that means of finding them.

She leaned back on the hood of the car, frustrated. Everyone else looked equally stumped. Were they all that stupid? Or was she just overthinking it? Jessie wouldn't make this rocket science. She'd want the clue to be solvable by the people who knew her: her family, friends, the team at HSS. It's not like she expected the guy who ran the auto body shop across the street to figure it out.

Suddenly, she sat up straight on the car.

"I know what the clue means," she said.

"What?" Ryan asked.

Kat stood up and pointed at the sign across the road.

"Car corpse," she said, " is a synonym for auto body."

*

"Are you Isaac?" Kat asked the huge guy standing at the gate of the auto body shop, who had been watching the action unfolding in front of his business.

"Yeah," he said, looking started at the question. "Am I in trouble?"

"Not if you answer our questions honestly," replied Ryan, who stood right beside Kat.

"Okay," Isaac said apprehensively.

"Do you just repair cars here?" Kat asked. "Or do you sell them too?"

"I refurbish some old ones and sell them," he said.

"Did you sell any in the last twenty-four hours?" Susannah Valentine wanted to know.

"Yes. I sold one to a woman first thing this morning. She walked in right when I opened at 8.am."

"Was this her?" Valentine asked, holding up a picture of Andy on her phone.

"Yeah, that's her," Isaac said, clearly doing his best to keep from losing it. "She said her name was Katherine Gentry."

Kat took an involuntary step back at that. This woman wasn't just running from them. She was screwing with them every chance she got. She knew they'd eventually find Isaac and had intentionally left the name just to twist the knife.

"Was there anyone with her?" Hannah demanded, refusing to be thrown by the manipulation. "Another woman, maybe?"

"No. She walked in alone, bought the car with cash, and drove off by herself. I never saw anyone else."

Everyone was quiet for a moment, stumped.

"We'll need a description of the vehicle she bought," Valentine finally said, "along with photos and the direction she went."

"Sure," Isaac said. "I have all that on the computer. As far as where she went, I remember she drove back west along Acacia Road, then turned south, but I didn't pay attention beyond that."

"Did the car have a GPS system in it?" Ryan pressed.

"Oh God, no," Isaac said. "It's a 1992 Mitsubishi. It doesn't have anything like that."

Kat felt the air drain out of her like a balloon.

"Did she say why she wanted such an old car?" Callum wondered.

"No. She just wanted to make sure that it was all wheel drive so that it could handle desert driving and that it would last a month or so. She also said it should have a trunk. Other than that, I don't remember her being too picky."

"Show us the photos," Ryan instructed.

Isaac headed back inside, with Ryan, Valentine, and Callum close behind. Kat didn't join them. Hannah, who had started to follow the others, noticed.

"Aren't you coming?" she asked.

"No, I think I'll stay out here," Kat said.

"Why?" Hannah pressed. "Don't you want to see what this car looks like?"

Kat leaned against the auto body shop fence, unable to come up with a good answer. Hannah walked back over.

"There's no point, is there?" the younger woman asked. "Andy got this car over twelve hours ago. She's had all that time to drive out to some hole in the desert. The vehicle has no GPS. It's worse than a needle in a haystack, right?"

Kat looked over at her, wanting to offer some words of hope. But Hannah was too perceptive to be deceived by platitudes and deserved better anyway. She had just voiced exactly what Kat had been thinking.

Despite all of Jessie's best efforts—scrawling a cryptic message in a dead man's blood, leaving her sandal behind as a clue for those in search of her—they were no closer to finding her than they had been this morning or last night. In fact, their chances felt somehow infinitely worse as they bumped up against the relentless precision of Andy's plan.

She shrugged and sighed heavily, then offered Hannah the only thing she had available: the truth.

"It doesn't look good, but that doesn't matter. We know what the haystack looks like. We know what the needle looks like. So, we keep searching. That's what Jessie would do. So that's what we'll do."

CHAPTER TWENTY FIVE

At least the meds had kicked in.

Jessie may have been cuffed to a rock in an abandoned mine where she was being held captive by an unstable murderer, but at least the full body throbbing sensation she'd felt since regaining consciousness after being drugged had subsided a little bit.

She hadn't had much to do for the last few hours other than watch Andy unpack supplies from the truck, take stock of the mine that she'd turned into a doomsday prepper shelter, and sit with her thoughts.

The more she studied the place, the more it became apparent that Andy intended for them to be here for the long haul. There were two additional generators in a back corner that Jessie hadn't noticed at first. In one of the large, plastic storage cabinets, there were enough canned goods to last over a year. And then there was the cabinet that appeared to house an entire cold weather wardrobe, suggesting that Andy expected to be here well into the winter. Considering that it was late March, that was a terrifying proposition.

As Andy unloaded the items, she continued to talk, sharing more about her life after what she bitterly referred to as her "special afternoon" here with Uncle Dan. Jessie let her go on uninterrupted, hoping that being a judgment-free sounding board would strengthen their connection and possibly reveal a weakness she could exploit.

"I kind of went off the deep end," Andy said, as she dragged a bag of flour across the floor toward the far end of the mine. "In the months after he died, I did more drugs than I ever did when I was sixteen. I would find the best late-night orgy in L.A. one night. Then I'd go to the country club the next day to play eighteen holes with three clueless women who would babble on about how hard it was to get their toddlers into the right preschool."

She pulled the bag of flour up onto the upper level of the cave and dropped it near the supply cabinet. As she did, the ground shook and Jessie noticed something she hadn't picked up on before: the section of rock holding the metal plate and ring that her handcuff was attached to rattled slightly and bits of gravel shifted.

Jessie gave a small tug and a little more rock broke free from the screws that had been used to embed the plate in place. It wasn't anything substantial. The plate was still solidly connected to the rock. But if she could get her hands on some kind of heavy implement, it might not take more than a few swings to loosen it enough for her to pull herself free.

"The funny thing is that none of it made me feel any better," Andy said as she walked back to the truck again. "Mostly it was an attempt to just feel anything, you know?"

Jessie was about to say that she did, but it wasn't necessary. Andy kept on going.

"After a while, even that didn't work. I was just bored all the time," Andy said. "I think that's why I stared the affair with Michael Missinger. Yeah, the sex was good. But mostly, it was the illicit nature of it that I got off on. And then, when Victoria found out, I had to take it up a notch by killing her. And after that, I didn't have a choice—I had to pin her murder on Marisol the maid. But truthfully, even that felt kind of rote until you entered the picture and spiced things up. Finally, I felt like I had met someone worthy of my gifts."

"Thank you," Jessie said.

"You're welcome," Andy said. "I need a little break from all this dragging stuff around. I was going to make myself a smoothie. You want one?"

"Sure," Jessie said, stunned that such a thing was even possible in this environment.

Andy walked over to a separate plastic cabinet and proceeded to pull out a blender. As she assembled it and grabbed various fruits from the fridge, she resumed.

"Anyway, that's why we're here. Because you are the one person that I think deserves this place. I really think that if we both commit ourselves to it, we can turn what used to be a house of horrors into a kind of new utopia…"

As she spoke, Jessie's thoughts drifted away. She'd heard Andy wax poetic about the new world they'd create in this mine multiple times and didn't need another go-round just now. Besides, something else the woman had said was sticking to the inside of her brain.

Andy had said that murdering a human being and framing someone else for it had felt rote until Jessie came along. That was a lot to process. But if she set aside the disturbing nature of the statement, she found that it was also quite revealing.

It occurred to her that she might have been misjudging this situation all along. After all, the two of them had genuinely hit it off from the first time they met. They had an easy rapport all the way up until the moment that Jessie realized that Andy was a killer. Under more normal circumstances, she could have seen them becoming friends.

All these years that Andy had been incarcerated, Jessie had assumed that her desire for friendship had simply curdled into something darker, a wish to control the woman who had uncovered her crime. It explained the need to have Jessie come to the prison to talk to her. It explained the kidnapping.

In the last few hours, she'd filled in the blanks of that theory, positing that Andy had simply replaced her obsession with her Uncle Dan with a fixation on her, because she always had to have someone to fuel her passion. And that might have been true at first.

But now she thought there might be more to it. The way Andy talked about their future was the way one half of a couple discussed their life together. Jessie wondered if somewhere along the way, Andy's fixation might have morphed into something more. She suspected that Andrea Robinson was in love with her.

The odd thing was that Andy didn't seem to realize it herself. She appeared to view the two of them as star-crossed lovers—Romeo and Juliet—but couldn't put a label to it. And then it hit Jessie like a thunderbolt—Andy was in love with her. She just couldn't admit it, either out loud or to herself.

If Jessie's life wasn't in danger, she might have been amused. After all, Andy had acknowledged multiple liaisons with women. She had talked about orgies and "girl toys" and there was little doubt that she'd used her sexual charms to manipulate her acolytes in prison. But apparently in her mind, those were just flings, or a means to an end.

This brilliant woman, who had engineered her release from prison and outsmarted all of southern California law enforcement to get to this mine, didn't seem to have any awareness of herself. She kept talking about how she wanted to be besties, like Kat, or sisters, like Hannah, but that's not what she really wanted. People don't generally kidnap folks they consider friends or sisters. They kidnap folks they're passionate about, either their children or someone they've attached some romantic significance to.

As she watched Andy dump the fruit and ice into the blender, Jessie knew what she had to do. She'd been thinking that she had to get Andy to let her guard down. But that wasn't going to happen by appearing to warm up to the situation in the mine. Andy would never believe that.

She needed to convince her captor of something more: that she accepted that she wasn't going anywhere and that, with that acceptance, she was starting to re-evaluate her feelings for the first time. She was starting to wonder if the wedding was the right thing for her after all, if she'd been so caught up in the planning that she'd forgotten to ask herself if that's what she really wanted, if there might be something more out there for her.

She would admit that something had been eating at her for a while, a feeling that her life could be fuller than what Ryan had to offer. She had kept ignoring that feeling, pushing it away. Only now, sore, exhausted, and face-to-face with herself, did she recognize it for what it was. She was scared but had to be open to exploring it.

It was important not to push too hard. If she was too obvious or clumsy, Andy would see right through it. Her comments had to be admissions about herself, realizations she was coming to about her own nature.

She couldn't suggest that Andy might now feel that way too, or ever had. As libertine as the woman was, it was clear that hinting to her that she might be in love with the woman she'd kidnapped could result in violent rejection. Jessie had to make herself vulnerable, open the door, and see if Andy peeked in.

If she did, then who knows what was possible. She didn't expect Andy to swoon with ardor and release her or spill her guts, but if she could cloud her head enough to get any kind of useful intel, it would be worth it. The question was, how far was far enough to convince Andy that she was sincere and how far was too far?

"Sorry," Andy said, yanking her out of her thoughts, "but this blender is a little loud. You might want to cover your ears."

Jessie nodded absently. But after a second, Andy's words flicked a switch in her head. Suddenly pumped with adrenaline, she resolved to do something very different with her hands.

She gripped the armrests of the patio chair she was seated in, waiting until Andy's back was turned. When her captor looked away and pushed the button to start the blender, Jessie stood up, lifting the entire chair with her, moved forward, and thrust it downward, using one chair leg's metal foot to whack at the spot where the metal plate and ring holding her cuff met the rock it was screwed to.

She got in six solid blows before Andy turned off the blender and the motor slowly came to a stop. The plate hadn't come free, but it was definitely looser. Jessie saw that at least two of the four screws holding it in place were wobbly. If Andy returned to unloading the truck, she might be able to twist them loose with her fingers.

She forced her eyes away from the plate and onto Andy, who was walking over with a large plastic cup. Jessie took it from her and tilted it back, allowing the liquid to slide into her throat.

"That's really good," she said, not kidding. "Where did you learn to make such good smoothies?"

"My mom taught me," Andy said. "She died when I was six. This is all I have left of her."

Jessie was surprised by the bluntness of the response but pretended not to be. Any personal revelation from Andy was a sign that the walls were coming down a bit.

"That's how old I was when my mom died too," Jessie said softly, pausing for a while, before switching to a more upbeat tone. "Anyway, if you spent less time on the kidnapping part and more on the smoothie-making, maybe we could find some common ground."

For a second, Andy looked like she was going to offer a snarky comeback, but then her face relaxed.

"I guess we've got lots of time for that now," she replied.

"I guess so," Jessie agreed with a sigh.

She watched her abductor's shoulders unclench slightly and knew that she'd opened the romantic door a crack. Now it was time to push just a bit harder. But before she could, a timer went off on Andy's watch.

"Give me a second," she said reluctantly. "I'll be right back."

She walked off to the far corner of the cave, pulled an orange duffel bag out of one of the cabinets, and placed it on the kitchen table. She unzipped it and pulled out what looked to Jessie to be a burner-style cell phone. Then she disappeared out of sight behind the sound-dampening curtains by the pickup truck. After a few seconds she started speaking.

Jessie couldn't hear what she was saying, but her tone was low and urgent. Jessie had thought that she was playing everything just right, but now she worried that she'd screwed up somehow, that Andy had seen though her attempt to woo her and was activating Operation Z.

She tried to tell herself that the timer had gone off independent of the conversation they'd been having, that whatever that call was had nothing to do with her attempts to seduce Andy, that she should continue with her plan, but it was hard not to worry that everything had just gone off the rails.

Andy pulled back the curtain, silently returned the phone to the orange duffel bag on the table, dropped the handcuff key still resting on the table in the bag as well, and then walked back over. Her face was a mask as she sat down in the patio chair opposite Jessie. Then she allowed herself a small smile.

"So where were we?" she asked.

Jessie smiled back as one thought took prominence over all the others in her head.

We're back in business.

CHAPTER TWENTY SIX

11:16 p.m., Sunday night

Susannah didn't mind the place.

They were back at the Best Restin' suite in Ehrenberg, adjacent to the travel center.

She'd worked in operation centers that were much more bare-bones than this. What she didn't love was trying to concentrate while maneuvering around ten other people from three different law enforcement agencies in a space intended for four people maximum.

She was sitting on an end table in the corner of the bedroom, listening in on a conference call with Ryan, Captain Decker, Detectives Bray and Nettles, and researcher Beth Ryerson as Jamil Winslow gave them more bad news.

"So just to be clear," asked Ryan, who was sitting on the bed across from her, "you've searched every freeway camera within 200 miles of Quartzsite for that Mitsubishi Galant and haven't come across one sighting of it?"

"I'm afraid not, Detective," Jamil said apologetically.

"This shouldn't come as a shock, people," Decker reminded them. "Based on what the auto body shop owner said, it sounds like Robinson intended to drive into the desert. So, we shouldn't have any expectation of freeway footage. The questions now are how long was she driving and how far did she get?"

Before anyone could offer a suggestion, one of the La Paz County deputies poked his head in from the other room.

"Sorry to interrupt, detectives, but we may have something," he said.

"What?" Ryan asked.

"We just got a 911 call," he said. "There was a sighting of two women entering a country and western bar called the Gold & Silver Mine just west of Tonopah a few minutes ago. One was blonde. The other was wearing a baseball cap and looked scared. According to the caller, they matched the descriptions of Robinson and Hunt that have been on the news."

"Are you hearing this, Captain?" Ryan asked, who had put his cell phone on speaker.

"Yes, where's Tonopah?"

"It's about an hour west of Phoenix," the deputy said, "and ninety miles east of here."

"Ryan," Susannah said, a thought springing into her exhausted brain, "do you remember what Corinne Bertans said when she was being questioned about where Andy might take Jessie—'all mine'? What if that wasn't a possessive thing? What if it was more literal than that—the actual name of the place that Robinson intended to take Jessie?"

"But why would she show up somewhere so public, where she could be identified?" Karen Bray asked from back in L.A.

"Maybe she didn't think anyone would notice," Susannah suggested, "or maybe she didn't care."

"What do you mean?" Decker asked.

"What if this is her last stand? What if she wants to go out in a blaze of glory? What better place to pick than public bar with lots of people with cell phones able to beam the show out to the world?"

Ryan turned back to the deputy.

"You said it's ninety miles away?" he confirmed.

"Yes, sir."

"That means the helicopter can get us there in a little over a half-hour," Ryan said. "I'm calling the pilot."

*

Hannah watched the helicopter lift off into the sky.

She was seated at the table in the coffee shop with Kat and Callum, where the three of them had been reviewing everything that they could find on 1992 Mitsubishi Galant VR-4s, the town of Quartzsite, and what connection Andy Robinson might have to either. So far, they'd come up empty.

Seconds later, Kat got a text.

"It's from Ryan," she said. "He says there was a possible sighting of Andy and Jessie at a bar near a town called Tonopah, about ninety miles east of here. They're taking the chopper to check it out."

"What makes him think this is any more legit than all the other false leads we've been chasing?" Callum asked.

"Apparently the bar is called the Gold & Silver Mine and they think it might be connected to what Corinne said about 'all mine.'"

"That seems like a stretch," Hannah said, surprised at her own cynicism in the face of the only positive news they had since the sandal lead fell through two hours ago.

"All the same, maybe we should go check it out," Kat said, starting to get up from the table.

"Come on, Kat," Callum said, gently grabbing her wrist, "you said it was ninety miles away. By the time we get there, the validity of the sighting will be borne out or not. Don't you think our time is better served here, looking for alternatives in case that falls apart?"

Kat sat back down, acknowledging that he was right without saying so. Hannah felt bad for her. She'd rarely seen the detective so down. She wished she could think of the right thing to say to buck her up, but as she didn't feel any more optimistic about the situation, she knew it would come across as false.

Mixed in with her despondency was a slow-bubbling frustration that Ryan, of all people, would really buy the idea that "all mine" could be a reference to some random bar in central Arizona. She understood the desire to latch on to something, but that just felt desperate.

Then again, they never had determined what the phrase meant. It clearly wasn't referring to Andy's Hancock Park mansion or Corinne's apartment, where they initially thought Jessie might have been stashed. Was it just about Andy's possessive feelings toward Jessie?

Dr. Lemmon had specifically said that she asked Corinne if Andy ever said where she planned to take Jessie and that Corinne's answer was "all mine." Maybe they had all been too dismissive of that response.

Maybe Corinne was telling the truth, in her own messed up way. Hannah opened the file again, sensing that she was missing something—something that she'd seen before but overlooked because it hadn't seemed important.

She pored over several pages before giving up. There was no way she'd ever find what she was after when she didn't even know what it was that she needed. It was like looking for a needle in a haystack when you didn't know what the needle looked like.

She stopped, mid-page-turn, frozen by small epiphany.

Suddenly Hannah glanced up, gazing at the top of Kat and Callum's heads, who were both staring down at documents of their own. It wasn't true—she *did* know what the needle looked like. And if she was right, she knew how to find it too.

"Kat," she said, trying to keep the excitement she felt from spilling out into her voice. "You scanned all the documents related to Andy Robinson, right? All the hard copies we're reviewing, you have in your laptop too?"

"Of course," Kat said, picking up on her tone, despite her best efforts, "why?"

"Can you run a keyword search?"

Kat nodded, her fingers waiting in anticipation just above the keyboard.

"What word?" she asked.

"Mine."

Kat looked at her quizzically but did it anyway.

"I come up with thirty-seven instances."

"Let's go through them," Hannah said.

They did, carefully and methodically. The first fifteen occasions didn't bear any fruit. But the sixteenth was interesting.

"It looks like the family has something called Rintoo Mining, just like the ranch," Kat said.

"Why didn't we come across it earlier, when we were searching the family holdings?" Hannah asked.

Kat studied the paperwork for a few seconds before answering.

"Because, just like the ranch and that house on Natucket, its ownership was passed through several holding companies, so unless you knew that the name 'Rintoo' was affiliated with the family, deciphering this stuff would require the help of a forensic accountant. If Erin Reed hadn't mentioned the origin of the name "Rintoo' to Ryan and Valentine, we still wouldn't know the connection."

"So, is that how their family got so rich?" Callum asked.

"Not initially," Kat explained. "Andrea's father, Thoreau, invented some polymer back in the nineties. That set them up for life. But apparently his brother, Dan, used some of that money to start this mining company. It looks like he died a few years back, but the business is still running. Four of the five mines are still working today. According to their financials, the whole operation brings in close to seven figures annually."

Hannah felt that same prickling sensation that she had gotten earlier in the evening when she realized that the ranch that Andy had spent her childhood summers at was somehow significant. It was a strange rush, not unlike the one she got when she'd killed the Night Hunter, only somehow lighter and less overwhelming.

"You said four of the mines were still operational," she noted. "What about the fifth?"

"It's called the Sunkist Mine," Kat said. "It looks like it was a bust. They shut it down in the late 1990s. It's been abandoned ever since."

"Does the family still own it?" Hannah asked.

"On paper, yes," Kat said. "They take it as a tax loss every year."

"Where is the mine located?" Hannah asked, the tingling now threatening to make her fingers and toes go numb.

Kat looked at the screen, then up at Hannah. It was clear that she was starting to get excited too.

"According to the documents, it's near where Plomosa Road and Sunkist Trail meet, not that far from the Quartzsite Rock Alignment."

"What does that mean in English?" Hannah asked.

Kat turned her laptop around. The red dot indicating the Rintoo Mine was in an isolated stretch of desert almost equidistant between the towns of Quartzsite and Bouse, where the Rintoo Ranch was.

"That's crazy," Callum said. "We've been hunting all day. Do you mean to tell me that Andy might have taken Jessie to an abandoned mine less than fifteen miles from here?"

"That might explain why she's been sending us all over the place," Kat suggested. "She distracts everyone by having them chase leads up to Nevada or over near Phoenix. Meanwhile, she finds a shady spot to hole up for most of the day, waits for everyone to go by, then slowly moseys her way up to the mine in a beat-up, thirty-year-old car that no one pays any attention to. All she needed was for the clunker to get her over some tricky terrain without dying and she was happy."

"Well, if she can do it, so can we," Hannah said. "Looking at that map, I'd say we can get pretty close in the car. Then we can hike the rest of the way. It shouldn't take us more than thirty minutes."

"At night? On poorly marked desert roads?" Callum challenged. "You're kidding yourself. It'll take way longer than that. Let's call in the cavalry and let them lead the way."

"Not a chance," Kat said. "If we're right and Andy is there, the cavalry is the worst possible option. If she hears sirens, do you think she's going to come out with her hands up? Or is she more likely to take herself out and Jessie along with her?"

"Kat's right," Hannah said, her resolve never stronger. "We have the element of surprise. Let's take advantage of it."

"What about Ryan?" Callum asked.

Hannah glanced at Kat before turning back to the retired detective.

"We'll call him, but not until we're closer. Helicopters are loud too."

CHAPTER TWENTY SEVEN

Jessie ignored her heavy eyelids.

For the last few hours, she'd ignored her body's demand that she give in to sleep for one main reason: Andy was talking.

As her captor unpacked the last duffel bags of supplies into the various plastic cabinets, she had shared all kinds of details about her life. She talked about her time in juvenile hall, her year at a European boarding school, and another one at a military academy. She talked about trying to follow in her father's footsteps by pursuing her master's in chemical engineering at Caltech, but how she dropped out after he died.

Jessie let her go on about all these things with a sympathetic, understanding ear. But the whole time, she was also carefully twisting loose the screws from the flat plate attaching the metal ring to both the mine rock and her handcuff. She had removed two screws entirely and was well on her way to finishing the third. The fourth screw was still embedded about halfway into the rock and would require several more minutes to come free.

"All done," Andy said as she snapped a cabinet closed.

"What?" Jessie asked, taken aback.

"Everything is finally in its proper place. Now we can just relax."

Andy came over and plopped down heavily in the patio chair opposite her, leaning back into it. Jessie looked at the woman, now dressed in blue jeans and a casual work shirt, with her blonde hair tied back in a ponytail, and tried to imagine that she could fall for her.

She tried to block out all the murders and manipulations, the kidnapping, drugging, and delusions. She tried instead to focus on Andy's charm, on her sense of humor, when it didn't involve cruelty, on the childhood pain that must have contributed to the person she was now. She tried to find a way to make herself care for Andy, so that her abductor would believe it.

"Can I tell you something?" she said quietly.

Andy's eyes, half-closed, popped open. The blue intensity bore into her.

"What?"

"I don't want you to jump on this or make more out of it than it is, okay? Promise me that you'll hear me out without any typical Andy Robinson snark."

Andy sat up, interested.

"I promise," she said.

"Okay, well, sitting here for the last few hours, I've had some time to think. And I've started to wonder if I was being a little hasty in my wedding planning—."

"Wait, what?" Andy asked, her tone scoffing.

"Forget it," Jessie said, looking away.

"No, go on," Andy insisted, sounding amused more than anything.

"You promised you wouldn't make fun," Jessie protested, pretending to be offended.

"But you're obviously screwing with me."

"Don't get me wrong," Jessie retorted indignantly. "I'm not justifying you kidnapping me from my bridal suite. That was criminal and proof that you never should have gotten out of that psych ward."

"Ah, there's the Jessie Hunt I know."

"I can hold two competing ideas in my head, Andy. What I'm saying is that you are unwell and should spend many years behind bars. But also, maybe, perhaps, it's also a tiny bit possible that I was so focused on the details of my big event that I didn't stop to ask myself if I really wanted it to happen at all."

"Do you really expect me to take any of this seriously?" Andy pressed, though her tone had lost its mocking, sarcastic edge.

Jessie put her head down, like she was uncomfortable with the topic and struggling to find the right words. But in her mind, she pictured herself losing Ryan for good and channeled that anxiety into the moment. When she looked up, she had tears in her eyes.

"Listen, it's just really confusing," she said. "Ryan saved my life many times. I felt tremendous loyalty to him, and yes, a certain kind of love. So, when he proposed, it felt like the natural thing to say 'yes.'"

"What are you telling me, Jessie?"

"I don't know," Jessie replied, letting the frustration in her voice take center stage. "Do you know how difficult it is to concede that I might have made a mistake? Especially to the person who removed me from that mistake *against my will*?"

"You're just messing with me, to try to get me to lower my guard," Andy said again, with a half-smile frozen on her face. But her eyes seemed to suggest that she wasn't so sure anymore.

"Never mind," Jessie said, sensing that pushing at this point would be counterproductive. "I shouldn't have said anything. I'm tired. I just want to go to sleep. If I have to sit in this chair all night, can you please at least get me a pillow?"

Andy looked at her curiously, then got up and went to the supply area. As she did, Jessie hurriedly undid the third screw on the metal plate with the ring. She hid the screw, then gave a tug. The contraption was definitely loose but would probably require another smoothie session to come completely free. Andy returned with the pillow and a blanket and handed them over.

"Sorry I don't have the cot made up for you, but the bedding for it is way in the back of the supply closet, and I just don't have the energy to get it tonight. But you'll have it tomorrow."

"That's fine," Jessie said with a hint of petulance in her voice.

"Don't give me that," Andy said irritably. "You can't really expect me to believe that after a few hours of being here, you've suddenly seen the light? That you know that you shouldn't have been marrying that lunkhead and that I rescued you from a life of suburban boredom. That's awfully convenient."

"I didn't say that," Jessie shot back. "I don't think you rescued me. I still think you're seriously unhinged. You killed an innocent man this morning. You had other former inmates commit unspeakable acts on your behalf. And I haven't forgotten that you tried to poison me a couple of years ago. But does that mean I can't also admit, in the isolation of some mine in the middle of nowhere, that I had doubts about my wedding? Is that not allowed?"

"What kind of doubts?" Andy demanded, unable to hide her interest.

"Look," Jessie said, leaning in, staring at the woman across from her, unblinking, "have you ever wondered if you're on the right road? Or if you're just following it because it's the one with the signs?"

"What do you mean?" Andy asked.

Jessie hesitated, as if what might come next was too personal to share even in the privacy of a cave.

"This is hard to say, but we both know there's always been a...connection between us. I felt it that first time we talked at the country club that day. And then that night, when I came to your place for drinks, I don't know what I expected exactly—obviously not for you to try to kill me—but I was...curious."

"For the record, I didn't want to poison you," Andy said, pushing the conversation away from the intimate. "I would have preferred you be a little dumber. If you'd never have figured out what I did to Victoria Missinger, who knows where we'd be now?"

"Yeah," Jessie said, "but if I was a little dumber, you probably wouldn't have found me so interesting."

"True," Andy conceded.

"So here we are now," Jessie said, "in this untenable situation."

"How so?" Andy asked, leaning in despite herself.

Jessie shrugged.

"I've acknowledged...interest," she said with a little lilt in her voice, "But I don't know what to do with that, especially since you're a murderer and I'm a law enforcement official. I've conceded that I'm drawn to you, which I'm ashamed of because you are an almost irredeemably bad person, Andy."

"That feels harsh," Andy muttered.

"But I don't know how to explore that organically when I'm your prisoner," Jessie said, pressing ahead, sensing she was finally getting somewhere. "I want to open up but how can I do that when the lives of my loved ones are under threat? You clearly want to spend more quality time with me, or you wouldn't have set up this whole arrangement, but you don't trust me. You want to believe that I'm sincere but fear that the second you let down your guard, I'll try to escape. How do we find a way past this?"

Andy shrugged in exasperation, pulling back. It was clear that she'd been wondering the same thing herself.

"I don't know," she said quietly. "I think it might take a while."

"Maybe," Jessie said. "But what if things go south? Maybe over time, I begin to resent the forced nature of all this even more."

"How do you propose we prevent that from happening?" Andy asked earnestly.

"What if we tried something else?" Jessie suggested. "What if we started fresh tonight?"

"What do you mean?"

This was where Jessie desperately wanted to ask her to call whoever was in charge of Operation Z and ask them to put a hold on it as a sign of good faith. But she knew she couldn't. Andy would see through it. They hadn't built a strong enough bond yet for her to even consider such a move.

"What if we tried this?" Jessie whispered as she leaned forward hesitantly, keeping her hands at her sides.

For a second, Andy seemed to hesitate too, but then she leaned in as well. Suddenly they were kissing. Jessie could feel the intensity coming off the other woman, knew that she'd been imagining this moment for years.

She took the lead, pressing her lips against Andy's before pulling back suddenly.

"I want to touch you," she whispered, "but I'm worried that you'll think I'm trying something sneaky."

"That's okay," Andy said, leaving her seat and coming over to Jessie's, "I'll touch you."

Andy was on her knees in front of her. Jessie closed her eyes as she felt the other woman's hands investigate her tentatively. She delicately ran her fingers through Andy's hair, making small ecstatic sounds, even as she tried to gauge how much farther to let this go before making her move.

She waited several minutes, allowing Andy to explore her more ravenously, hearing the other woman's breathing get faster and shallower. She almost felt guilty for her lack of genuine reciprocation. She knew this was a powerful moment for Andy, but for her it was mostly a performance.

Even if she hadn't been in love with Ryan, it was nearly impossible to give herself over to the physical sensations Andy was trying to provide. Her insides were a knot of nerves, and her senses were focused on the task in front of her. Everything else was a distraction. It was just as Andy began kissing her stomach and started to lift the Barry Manilow shirt off her that she decided the time had come.

It was still risky, but she couldn't chance waiting until after they had consummated something. She needed Andy anticipating the deepest throes of passion, but not yet there, when she made her decision.

"I need to ask you for something," she whispered breathily.

"Anything," Andy said, licking the skin just below her navel.

"I need you to call off Operation Z."

Andy stopped licking. Her head popped out from under the shirt. Her hair was a mess, and her eyes were wild.

"What?" she said.

"Andy, for me to feel comfortable doing this, you need to call it off."

CHAPTER TWENTY EIGHT

Andy was torn.

Part of her was filled with a voracious desire to rip Jessie's shirt and pants off and ravage her. But another part was on high alert, sensing that this was a piece of a long con that Jessie had been conceiving for hours.

"Why would I call off the operation?" she asked.

Her brain was trying to catch up to her body, which was prickling with excitement. She knew she was in a dangerous place, where passion might trump good sense, and was tempted to shut off the former completely. But she was reluctant to do that. She'd waited so long to get to this point.

"Andy," Jessie told her, looking down at her with those green eyes that always made her quiver slightly, "you know why. I can't fully embrace…whatever this is…if the people I care about are in danger."

Andy looked at the belly button she'd just been licking longingly, before tearing her eyes away to study Jessie's face again. She didn't appear deceptive. She was simply stating a truth.

"But I told you that as long as you stayed here, they'd be safe," she reminder her.

"You know that's not enough," Jessie implored her. "What if something happened to your burner phone one day and you couldn't get through to tell your contact that you were alive? Or what if she just got tired of waiting for her big moment and decided to take matters into her own hands? Not everything is in your control, Andy. But that's not even the point."

"What is the point then?"

Jessie bent down, cupped her cheeks in her hands, and kissed her gently. As she did, her handcuff rattled slightly.

"The point is that I can't fully give myself over to this if I know other people are in danger. It's one thing if *I'm* out here with you. That's me, making a conscious choice to let this happen. But those are people I care about, not to mention all the other innocents throughout the city that you said would pay as well. I can't be open to whatever this is while knowing that they could be at risk."

Andy leaned back, away from Jessie's lips and her sweet scent. She shook her head.

"You're asking me to give up the only thing I have keeping you here," she said. "Do you really expect me to do that?"

"No, I'm not," Jessie insisted. "Look, I'm here. I'm chained up. I'm in a frickin' abandoned mine, Andy. Where am I going to go? You said it yourself. It's too far for me to walk anywhere from here, and that's even if I knew where I was going, which I don't. I'm not going anywhere."

Andy stood up. For a second her vision went dark, and she thought she might pass out, but the feeling subsided.

"I want to believe you," she said quietly. "Obviously, that's why I brought you out here in the first place—to build something together. But how can I trust that once I make that call you won't try to kill me or make a run for it?"

Jessie smiled at her with an unexpected patience and warmth.

"There are two ways to look at this," she said. "First, let's be practical about it. I understand that my request is a big one. That's why I'm not asking you to release me from the handcuff. I know that would be too much. So that means I'm still tied up. I can't get to the handcuff key. I'm not going to make a run for it because I can't run anywhere. So, killing you wouldn't do me any good. I'd just end up sitting in this patio chair, or maybe on a cot, slowly withering away from lack of food. That doesn't sound fun. That's the practical way to look at this. But there's another way. Would you like to hear it?"

"I'm listening."

"I just made a confession to you, a pretty raw one," she said. "I admitted that I didn't love the man I was about to marry and that I have feelings for you, the woman who once tried to kill me and who just kidnapped me. I consider that a pretty big step. But I guess I was just tired of denying the feelings that were eating away at my insides. I reached out to you, even though it made me vulnerable, even though it put me in an emotionally precarious place. Now I think it's your turn."

Andy wasn't sure how to respond to that. It sounded almost like an accusation.

"What do you mean by that?"

"I mean that I took a step toward you by being honest about something really difficult for me," Jessie said. "If this is ever going to work, you have to take a step toward me. If we're going to build something together, you have to show some kind of trust in me. And this is how I'm asking you to do it—by calling off the operation."

"You think that's going to just wipe the slate clean between us?" Andy asked, fighting back a bitter laugh.

"Of course not," Jessie said. "But it would be a huge step. Think about it. If I knew that you had given up this thing that you're holding over me, that would tell me that you're willing to give this a real chance. It would also earn you a hell of a lot of goodwill. If I knew that my sister was safe, that Ryan was safe, and that the people of Los Angeles were safe, it would tell me a lot. It would say that having me is more important than punishing them. That would go a long way, Andy. Remember, my job is to help people, to keep them safe. Do you think I'll ever be able to genuinely commit to being here with you if I'm constantly worried about what might happen to them? If it's just you and me, then I can find a way to feel okay about however things turn out because there's nothing else in the way."

Andy sat with that for a minute, trying to calculation the different permutations. Eventually she gave up.

"If I did that, how could I ever know you'd keep your word?" she asked. "If I don't have that over your head, how do I know you won't try to bail when we have an argument?"

Jessie laughed, but not in a mean way.

"I could ask the same thing of you," she said. "If we had an argument and you got especially upset, how could I be sure you wouldn't have my sister killed? That's the whole point, Andy. In a mature relationship between two adults—two equals—you never know when one of them might bail. That's the risk you take when you offer your heart to someone, that they might leave it in shreds when they walk out the door."

Andy couldn't think of a comeback for that one. She'd never actually been in a mature, adult relationship, not with anyone, certainly not with a woman. She averted her gaze, slightly embarrassed that this person was treating her like someone worthy of this conversation.

"Luckily for you," Jessie continued. "We're not exactly equals because I *can't* physically walk out the door. Even more, I'm telling you I won't even try. I'm not asking you to uncuff me or release me. I'm not asking to go. I'm just asking you for this one thing, to remove the threat to other people. If you want this to work, if you want us to have any chance at a future together, this is the leap you have to take for me."

When Andy finally looked up again, she saw tears streaming down Jessie's face. The profiler made no attempt to hide them or wipe them away. Her expression was one of pleading, of longing, of hope. It was everything Andy had dreamed of when she first put this plan together.

"I'll make the call," she whispered.

Jessie nodded but said nothing, instead finally wiping her face with the sleeve of her shirt. Andy turned and headed back to get the burner phone from the duffel bag on the counter. It was late at night to be reaching out to Zoe, but this was important.

How would she explain it? Did she even need to? All she really had to do was speak the phrase, "The day has ended. Let us all sleep peacefully." That was the official indicator that Operation Z was to be permanently shut down and that Zoe should resume a normal life. Nothing more should be necessary.

But Zoe would surely be disappointed. She knew that her fellow acolytes had all gotten to complete their tasks. Of course, those tasks had been in the service of getting Andy out of prison so that she could be in this very moment now, with Jessie. There was no need for further missions. Zoe would just have to accept that. In an ideal world, she should be thrilled that Andy was getting her happy ending.

She picked up the phone, then glanced back at Jessie, who was still sitting in the patio chair, looking back at her with a mix of pride and affection. It was perfect. Maybe too perfect.

Am I making a mistake? Am I being played? Think about it. This woman's job is to reach into my psyche and use it against me. Was what just happened real, or did she just try to seduce me to fuzz up my brain? What's to stop her from breaking my neck once I make that call? She endured three days tied up in a snowy cabin with her dead mother's body. Why would she be afraid of being stuck in a mine with me rotting beside her? She'd chew off her own arm if she had to in order to survive. And if she knew the truth—that there was actually a road less than two miles from the entrance of this mine, she'd crawl out of here in a second. Jessie Hunt isn't to be trusted.

Andy felt something inside her break. It was almost audible, like a small twig, but she knew what it was: the last remnant of her hope and faith that this experiment could work, along with her heart. Jessie Hunt had snapped all of them in half with her lies, her manipulations, her attempts to twist Andy's brain into a pretzel of base, venal desire.

"I changed my mind," she said, turning around.

"What?" Jessie asked, clearly stunned. "Why?"

Andy dropped the phone back in the duffel bag and stared at the woman across the room. Then she picked up another item from the same bag—a grenade—and put it in her jacket pocket. Right about now, she was tempted to shove it in Jessie's mouth. But she'd have to settle for scaring her with it when the time was right.

"I thought about it," she said, "and it occurs to me that the brilliant profiler may be trying to mess with my head. First you start telling me how you want to have a relationship with me. You make me think that's what I want too—some kind of domesticated lesbian fantasy. Then you start getting all hot and heavy, using my urges and my vulnerability against me, so that my judgment gets clouded."

"Wait," Jessie said, holding up her uncuffed hand. "I'm confused. Your urges and vulnerability? Domesticated lesbian fantasy? *You* kidnapped me. You brought be here to be with you. I finally open up and admit that I'm not appalled by the idea, and this is your reaction? Isn't this what you wanted?"

"You're manipulating me, Jessie, using what happened to me as a girl to make me think I should be with you now."

"Why are you suddenly rejecting your true feelings, Andy?" Jessie asked. "There's no one here but us. You don't have any image to live up to. You're not disappointing anyone. Your father is dead. Your horrific uncle is dead. You can be honest about who you are and what you want. I'm not sure where this sudden denial is coming from. You've already shown me how you feel."

Andy shook her head violently, refusing to let the profiler play her games, get in her head.

"You're trying to make me go soft so that I give up the one tactical advantage I have. You're playing me."

Jessie pushed on the armrests of the patio chair and stood up. She looked hurt and defeated.

"I don't know what to say," she replied quietly. "I feel like I shared my deepest self with you and now you're throwing it back in my face. But you know what hurts the most? That you think it was all an act."

"Well, I'm sorry you feel that way," Andy said. "If I misjudged you, you'll have many months to prove me wrong. Now sit back down."

"I can't," Jessie said. "My leg is cramping up and standing up is the only way to stop it, unless you have a Gatorade or something in that fridge back there."

Andy was inclined to let her suffer through the cramp but some small part of her still couldn't bear the though of Jessie's green eyes cringing in avoidable discomfort.

"Hold on," she said.

She walked to the back fridge and was rummaging through it when she first heard the banging sound. At first, she thought it might be the initial stage of a cave-in, but the sound was too regular and clean. She turned around.

Across the open space, Jessie Hunt was slamming her patio chair against the rock next to her. It only took a fraction of a second for Andy to understand what Jessie was doing. She immediately sprinted back toward her captive.

She didn't know if Jessie was actually close to getting free or if this was just the desperate move of a trapped woman, but she didn't care. It had to be stopped.

Andy closed the ground between them quickly, making her way toward the treacherous, backstabbing bitch in mere seconds. Jessie saw her coming and gave one last whack at the rock just as Andy launched herself into the air.

She slammed hard into Jessie's chest and they both fell backward with a thud. As they did, Andy heard another, less welcoming sound. The metal plate holding the ring and handcuff that kept Jessie attached to the rock snapped with a loud thwack that echoed throughout the cavernous mine.

Jessie Hunt was free.

CHAPTER TWENTY NINE

12:01 a.m., Monday morning

"Clear!"

With that last shouted phrase, Ryan saw their latest lead dry up, just like all the others had.

Along with the Maricopa County Sheriff's department and help from the Phoenix FBI field office, they'd just conducted a raid of the Gold & Silver Mine bar that turned up absolutely nothing. He was about to call Decker and the others to inform them when Agent Bland came over to him and Valentine.

"We just got word that the 911 call about this place came in on a burner phone," he said. "My guess is that it was Robinson calling to throw everyone off again."

Susannah Valentine shook her head in frustration.

"At this point why would she do that?" she demanded. "She's just rubbing our faces in it now."

"No way to trace it?" Ryan asked, though he knew the answer already.

Agent Bland shook his head.

"No," he said. "The call was too short."

Ryan nodded in resignation. He could feel tendrils of hopelessness reaching out for him, telling him that it was time to give up, to accept the inevitable. Glancing over at Valentine, he saw that she was on the verge of giving in to the same feeling.

He forced his face into a mask, refusing to let her see his doubt. If Valentine saw it, that made it real, something he had to deal with, talk about. He wasn't ready for that. In his heart, he knew he would never be ready for that conversation.

He cleared his throat, hoping to hide his despair. Something about hearing the hitch in his own voice filled him with disgust. Jessie would never give up on him. What was he doing, even considering doing the same to her?

With barely controlled fury, he pulled out his phone. He was about to call HSS to update Decker and the others when he saw that he had two voicemails and a text from Kat. With the noise of the helicopter and the subsequent raid of the bar, he had missed them all.

The first voicemail was from twenty-five minutes ago. He pressed the phone hard against his ear to block out the surrounding noise from the parking lot as he listened to the message. It said: "Ryan, we're following up on a lead. Andy Robinson's family owns an abandoned mine not far from the Rintoo Ranch called the Sunkist Mine, as in "all mine." It's about halfway between Quartzsite and Bouse. We think Andy may have taken Jessie there. We're headed that way now. I know you'll want to meet us when you get this but don't come in heavy. It's isolated territory out there. If Robinson hears sirens or a chopper or a parade of squad cars, then we lose our advantage. I'll keep you posted."

He immediately started running for the helicopter. Valentine chased after him, yelling "what the hell?"

He ignored her as he listened to the second voicemail from ten minutes ago. It was static-y but he got the gist: "Leaving the car. Terrain…rough. Hiking the rest…way. I…signal…bad…hills."

The lone text was from the same time as the second voicemail and said simply: *check your VM. Possible lead. Sunkist Mine. Almost there now.*

He arrived at the chopper, where Rusty was seated, sucking on a milkshake that he'd secured from the travel center earlier in the evening.

"I need you to punch a location into your map," Ryan instructed. "Sunkist Mine, halfway between Quartzsite and Bouse."

"I don't need to punch it in," Rusty said indignantly. "I know where that is. It's not too far north of the Quartzsite Rock Alignment."

"How long does it take to get there?"

"Maybe forty-five minutes?"

Ryan grimaced as he got in and slammed the door shut.

"We need to go now," he ordered. "And if you can cut fifteen minutes off that time, that'd be great."

Valentine had barely closed her door before Rusty was flicking buttons and the chopper was revving up.

"Are you going to fill me in on what's going on?' she shouted as they put on their headsets.

Ryan strapped on his belt and indicated that she should do the same. By the time he responded, the chopper was already lifting off.

"I'll fill you in along with everyone else," he said as he dialed the number for HSS. "I just hope that by the time I'm done, it's not too late."

CHAPTER THIRTY

Jessie could barely breathe.

After the momentary high that came from realizing the ring connecting her handcuff to the rock had snapped, she was faced with the brutal reality of Andy Robinson landing on top of her, sitting astride her chest, and punching her relentlessly.

After the shock of the first few blows to the face, she was able lift her forearms and use them as shields, letting them take the brunt of her attacker's fury. She could hear Andy's guttural screaming in between gulps of air.

"It was all a lie!" she shouted, spittle dripping down her lips into Jessie's hair. "I shared the worst thing that ever happened to me, and you used it against me!"

Jessie could feel the savagery of the strikes getting less powerful as the first rush of adrenaline flushed through Andy's system. But her voice lost none of its venom.

"You used my pain to make me doubt myself, just like Uncle Dan did!" Andy spat, her voice cracking slightly.

Jessie ignored the accusation that she'd used Andy's child rape as a tool to escape. This wasn't the time to defend herself against rabid charges. She just had to defend herself.

She waited for the moment she knew would inevitably come when Andy would have to stop punching and screaming in order to regroup and take a breath. It came just seconds later. She sensed Andy's legs loosen their grip around her waist slightly as she inhaled deeply. That's when Jessie acted.

With all her strength, she kicked up with her legs, as if she was a horse bucking her rider off. At the same time, she extended her arms and shoved Andy in the ribs, sending her toppling off to the side. For the briefest of moments, she considered using her advantage to take the fight to her captor, but she sensed that her body just wasn't up to the task.

Instead, she pushed herself upright, got to her feet, and without looking back, started running toward the sound-dampening curtains, to Old Betsy the pickup truck, and to the mineshaft entrance beyond.

Her legs silently shrieked in revolt. Though she typically ran five miles a day, this was a different matter. After over twenty-four hours of cramped confinement in back seats, trunks, and patio chairs, her body wasn't prepared to go into full sprint mode. To make it worse, her balance was uneven, barefoot on one foot and a sandal on the other. She pretended not to notice as she fixed her attention on her path to freedom.

She felt a twinge in her left calf just as she pushed through the curtains and a tightening in her right thigh as she stumbled past Old Betsy. It didn't help that she had a heavy, foot-long collection of metal dangling from her wrist, including the handcuff, the ring, and what was left of the metal plate that had been screwed into the rock.

Jessie heard a scraping sound behind her and glanced back to see that Andy, who wasn't far behind, had grabbed a crowbar from the bed of the pickup and was clutching it above her head. Jessie returned her attention to the shaft in front of her, ignoring the fact that each step away from the main cavern led her further into darkness and toward a gate that was padlocked shut.

Suddenly a searing pain in her left ankle made her leg buckle and she tumbled to the ground. She looked back and saw Andy laying in the dirt behind her. She must have dived after her, swinging the crowbar and making contact as she fell.

Jessie's eyes watered in agony as she clutched her ankle, wondering if it was broken. Through her blurred vision, she saw Andy crawl toward her. All of the woman's charm had been drained away. The creature moving toward her seemed more animal than human, her piercing blue eyes blazing with hate and pain Without warning, Andy, still on her knees, dropped the crowbar, grabbed her by the hair and began dragging her back toward the big cave.

Though both her foot and her head were in anguish, neither could compare to the anger Jessie felt at this indignity. Without even thinking, she swung her arm backward, hoping to make contact. She missed, but her metal companion didn't. One edge of the steel plate slammed hard into Andy's temple, causing an echo throughout the mineshaft.

Andy let go of Jessie's hair. For a second she did nothing other than stare down at her. Then she slowly reached up and touched the spot where she'd been hit. It was already bleeding profusely, running down the left side of her face, just outside of her eye.

"Is it bad?" she asked.

"I don't know," Jessie answered honestly.

"There's a first aid kit back in the main cavern."

Jessie sighed.

"If you tell me where the keys to Old Betsy are, I can put you in the passenger seat and we'll go to the nearest hospital."

Andy chuckled softly, oblivious to the blood that splattered off her head onto the nearby dirt. She stood up, seemed to briefly lose her balance, then steadied herself against the mineshaft wall.

"It's never going to work, is it?" she asked. "You'll never just be with me."

Jessie was dumbfounded. This was the question on her mind at the moment? Hadn't she been denying that being together was what she wanted mere moments ago? Andy's mind seemed to be unraveling more intensely with each passing second.

But maybe the fact that she was asking this question was a good thing. Did it mean there was still a way out of this? Could she still be talked down? Jessie tried to think fast, to come up with the best answer.

"I said that I would, but you wouldn't take 'yes' for an answer."

"Don't lie now, Jessie," Andy said, leaning her back against the wall of the shaft for support. "It's unbecoming."

Jessie, her hair still tingling and her ankle throbbing, did her best to shrug. She wasn't sure what the woman wanted her to say. She doubted that Andy even knew anymore. And she worried that guessing wrong would make her pick up that crowbar again. She tried to answer carefully.

"No, Andy, I was never going to be with you by choice," she admitted, "but I would have been with you out of duty. If you had agreed to let all the others go free, I would have done that. I still will."

"You're still lying," Andy hissed. "That's all you do is lie. You say I'm a bad person but here I am at my darkest moment, and you still won't be straight with me. You're still manipulating and conniving and angling to use my most broken parts against me. If I'm bad, what does that make you?"

Jessie chose not to answer that question, refused to even let herself acknowledge if it had merit. Instead, she asked one of her own.

"What do you want, Andy? If I bare everything to you, will you let the people I care about live?"

Now it was Andy's turn to shrug.

"You've got a better shot that way than the path you're currently on," she said as blood dripped off her chin, creating a small puddle in the dirt at her feet.

Jessie took a deep breath in and exhaled slowly. She'd tried to outsmart Andy. She'd tried to seduce her. She'd tried to escape. All had failed. None of those tactics would work again. She was out of moves. All she had left was the truth and the hope that somewhere deep in Andrea Robinson's soul was a kernel of decency left, one that would prevent her from making anyone else suffer unnecessarily.

"Okay, here's the truth," she said quietly. "I was never going to be with you. I love Ryan Hernandez. I'm *in love* with him. I want to spend the rest of my life with him. And I love my sister and my best friend. And I care about the people of my city. So, I was willing to stay here with you in order to keep them safe. But when you wouldn't make that concession—to promise to let them live—what choice did you leave me but to fight back? I'm not going to just be your plaything, forever worried that one wrong word will put countless lives in danger. I can't live like that."

Andy, half of her face now smeared in blood, smiled down at her.

"You won't have to," she said.

"What do you mean?" Jessie asked nervously.

Andy pulled something out of her jacket pocket, keeping it cupped between her hands.

"Do you remember earlier, how you said that if I ended Operation Z, it would prove that having you was more important to me than punishing all of them?"

"What are you holding, Andy?" Jessie demanded.

"You misunderstood my purpose," Andy continued, ignoring the question. "Operation Z was never about punishing them. It was about punishing *you*, leaving you to live with the everlasting pain of your loved ones' deaths, of the deaths of countless others, all of which you could have prevented, all their blood on your hands."

"What are you holding?" Jessie repeated.

Andy opened her hands like a magician revealing a trick. Resting in her palms was a grenade.

"Why do you have that?" Jessie asked, her voice calmer than her nerves.

"I'm saving you from that pain," Andy said coolly, "at least part of it. We'll die here, together. Of course, that means that my contact won't hear from me, and Operation Z will be activated. So, I guess you *will* have to live with that knowledge and pain. But not for much longer."

Before Jessie could respond, Andy yanked the pin from the grenade and dove on top of her, wrapping one arm around her as she clutched the grenade tightly in the other hand.

*

Maybe it was because her life had flashed before her eyes before on more than one occasion, but for whatever reason, it didn't shock Jessie when, as Andy grabbed at her, time seemed to slow down.

She'd had guns pulled on her and knives too. She'd been near death before and seen others she loved die in front of her. And those last seconds always seemed to play out like molasses. So, she wasn't surprised when her brain seemed to click into slow motion as Andy's body fell on hers.

She suddenly flashed back to one of her earliest encounters with Andy, over two years ago, back before she knew the woman was a killer. She recalled Andy meeting her at Coffee Klatch, dressed casually in sporty sweatpants, a light sweater, and a windbreaker. She was wearing a Dodgers baseball cap with a blonde ponytail poking through the hole in back. They'd talked about college spring break hijinks and complicated fathers. Jessie had thought she'd made a new friend.

The memory evaporated in an instant, but the world still seemed to be moving at a snail's pace. Even as she felt the weight of the collision with Andy, she had accepted that these could be her last seconds on Earth and that nothing she did in them was certain to alter that outcome. But that didn't stop her brain from kicking into action.

She immediately eliminated the idea of trying to use Andy as a human shield against the grenade. If Andy died, so did Hannah, Ryan, and who knows how many others? She needed to live, which meant moving the grenade.

That's why, even as she grunted in pain at the force of Andy's body slamming into hers, she welcomed the momentum because it meant Andy's nose was heading straight toward Jessie's waiting, extended elbow. When the two collided, Andy's hand, involuntarily released the grenade. Jessie grabbed it and, expecting to see her arm disappear in a red mist at any moment, flung it as far as she could back toward the main cavern they'd come from.

It was only when she heard it land that time seemed to return to its normal speed. The thing rolled for several more seconds. She looked over at Andy, whose face was filled with blood-soaked disappointment. Jessie, clinging to the prayer that it was a dud, started to exhale. That's when it exploded.

Even though she was lying on the ground, the force of the blast shot Jessie up and back several feet. She thought she might have been knocked out briefly but couldn't be sure. Either way, her ears were ringing, and her vision was fuzzy. She blinked several times before the latter began to clear up.

Despite the ringing, she heard a groan nearby and glanced over to see that Andy was still beside her, having also been sent flying. She looked dazed. Suddenly her groaning was overwhelmed by a louder noise, a grumbling that seemed to be coming from the Earth beneath them. Small bits of dirt and gravel on the ground began to shake, like popcorn kernels just getting warmed up.

And then, without warning, the Earth beneath them both gave way.

CHAPTER THIRTY ONE

12:06 a.m., Sunday morning

Hannah was knocked right off her feet.

The first, much smaller explosion a minute earlier had made her lose her balance. But at least that had helped direct them to the mine after minutes of wandering around in aimless frustration.

But this second one, just after they'd discovered the well-hidden, padlocked gate to the Sunkist Mine, literally tossed her off the surface of the Earth for a couple of seconds before she landed hard on her butt.

"What was that?" she asked. "An earthquake?"

"No," Kat said, "A cave-in."

"Step back," Callum instructed, pulling out his gun and pointing it at the padlock. "I think whatever's going on in there means we can dispense with the stealth element of our plan."

He fired at the lock, destroying it. Kat yanked opened the ancient gates. Hannah started to rush through when the older woman grabbed her arm.

"Stay out here," she ordered.

"Not in a million years," Hannah told her. "I'll let you go first and try to stay behind you. That's all I'm willing to promise."

Kat looked conflicted for half a second.

"Fine," she muttered. "But please be careful."

Hannah nodded. Kat took the lead, using her flashlight to guide them through the pitch-black mineshaft. Hannah and Callum followed, both using the lights on their phones, which were far weaker. As they moved deeper into the mine, the rumbling got louder and closer. It felt like the whole place might collapse at any second.

They rounded a bend and saw what looked to be a dim light in the distance.

"You see that?" Callum whispered.

"I do," Kat replied. "Approach with caution."

As they moved forward, the groaning bowels of the cave paused. There was a moment of brief, total silence, and then a voice.

"Hello?" a woman called out in a raspy voice, barely audible somewhere in the dimness up ahead. "Is someone there?"

They all froze. Everyone knew it could be a trap. But Hannah also knew that they were in a crumbling mine that might be hiding her sister. She didn't agree with Kat—now wasn't the time for caution.

"Who's there?" she shouted.

"My name is Jessie Hunt. I'm trapped. I need help."

Hannah was running toward her before she'd even completed the sentence. She couldn't see very well despite her phone's flashlight and stumbled several times. She knew she was close when she suddenly felt a powerful hand grip her shoulder and yank her back like she was a rag doll.

"What the—?" she started to object when she saw that it was Kat who had stopped her. But then she saw why. She was just feet from falling into a massive chasm in the shaft. She shined her light on the gap, following its path and saw that it blocked much of the rest of the way into the mine. But she didn't see her sister.

"Jessie," she yelled, "it's Hannah. Where are you?"

"Hannah!" Jessie shouted back from startlingly close, sounding equal parts, excited, shocked, anguished, and weak. "I'm here. Hurry."

Hannah looked to her right, just past a forlorn crowbar lying in the dirt, and for a moment, she couldn't process what she was seeing. Her sister, who for some reason had platinum blonde hair, was dangling over a section of the chasm. The only thing that seemed to be preventing her from falling in was a handcuff attached to a metal ring, which was hooked around an old mine cart track spike buried in the dirt.

Before she could do or say anything, Kat had dropped onto the ground beside her sister, and clutched her forearm, helping take some of the weight off her clearly broken wrist.

"Give me your other hand and I'll pull you out," she said with quiet calm that Hannah admired.

"I can't," Jessie grunted, nodding down into the chasm, "look."

Just then, Callum finally caught up, breathing heavily. With her free hand, Kat shined her flashlight into the darkness. At first, Hannah was shocked by what she saw. But her shock quickly turned to fury.

Jessie was clinging to Andy Robinson, preventing her from falling to her death. Somehow, she'd hooked her own elbow under Andy's armpit, looped her arm back over it and clasped her hand onto the other woman's shoulder, basically supporting all Andy's weight on her own broken, manacled, wrist, which was only secured to the world above by a ring and a rusty post.

Andy's eyes were open, but she only looked semi-conscious. One half of her face was covered in blood, caused by a gash near her left temple. Her head was lolling about, her eyes were cloudy, and she wasn't speaking.

Hannah had no idea why her sister was trying to save the life of the woman who had kidnapped her. Maybe some kind of Stockholm Syndrome had developed in their short time together. Maybe this was part of Jessie's sense of obligation to save everyone, even those who had wronged her. Either way, Hannah aimed to remedy it.

She glanced over at the crowbar on the ground. It was long enough that she could get a solid swing at Andy's skull and knock her out so that she couldn't cling to Jessie. Or maybe she could do more than knock her out. With a couple of blows, she could split the skull open, help the brains ooze out, and make it useless for Jessie to hold on to her. She knelt down and wrapped her hand around the bar.

"Just let go of her," Kat pleaded.

"I really can't," Jessie muttered through gritted teeth. "Listen, she's got a backup plan. It's called Operation Z. If she dies, one of her minions who got released from prison is supposed to put it into effect. I don't know the details, but she said it includes killing you, Hannah, Ryan, and a *lot* of other innocent people. She has to stay alive so we can find this person and stop her. Help me get her out."

"Okay," Kat said as she got on her knees to gain better traction. "Hannah, hold me in place."

Hannah didn't want to let go of the crowbar. She still felt the strong urge to punish the woman who had done this to her sister, to bash Andy's skull in, to feel the bones soften and turn to mush and watch her eyes go dim. The bloodlust coursed through her veins.

But that wouldn't help Jessie. Her sister didn't need vengeance right now. She needed someone to hold onto Kat, so they didn't all fall into nothingness. Reluctantly, she let go of the bar.

"I've got you," she said, wrapping her arms around Kat's waist.

"Callum, shine this in there," Kat said, tossing him her flashlight. He caught it and pointed it into the hole.

What it showed startled all of them. Andy's eyes were no longer cloudy. They were clear and bright. She was staring at Jessie. And she was smiling.

"You do care," she said.

"What?" Jessie replied, confused, before saying, "Of course I care. I don't want you to die, Andy. Let me help you. Reach up with your other hand and Kat will grab you."

Kat looked over her shoulder.

"Considering that plan," she muttered, "I assume the hand without the flashlight has a gun in it, Callum."

"It does," he assured her.

Kat extended her hand down, but Andy made no attempt to reach up to grab it.

"Come on, Andy," Jessie pleaded, "My elbow's starting to give out. I can't support your weight much longer. Take Kat's hand."

"No," Andy said. "This is better."

"What?" Jessie asked, clearly straining to talk and hold on to her at the same time.

"If I live, then I'll go back to Twin Towers or someplace like it. You'll eventually forget me. But if I die, then so will everyone else you love. You won't know how or when death will come for them. But it will, and it will haunt you forever. And in that way, I'll control your soul forever."

"Wouldn't you rather try to control the real me, Andy?" Jessie begged. "Reach out your hand."

Hannah could hear the desperation in her sister's voice and knew right away that her plea wouldn't work. Instead of reaching up, Andy reached down and pulled something out from under the cuff of her jeans. When she lifted it into the light, the point of a four-inch switchblade gleamed.

"Don't even think about it!" Callum barked from behind them.

"I was saving this," Andy said. "I could have used it on you earlier, but I didn't want it to end this way for us. It's so pedestrian. But if you don't let go of me, I'll have to use it now. I swear I'll cut you open, right at an artery. You'll bleed out before help can arrive."

"You make a move toward her, and you lose a hand," Kat warned.

"I can't let go of you," Jessie said, clearly straining, her elbow starting to unfurl under the weight of Andy's body. "I can't let you die. Not if it means letting you kill all those people too."

"They're going to die no matter what," Andy said. "It's just a question of whether you'll join them."

Hannah considered letting go of Kat to grab the crowbar and whack the knife out of Andy's hand but feared that might send the woman tumbling into the chasm.

"You won't kill me," Jessie said quietly. "You love me."

Andy stared up at her with those brilliant blue, piercing eyes, like cobalt lasers burning into her sister.

"I do love you," she said, "but we always hurt the ones we love."

Without another word, she flung her body upward, swinging the knife toward Jessie. But before it reached her a shot rang out. Hannah saw a hole slam into her chest as the knife dropped from her hand. Her whole body slumped and seemed to slide out from under Jessie's arm like it was melting. Her eyes stayed fixed on the woman above her as she fell. One word escaped her mouth in a ghastly whisper as she disappeared into the darkness below.

"Jessie."

Hannah looked over her shoulder to see Callum Reid still pointing his gun at the empty space where Andrea Robinson had been only moments earlier. For several seconds there was no sound other than the endless echo of the gunshot.

Then the rumbling in the mine returned.

CHAPTER THIRTY TWO

Hannah stared at Callum, who seemed frozen in place. She wanted to say something to snap him out of it but couldn't come up with the right words.

"I couldn't risk aiming for her hand," Callum finally said quietly. "I couldn't take the chance that she'd get Jessie with that knife."

"We'll deal with that later," Kat barked. "Right now, we have to get out of here. This place is on the verge of complete collapse."

With Jessie no longer fighting them, they were able to pull her up in seconds. Kat tried to unhook the ring from the spike in the ground, but it was snagged on a corroded notch.

"Where's the key to the cuffs?" she asked Jessie. "We can just untie you from the ring that way."

"It's in an orange duffle bag on a kitchen table in the main cavern back there."

"It's too dangerous to go back there now," Callum said, "Let's just shoot the cuff off and be done with it."

"But that might trigger the collapse," Kat protested.

"We have to go back," Jessie insisted. "That bag also has the burner phone I think Andy was using to communicate with whoever is in charge of Operation Z. Now that she's dead, it's our only link to this woman. Maybe we can use it to find her. Without it, we've got nothing. And once she hears about Andy's death, there won't be anything to stop her from putting the plan into motion."

"Okay," Hannah said. "I'll go get it."

She started to get up when Kat grabbed her.

"No way," she chided. "Stay with your sister. Keep working on getting the ring loose. I'll be right back."

She stood up before Hannah could protest. That's when they both noticed that Callum had already traversed the narrow gap in the path and was hurrying toward the big cavern.

"I thought you said it was too dangerous to go back there," Hannah called after him.

"It is," he yelled back. "But I'm a seasoned professional."

As he faded from view, Kat returned her attention to the ring, trying again to tug it free from the snag without success. Hannah looked at her sister, who seemed to be trying to hold it together, despite clearly being on the verge of shock.

Her face was bruised. Her breathing was shallow. Her wrist was ugly—purple and swollen. And looking at her feet, Hannah saw that she was wearing one sandal. The ankle of her other, bare foot looked as bad as her wrist.

"What happened there?" she asked.

"Crowbar," Jessie mumbled, clearly trying to keep it together. "How bad is it?"

"Not as bad your hair," Hannah said, hoping to take her mind off the pain she was clearly feeling. "I get that you're jealous of your younger, blonde, sister, but this seems excessive."

"Believe me," Jessie replied through gritted teeth, "this is *not* my dream look."

"Found it," Callum called out from somewhere in the distance.

"Good," Kat yelled back. "Hurry!"

Almost as soon as she got the words out, the rumbling returned, this time louder than before. The hole beside them started to expand. Rocks began falling from above them.

"We can't wait—I'm shooting the cuff!" Kat yelled. "Be ready to pull her away by the legs as soon as I say 'go!'"

"Okay," Hannah said, ignoring the coffee mug-sized rocks hitting her back and Jessie's wince as she clutched her by the ankles.

The gunshot came within seconds, as did the shouted "go!" She yanked hard and dragged her sister as fast and as far as she could before the mine erupted, coughing her up into the air. She was off her feet again, just as she had been outside the mine. This time she landed on her face. Without pausing, she shot back up to look for Jessie. It wasn't hard to find her.

The last tremor had opened up a chunk of the roof of the mine the size of a picnic table and the night sky was pouring in, illuminating the shaft in bright starlight. Jessie appeared to be okay. There was debris around her but no major pieces on top of her. Kat too was getting to her feet, brushing herself off. After checking on Jessie, she looked around.

"Where's Callum?" she asked.

"I'm here," he called out from somewhere behind them.

They looked back in the direction of the voice. The dust started to clear, and they could see him about twenty feet back, holding the orange duffel bag that Jessie had described. It took a few more seconds for it to become apparent why he hadn't come any farther.

There was a huge gap spanning the entire distance between them, which took up the whole mineshaft. There was no way around it. Hannah tried to calculate if it might be possible to jump the gap, but almost immediately stopped herself. It would be impossible for someone in good shape to jump half that distance. There was no way Callum could clear all of it.

The mine rumbled again, as if mocking them. Several rocks, one the size of a toaster, fell just to the left of Jessie. Hannah and Kat rushed over to her and helped pull her to her feet. As they did, she spoke.

"Listen, Callum," she tried to shout, though her voice was weak. "I saw Andy put some cordage in one of those plastic bins back there. Go get it. Wrap one end around your chest just under the armpits. Toss the other end to us. Jump across and we'll pull you up. We'll use the gate at the mine entrance to tie off for extra support."

More rocks tumbled around them as the ground shifted beneath their feet. Callum nodded.

"Okay," he said. "First, let me get this bag across to you. You sure it's the right one? Because I didn't search it for the phone."

"She only had one orange duffle bag," Jessie assured him.

"Okay then. Here it comes."

He flung it. They all watched as it spun endlessly across the starry night until it landed in the dirt not far from Hannah's feet.

"Good toss," Jessie commended him. "Now go get that rope."

"You know that's not happening, Jessie," he said with a sad smile.

"Of course, it is," Jessie told him. "I think it was in the cabinet on the far right."

"Let's be real, my friend," he said, sitting down on the dirt at the end of chasm.

Something about seeing him do that made Hannah's chest start to ache. Next to her, she could feel Jessie falter slightly.

"I'm too old and fat to make that jump," he said. "I'd pull you ladies right there down with me. Besides, by the time I find that rope and you tie it off to the gate, this whole section of Earth is going to be under a mountain of rubble. That could happen at any second, which is why you have to go now."

As if to confirm his concerns, the mine seemed to gargle and belch all at once. More rocks fell. This time, one about the size of a houseplant landed on Kat's shoulder. She grunted softly before turning to Jessie.

"He's right," she whispered. "If we don't go now, we all die and this whole thing was for nothing. His sacrifice was for nothing. And this Operation Z, whatever it is, gets activated. We have to get out, Jessie."

Jessie looked at her best friend for a second, then turned back to Callum.

"You're not even supposed to be here," she yelled at him, her voice cracking. "You're retired. What the hell are you doing here anyway?"

He gave her a little smile, then shrugged.

"I was looking out for my friend," he said. "Just like she always did for me. Now please go, if not for me or yourself, for that little sister of yours. She's pretty impressive in case you didn't know."

The ache in Hannah's chest burst open and she thought she might choke on the pain.

"I know," Jessie said, and Hannah could feel her sister's body quivering beside her. Then all at once the shaking stopped and Jessie seemed to straighten up slightly. "Thank you, Callum."

"Tell Tanya and the kids I love them."

"I will," she promised, before taking a deep breath and turning to face Hannah. Her eyes were wet but focused. "I appreciate the help, but I think I'm going to ask the former Army Ranger to drag me out of here. You grab that bag. Don't let go of it, no matter what, got it?"

"Got it," Hannah said, inexplicably reassured by her sister's take-charge energy. She picked up the bag and flung it over her shoulder.

The mine didn't seem as enthused by her confidence. Its constant, slow rumbling was growing deafening, just as it had before the last two giant quakes.

"Kat," Jessie said. "My ankle's shot. You're going to have to do most of the work here."

"Not a problem," Kat said, swinging her shoulder under Jessie's armpit and nearly lifting her off the ground as she started toward the mine entrance, "Let's move!"

Even though her load was lighter, Hannah had to hurry to keep up with them. The roar of the mine was so loud now that she couldn't even hear the chunks of rock as they landed on the ground nearby. As she followed Kat and Jessie around the bend that led to the entrance, she cast one last look back.

Callum was still sitting at the edge of the chasm. He stared back at her, a peaceful look on his face, a half-grin playing at his lips. He gave her a small wave. And then, in an instant, the ground beneath him gave way, and he was gone.

Hannah turned back around, blocked out everything but the gate in the distance ahead, and ran.

CHAPTER THIRTY THREE

She wanted to fall asleep but knew there was a reason she couldn't.

Something was itching at the inside of Jessie's brain and until she could scratch it, she was afraid to let her mind rest.

"Listen," Ryan said, "the medivac copter will be here in less than a minute. They'll have something for the pain. Can you hold out a little bit longer?"

She nodded, even though she wasn't sure that she could.

It had been about a half-hour since the mine completely collapsed. She had waited, lying on her back on a pile of soft dirt, with Kat and Hannah during that time, slipping in and out of consciousness as they called for help. While she was awake, they told her about the search for her, including the fact that she was in the Arizona desert, only about forty-five miles from the California border. She got the impression that they were leaving some details out because of her diminished state.

Ryan and Susannah Valentine had arrived about ten minutes ago in an FBI-contracted helicopter. Apparently, the FBI, U.S. Marshals, and multiple Sheriff's departments had all been working together to find her. Jessie was honored to have earned such a big response and decided to even give Valentine the benefit of the doubt this once, especially when the woman insisted on going back to the mine to search for Callum.

The group had considered just transporting her in the FBI chopper, but the pilot was resistant and apparently Decker insisted they wait for the medivac, especially once he heard about the extent of her injuries, including a possible concussion.

"Where are Hannah and Kat?" she asked, unable to see them from her position, lying on her back.

"We're right here," Hannah said from just out of sight.

"Did you check the orange duffel bag for that phone?" Jessie pressed. "Did I already ask you that?"

"You did ask and it's in there," Hannah assured her as a helicopter appeared over the ridge and came their way.

"Remember," Ryan said gently, "We're just leaving it in the bag for now until the tech experts can get their hands on it."

"Sorry if I'm repeating myself," Jessie said.

"It's okay," Kat replied. "You've been through a lot. It's to be expected."

"Just make sure that it gets to Jamil," Jessie told Ryan. "It could be key to stopping Operation Z."

"Operation what?" he asked.

"I didn't mention that yet?"

He shook his head, confused.

Jessie sighed at the challenge of explaining the whole thing to him.

"We'll catch him up," Kat promised in a soft, reassuring voice. "You just rest."

The helicopter was landing, making it too hard to hear anything anyway. Once it touched down the EMTs came over, transferred her to a stretcher, inserted an IV, and asked a series of questions. She did her best to answer them but was glad that Kat and Hannah were there to fill in the blanks. She was troubled that there were blanks.

"How is Callum doing?" she asked when they were done.

Both Kat and Hannah gave her dismayed looks and she realized her mistake.

"Right," she corrected herself, "he didn't make it. I'm a little fuzzy."

"Part of that might be the medication we just gave you, Ms. Hunt," one of the EMTs said. "It should help with some of your discomfort. It might also make you a little sleepy. We're going to move to you to the chopper now, okay?"

Just then, Valentine came running up, breathing heavily. For a moment, Jessie was confused as to why. But when she saw the distressed look on the detective's face, she remembered.

"I couldn't find any sign of Callum's body," she said between huffs, "or Robinson for that matter."

Hannah raised her hand hesitantly as if she was answering a tough question in class.

"I saw then both disappear into a massive hole in the Earth," she said quietly. "I don't know if we'll ever find them."

"I'm sorry," the EMT interrupted, "but we really have to get moving."

"Okay," Jessie said, already sensing the agony in her wrist and ankle start to subside a bit as a result of the meds she'd been given. Her eyelids felt a bit heavy too. But she fought to keep them awake, again sensing that there was some crucial, unfinished business she had to complete before she could rest.

"Who's accompanying her?" the EMT asked. "Family only."

"I am," Ryan said.

"Me too," Hannah said.

"I'm afraid we can only accommodate one family member."

Jessie stared up through thick eyes as Ryan and Hannah looked at each other. Then Ryan turned to the EMT.

"You're making an exception in this case," he said firmly.

The EMT opened his mouth to protest, then seemed to think better of it.

"Okay then," he said.

They started to lift her when Jessie remembered what she'd been forgetting.

"Wait," she said, grabbing Ryan's wrist. "Andy's not dead."

He looked down at her with a mix of affection and concern.

"Jessie," he said comfortingly, "you don't have to worry. Based on what Kat and Hannah told me, she absolutely is."

"No," Jessie said, clutching him tighter and opening her eyes as wide as she could and trying to enunciate each word clearly. "You don't understand. She can't be dead."

Ryan extricated his wrist and patted her arm gently.

"Okay, we'll clear it all up later," he assured her.

Panic rose inside her. She had to make him understand. If he didn't, he would die. So many people would die. But she could feel herself fading. She couldn't explain it to him. She looked around for anyone who could help her. Finally, her eyes locked on Hannah's, and she licked her lips. Her sister seemed to understand that meant that she needed her to lean in and put her ear close to Jessie's mouth.

"Andy must be alive," she murmured, unsure if her words were even coming out coherently. "Only way to stop Z. Understand?"

Hannah lifted her head and looked down at her. Then she nodded.

Jessie let her eyes close.

CHAPTER THIRTY FOUR

3:59 p.m., Tuesday afternoon

Jessie made sure not to push the button on the remote too hard.

If she did, the hospital bed would go up higher than she wanted and her ribs would ache, despite the pain medication she was on. She'd already made that mistake once when she first woke up around midday but was still too drugged up to figure the thing out. Luckily a nurse was there to help ease her back down or she'd have been stuck that way—bent over with cracked ribs—for who knows how long.

But she was much more clear-headed this time around. In fact, now it was Ryan who was zonked out, slumped in the uncomfortable-looking chair next to the bed, wearing a ridiculous trench coat like a wannabe Sam Spade. She wondered why. After all, it was late March already. Was it that cold in here? Maybe she was more drugged up than she realized.

The doctor had told her earlier that he'd be keeping her on the morphine drip for another day, despite her objections. That was because, in addition to the two cracked ribs, she had the broken wrist, the fracture in her ankle bone, multiple facial, back, and leg bruises, and at least one concussion. That last diagnosis was why he was refusing to discharge her for at least another forty-eight hours. She still remembered how cagey he'd been about it at first.

"We're still waiting for some test results," he'd said.

"Can't I just come back when you have them, and we'll go over them then?" she remembered asking. "There's a funeral for a friend of mine tomorrow afternoon and it's important that I be there, even if I'm wheelchair-bound."

"That won't be possible," the doctor had said. "We need to keep you under close observation in the interim."

"I'll come right back, Doc," she had said, flashing her most charming smile, "It won't be more than a couple of hours."

"I'm afraid it's non-negotiable," the doctor had said flatly.

Jessie could tell from his tone that he meant business. And when she looked over at Ryan, who had hadn't tried to argue her case, she knew she wasn't going to win this one.

"Okay," she had said, leaving it at that, unwilling to ask the obvious follow-up questions that she would have pursued if this were an interrogation. In that moment, she wasn't sure she wanted to hear the potential answers.

She'd have to wait to talk to Tanya Reid, Callum's widow, later. Maybe it would be better that way anyway. Tanya had enough to deal with at the moment, now that she was suddenly a single mother to two kids. Hell, she wasn't even able to bury her husband properly.

His coffin would be empty because, like Andy's, his body had never been found. Besides, Jessie wasn't even sure what to say to the woman, much less the kids. Tired of thinking about it, she looked for the other remote that operated the TV. It was 4 p.m. and the local news was about to start.

This was the first time she'd be coherent enough to watch it since being brought to the hospital last night and she was curious to see how they were reporting recent events. When the screen clicked on, the anchor was already throwing to an attractively statuesque, black reporter, standing outside police headquarters.

"...still a lot of confusion in the wake these events, Calista," he said.

"That's right, Stan," Calista agreed conversationally, before switching into informational mode. "There are still as many questions as answers surrounding the last few tumultuous days for southern California law enforcement. What we know for sure is that a multijurisdictional unit led by the Los Angeles Police Department and incorporating the resources of Los Angeles and Phoenix FBI field offices, the U.S. Marshals Service, and Sheriff's departments from two states and four counties all worked together in a non-stop search to locate kidnapped criminal profiler Jessie Hunt."

As she continued, the screen then cut to a drone shot of the Peninsula resort.

"Viewers will remember that Hunt was abducted on her own wedding night from The Peninsula Resort and Spa, just before she was about to exchange vows with Detective Ryan Hernandez, also of the famed Homicide Special Section Unit. While it was quickly determined that the kidnapper was recently paroled, convicted murderer Andrea Robinson, finding the two women wasn't as simple."

The resort was replaced with a series of video clips, including footage from the Flying Y travel center, a freeway chase involving a flipped car and a helicopter, a bar raid, and multiple stock images of endless desert, culminating in a long shot of the Sunkist Mine, all narrated by the reporter.

"In the end, despite all the shared resources and teamwork, it wasn't the professionals who found Jessie Hunt. Rather it was Hunt's best friend—a private detective and former Army Ranger—along with her teenage stepsister, and a retired LAPD detective, Callum Reid, who died in the in the effort and will be laid to rest tomorrow."

The camera returned to the image of the reporter, who stared gravely at everyone watching.

"That's what we know," she said. "But there's a lot we don't. Questions still being asked by many include: What took Mayor Alvarez so long to replace Chief Richard Laird in light of the failures he outlined in his press conference last night? Would any of these events have even occurred if Laird had been removed earlier, likely preventing Andrea Robinson from ever being released in the first place? How long will Roy Decker remain as interim chief before a permanent chief is named and who will take over the reins of Homicide Special Section from him? Interim Chief Decker has promised that he will have an answer on that last question 'soon.'"

The camera, which had been in a medium shot, now moved into a close-up, suggesting that the best was yet to come.

"Lastly," the reporter said, her tone grave, "and perhaps most importantly, the question remains: where is Andrea Robinson? Authorities acknowledge that when Hunt was discovered, Robinson was nowhere to be found. According to unconfirmed reports, Hunt herself said that she awoke in the Sunkist Mine alone after having been drugged, without any idea where Robinson was or how long she had been gone. Some investigators reportedly believe that Robinson may have set the mine to explode, hoping to trap Hunt and those who found her in a rocky tomb. On that front, luck may have been on the side of the angels, as the mine didn't cave in until they had gotten out. But it leaves open the very troubling concern that Andrea Robinson is still out there, plotting her next act of violence against Jessie Hunt and the people of Los Angeles. Live from Police Headquarters, this is Calista Dunphree, Eye in the Sky News."

"That's as close to alive as we could get."

Jessie jumped slightly at the sound of the voice to her left. It was Ryan, now awake, with a drowsy grin on his face. She turned off the television.

"It's pretty good," Jessie said. "I especially like the idea that Andy tried to lure people into the mine to blow us all up when they found me. It sounds like her. Very believable. It almost makes me think she's still out there."

"That was your sister's idea," Ryan said. "Once she explained what this Operation Z was and what you meant about Andy needing to still be alive, we put together a cover story quickly. But she came up with the most convincing grace notes. She knows how to think like these people. Kind of reminds me of someone else I know."

Jessie felt a mix of pride and anxiety at hearing that and pushed past it for now.

"Well, I think it will hold off whoever's running Operation Z, at least for a little while. The problem is that Andy dying might not be the only way the operation gets activated."

"What do you mean?" Ryan asked.

"Knowing Andy, there's always a contingency plan," Jessie said. "She might not have foreseen us covering up her death, but she likely anticipated something going sideways. We have to assume that she set up some sort of standard check-in with this acolyte. Otherwise, why have the burner phone at all? Maybe she's supposed to call the woman every week or even every month, just to let her know to stand down. But if the acolyte doesn't get that call, she knows something's wrong, even if she hasn't gotten word of Andy's death, and she activates Operation Z. If I'm right, that means there's a ticking clock on this thing. We just don't know how much time it has left."

Ryan tried to hide his concern with a smile, but Jessie knew him too well. His eyes gave him away.

"We're on it, Jessie," he said. "Jamil's been poring over the phone since he got it. Plus, Kat, Hannah, and Callum found some interesting stuff in the medicine cabinet at the apartment of Corinne Bertans, the woman who took your place at the wedding. It was connected to the various acolytes. We're doing some pattern analysis on it. There are leads, Jessie. I promise we're not twiddling our thumbs over there at HSS."

She could tell that her agitation was worrying him and decided not to press the issue. Between Operation Z and whatever concern had the doctor keeping her under observation, he was under as much stress as she was. And she doubted he'd gotten a night's worth of morphine-aided sleep. She decided to ease up.

"So, who's 'we?'" she asked playfully.

"What?"

"You said 'we're' on it," she reminded him. "Who's making those decisions? Is it still Decker? According to Calista from Eye in the Sky, now that he's chief, he's choosing his HSS replacement soon. Care to loop me in?"

"He doesn't just have to choose who runs HSS," Ryan said quietly. "Remember, he's got to pick a new captain for all of Central Station. That place won't just run itself."

Jessie frowned.

"But Listovich has been his second in command since forever," Jessie said. "I just assumed he'd take over."

Ryan shook his head.

"Remember, when Mayor Alvarez dumped Laird, all his cronies had to go too. That means Decker needs people he knows and trusts with him in positions of power at headquarters. That almost certainly includes Listovich."

"So, who would lead Central then?" Jessie asked, stumped.

Ryan looked down at the floor and shrugged silently. Jessie suddenly felt very uneasy.

"Wait, are you serious?" she asked.

He looked up.

"Nothing's been determined," he replied. "But it's been mentioned as a possibility. I've been the de facto day-to-day leader of HSS since its inception. It wouldn't be that huge a leap. How would you feel about it if I got discussed more seriously?"

Jessie's gut was tumble of mixed emotions, all of which she set aside. This moment wasn't about her, and she didn't want him to remember her as being anything other than supportive.

"You definitely deserve it," she said. "You're more than qualified. And think of the billboard material. Hero cop goes from coma to captain in less than year. It's inspiring. Officers would run through walls for you, Ryan."

He shook his head.

"Yeah, but how would you *feel* about it?"

It was her turn to shrug.

"I just suffered a head injury so you can't hold anything I say against me, right?"

"Right," he promised.

"Okay," she said. "I would be incredibly proud of you. I would support you without question. But the selfish part of me is worried about what would happen to me. I'm supposed to start back with the department full-time soon, assuming that doctor gives me the 'all clear.' Does that mean we're not working cases together anymore? Would you be my boss? How would that work at home? And who would I partner up with—Karen? Nettles? Dear God, would I have to partner with Susannah Valentine?"

He held up his hands.

"Let's not get a head of ourselves," he said. "Nothing's happened yet, and it might not. The idea was just floated. By the way, not to defend her or anything, but just so you know, it was Valentine who stopped Corinne Bertans from throwing herself off that cliff at the wedding. She snagged her from behind just in time. If she hadn't, we never would have gotten the clue that led to finding that mine and saving you. Just something to think about."

Jessie nodded, taking in the information, which was new to her.

"I'll have to thank her for that," she said, before adding, too quietly for him to hear, "I guess that makes up for *one* of the dozen times I saw her flirting with you."

"What was that?" he asked.

"Nothing," she told him. "Just talking to myself."

He gave her an odd look, then pushed himself up from the chair. He suddenly looked nervous.

"I have to step out for just a second," he said. "I'll be right back."

"Are you off to buy a fedora to go with that trench coat?" she teased.

"You don't like the coat?" he asked.

"It's almost April in Los Angeles, Ryan."

"I think you're just trying to deflect attention away from that platinum blonde hair that you obviously asked Andy to give you," he needled, proving that he wasn't going to let her get the upper hand all the time, even if she was bedridden.

"Mocking an invalid?" she replied, feigning deep offense. "What kind of man are you?

He grinned sheepishly.

"No fedora, I swear," he said.

Jessie suddenly had a terrifying thought.

"You're not going to bring Valentine in here to have a special moment with me, are you?" she asked.

"No, Jessie," he said, sighing. "Don't worry."

He stepped out, almost tripping over his trench coat as he left the room. She felt a tiny bit of pleasure at the sight before guilt quickly took over. She knew it wasn't fair to be upset with him for sticking up for Valentine. Of course, that wasn't what really irked her.

If she was honest, it was something equally unfair. She found herself blaming Ryan for not rescuing her. As she had learned, while Kat, Hannah, and Callum were closing in on the Sunkist Mine, he was off raiding a country and western bar in another part of the state, completely snowed by one of Andy's many misdirections.

Of course, Andy had fooled everyone multiple times and he had done everything that he possibly could at every step along the way. But when the moment came, when she was dangling from a spike over a vast emptiness, he wasn't the one who called out to her in the darkness, who came running to her aid. It wasn't his fault, but it was true. And it ate at her.

That wasn't the only thing eating at her. She still remembered Andy calling out her name as she fell into the gaping hole in the earth, her blue eyes penetrating her even after they had disappeared into the blackness.

Just as troubling, she remembered Andy's final accusation, minutes earlier, as she stood over her in the mine, bloody-faced and vengeful—her allegation that Jessie was using her childhood rape to get a tactical advantage.

"You say I'm a bad person, but here I am at my darkest moment," she had charged, "and you're still manipulating and conniving and angling to use my most broken parts against me. If I'm bad, what does that make you?"

Had she used Andy's most traumatic moment as a tool to weaken her? If so, did the ends justify the means? Had she crossed some line that now made her as irredeemable as the people she hunted?

It was a question she wasn't sure she was equipped to answer in her current condition. And even though deep down, she knew that she was using her injuries and exhaustion as a justification to avoid addressing it, she leapt at the excuse to put it out of her mind.

The door opened and Ryan stepped back inside. He was no longer wearing the trench coat. Instead, he had on a simple black tuxedo. His face was beet-red. He pulled the door shut behind him.

"What the—?" Jessie started to say.

"Jessie," he interrupted, "I'm tired of waiting. I know we can reschedule something with our family and friends. I'd like to do that. But I want to be married to you, not in another month, or week, or even a day. I want to be married to you right now."

"Is this why the doctor wanted to keep me under observation?" Jessie asked disbelievingly, "because I'm not sure that I totally understand what's going on."

Ryan walked over and took her hand, the one not in a cast, squeezing it tight.

"The hospital chaplain is right outside," he said. "So is your nurse, so we have someone to take pictures. If you're willing, we can do this right now. We've already had too much time stolen from us. I don't want to lose another minute."

Jessie could feel tears forming in her eyes as she tried to come up with the right words to say. For one of the few times in her life, she was speechless. Ryan frowned uncertainly.

"I know this is dramatic," he whispered. "If it's too much or your head's not right or the meds are getting in the way or this just isn't how you want to do it or…if you're having second thoughts, I can just tell them to go away. No harm done. I just…I love you and I want to be with you and…that's all I guess."

Jessie took a deep breath and exhaled loudly before trying to speak.

"The thing is," she said, "I have this ridiculous hair and all these bruises on my face."

Ryan nodded and lowered his head.

"I understand," he said.

"So, we'll have to photoshop those out later."

He looked up again.

"What?"

"Call them in," she said, smiling.

"You're serious?" he asked, his eyes now welling up.

"I am," she told him, pulling him toward her and giving him a soft kiss on the lips, "except for one thing."

"What?" he asked.

"The photoshopping—we're not doing it."

"No?" he said.

"You know me better than that. I'll deal with the hair. And as far as the bruises go, I consider them a badge of honor."

EPILOGUE

Zoe turned off the television.

As she walked into the kitchen to do the dishes, she replayed the news story in her head. Things certainly hadn't gone as she'd expected, or as Andy had predicted they would. It was all a little unsettling.

She turned on the water, soaped up a dish rag, and reached for the first plate, which promptly slipped out of her hand and shattered onto the floor. She turned off the water, dried her hands, and pressed them hard against the kitchen counter.

At times like this it was important to be honest with herself. This situation was more than unsettling. It was downright disappointing. She'd been so excited, anticipating what seemed like a certainty. She would finally get to complete the mission she'd been planning for months. But she hadn't prepared for the letdown that would come from no resolution at all.

It had been over twelve hours since Jessie Hunt was discovered and there hadn't been a word from Andy. Zoe was stuck in this infuriating holding pattern. She didn't know what she could and couldn't do.

If Jessie had been officially rescued, that meant Operation Z could be activated. But it wasn't clear if Jessie had been rescued or if Andy had simply abandoned her in the mine or perhaps given the location to searchers herself to draw them in and trap them in an explosion. Until that crucial distinction was clarified, she couldn't assume anything or take any action.

But right now, Andy could be on the run, in hiding, perhaps injured, unable to reach out. Her status was unknown. And until she reached out with an update, Zoe was in limbo too, unsure when, or even if she would ever get the chance to put her masterwork into effect.

Suddenly Zoe relaxed her hands on the countertop as she remembered that wasn't quite true. Yes, she was in limbo for now, but not forever. There was a date by which Andy was obligated to contact her. It was set in stone. If Zoe didn't hear from Andy by then, she was to assume that The Principal was dead, and that Operation Z was officially active.

She hoped she got word before then. She wanted to hear Andy's voice again, to imagine it was right next to her, whispering in her ear, tickling the hairs on her neck. But if that call didn't come, then Zoe would honor The Principal's legacy by completing the mission she'd been assigned.

She got a pen and circled the date on the wall calendar. Then she got down on her knees and began picking up shards of the shattered plate on the floor with her hands. Bits of the sharp edges cut her, and blood started to trickle down her fingertips, but she didn't mind.

Pain clarified. Blood purified. Soon enough, everyone would know those simple truths.

NOW AVAILABLE!

THE PERFECT MASK
(A Jessie Hunt Psychological Suspense Thriller—Book Twenty-Four)

When high-society women are found dead in their opulent California homes, Jessie Hunt is summoned to crack the case. With little to connect them—other than hidden scandal—Jessie is at a loss. Why are they being targeted? And who is next?

"A masterpiece of thriller and mystery."
—Books and Movie Reviews, Roberto Mattos (re Once Gone)

THE PERFECT MASK is book #24 in a new psychological suspense series by bestselling author Blake Pierce, which begins with *The Perfect Wife*, **a #1 bestseller (and free download) with over 5,000 five-star ratings and 1,000 five-star reviews.**

These wealthy wives and moms are unlikely targets, and with no sign of foul play, connecting the dots seems impossible.

Yet Jessie digs deep, plumbing this exclusive world for clues, finding out more than she wished she'd ever knew.

But every society has a dark side.

And Jessie may just be about to step into a killer's arms.

A fast-paced psychological suspense thriller with unforgettable characters and heart-pounding suspense, the JESSIE HUNT series is a riveting new series that will leave you turning pages late into the night.

Book #25—THE PERFECT RUSE—and Book #26—THE PERFECT VENEER--are now also available.

"An edge of your seat thriller in a new series that keeps you turning pages! ...So many twists, turns and red herrings... I can't wait to see what happens next."
—Reader review (Her Last Wish)

"A strong, complex story about two FBI agents trying to stop a serial killer. If you want an author to capture your attention and have you guessing, yet trying to put the pieces together, Pierce is your author!"
—Reader review (Her Last Wish)

"A typical Blake Pierce twisting, turning, roller coaster ride suspense thriller. Will have you turning the pages to the last sentence of the last chapter!!!"
—Reader review (City of Prey)

"Right from the start we have an unusual protagonist that I haven't seen done in this genre before. The action is nonstop... A very atmospheric novel that will keep you turning pages well into the wee hours."
—Reader review (City of Prey)

"Everything that I look for in a book... a great plot, interesting characters, and grabs your interest right away. The book moves along at a breakneck pace and stays that way until the end. Now on go I to book two!"
—Reader review (Girl, Alone)

"Exciting, heart pounding, edge of your seat book... a must read for mystery and suspense readers!"
—Reader review (Girl, Alone)

Blake Pierce

Blake Pierce is the USA Today bestselling author of the RILEY PAGE mystery series, which includes seventeen books. Blake Pierce is also the author of the MACKENZIE WHITE mystery series, comprising fourteen books; of the AVERY BLACK mystery series, comprising six books; of the KERI LOCKE mystery series, comprising five books; of the MAKING OF RILEY PAIGE mystery series, comprising six books; of the KATE WISE mystery series, comprising seven books; of the CHLOE FINE psychological suspense mystery, comprising six books; of the JESSIE HUNT psychological suspense thriller series, comprising twenty six books; of the AU PAIR psychological suspense thriller series, comprising three books; of the ZOE PRIME mystery series, comprising six books; of the ADELE SHARP mystery series, comprising sixteen books, of the EUROPEAN VOYAGE cozy mystery series, comprising six books; of the LAURA FROST FBI suspense thriller, comprising eleven books; of the ELLA DARK FBI suspense thriller, comprising fourteen books (and counting); of the A YEAR IN EUROPE cozy mystery series, comprising nine books, of the AVA GOLD mystery series, comprising six books (and counting); of the RACHEL GIFT mystery series, comprising ten books (and counting); of the VALERIE LAW mystery series, comprising nine books (and counting); of the PAIGE KING mystery series, comprising eight books (and counting); of the MAY MOORE mystery series, comprising eleven books (and counting); the CORA SHIELDS mystery series, comprising five books (and counting); of the NICKY LYONS mystery series, comprising five books (and counting), and of the new CAMI LARK mystery series, comprising five books (and counting).

An avid reader and lifelong fan of the mystery and thriller genres, Blake loves to hear from you, so please feel free to visit www.blakepierceauthor.com to learn more and stay in touch.

BOOKS BY BLAKE PIERCE

CAMI LARK MYSTERY SERIES
JUST ME (Book #1)
JUST OUTSIDE (Book #2)
JUST RIGHT (Book #3)
JUST FORGET (Book #4)
JUST ONCE (Book #5)

NICKY LYONS MYSTERY SERIES
ALL MINE (Book #1)
ALL HIS (Book #2)
ALL HE SEES (Book #3)
ALL ALONE (Book #4)
ALL FOR ONE (Book #5)

CORA SHIELDS MYSTERY SERIES
UNDONE (Book #1)
UNWANTED (Book #2)
UNHINGED (Book #3)
UNSAID (Book #4)
UNGLUED (Book #5)

MAY MOORE SUSPENSE THRILLER
NEVER RUN (Book #1)
NEVER TELL (Book #2)
NEVER LIVE (Book #3)
NEVER HIDE (Book #4)
NEVER FORGIVE (Book #5)
NEVER AGAIN (Book #6)
NEVER LOOK BACK (Book #7)
NEVER FORGET (Book #8)
NEVER LET GO (Book #9)
NEVER PRETEND (Book #10)
NEVER HESITATE (Book #11)

PAIGE KING MYSTERY SERIES

THE GIRL HE PINED (Book #1)
THE GIRL HE CHOSE (Book #2)
THE GIRL HE TOOK (Book #3)
THE GIRL HE WISHED (Book #4)
THE GIRL HE CROWNED (Book #5)
THE GIRL HE WATCHED (Book #6)
THE GIRL HE WANTED (Book #7)
THE GIRL HE CLAIMED (Book #8)

VALERIE LAW MYSTERY SERIES
NO MERCY (Book #1)
NO PITY (Book #2)
NO FEAR (Book #3)
NO SLEEP (Book #4)
NO QUARTER (Book #5)
NO CHANCE (Book #6)
NO REFUGE (Book #7)
NO GRACE (Book #8)
NO ESCAPE (Book #9)

RACHEL GIFT MYSTERY SERIES
HER LAST WISH (Book #1)
HER LAST CHANCE (Book #2)
HER LAST HOPE (Book #3)
HER LAST FEAR (Book #4)
HER LAST CHOICE (Book #5)
HER LAST BREATH (Book #6)
HER LAST MISTAKE (Book #7)
HER LAST DESIRE (Book #8)
HER LAST REGRET (Book #9)
HER LAST HOUR (Book #10)

AVA GOLD MYSTERY SERIES
CITY OF PREY (Book #1)
CITY OF FEAR (Book #2)
CITY OF BONES (Book #3)
CITY OF GHOSTS (Book #4)
CITY OF DEATH (Book #5)
CITY OF VICE (Book #6)

A YEAR IN EUROPE
A MURDER IN PARIS (Book #1)
DEATH IN FLORENCE (Book #2)
VENGEANCE IN VIENNA (Book #3)
A FATALITY IN SPAIN (Book #4)

ELLA DARK FBI SUSPENSE THRILLER
GIRL, ALONE (Book #1)
GIRL, TAKEN (Book #2)
GIRL, HUNTED (Book #3)
GIRL, SILENCED (Book #4)
GIRL, VANISHED (Book 5)
GIRL ERASED (Book #6)
GIRL, FORSAKEN (Book #7)
GIRL, TRAPPED (Book #8)
GIRL, EXPENDABLE (Book #9)
GIRL, ESCAPED (Book #10)
GIRL, HIS (Book #11)
GIRL, LURED (Book #12)
GIRL, MISSING (Book #13)
GIRL, UNKNOWN (Book #14)

LAURA FROST FBI SUSPENSE THRILLER
ALREADY GONE (Book #1)
ALREADY SEEN (Book #2)
ALREADY TRAPPED (Book #3)
ALREADY MISSING (Book #4)
ALREADY DEAD (Book #5)
ALREADY TAKEN (Book #6)
ALREADY CHOSEN (Book #7)
ALREADY LOST (Book #8)
ALREADY HIS (Book #9)
ALREADY LURED (Book #10)
ALREADY COLD (Book #11)

EUROPEAN VOYAGE COZY MYSTERY SERIES
MURDER (AND BAKLAVA) (Book #1)
DEATH (AND APPLE STRUDEL) (Book #2)
CRIME (AND LAGER) (Book #3)
MISFORTUNE (AND GOUDA) (Book #4)

CALAMITY (AND A DANISH) (Book #5)
MAYHEM (AND HERRING) (Book #6)

ADELE SHARP MYSTERY SERIES
LEFT TO DIE (Book #1)
LEFT TO RUN (Book #2)
LEFT TO HIDE (Book #3)
LEFT TO KILL (Book #4)
LEFT TO MURDER (Book #5)
LEFT TO ENVY (Book #6)
LEFT TO LAPSE (Book #7)
LEFT TO VANISH (Book #8)
LEFT TO HUNT (Book #9)
LEFT TO FEAR (Book #10)
LEFT TO PREY (Book #11)
LEFT TO LURE (Book #12)
LEFT TO CRAVE (Book #13)
LEFT TO LOATHE (Book #14)
LEFT TO HARM (Book #15)
LEFT TO RUIN (Book #16)

THE AU PAIR SERIES
ALMOST GONE (Book#1)
ALMOST LOST (Book #2)
ALMOST DEAD (Book #3)

ZOE PRIME MYSTERY SERIES
FACE OF DEATH (Book#1)
FACE OF MURDER (Book #2)
FACE OF FEAR (Book #3)
FACE OF MADNESS (Book #4)
FACE OF FURY (Book #5)
FACE OF DARKNESS (Book #6)

A JESSIE HUNT PSYCHOLOGICAL SUSPENSE SERIES
THE PERFECT WIFE (Book #1)
THE PERFECT BLOCK (Book #2)
THE PERFECT HOUSE (Book #3)
THE PERFECT SMILE (Book #4)
THE PERFECT LIE (Book #5)

THE PERFECT LOOK (Book #6)
THE PERFECT AFFAIR (Book #7)
THE PERFECT ALIBI (Book #8)
THE PERFECT NEIGHBOR (Book #9)
THE PERFECT DISGUISE (Book #10)
THE PERFECT SECRET (Book #11)
THE PERFECT FAÇADE (Book #12)
THE PERFECT IMPRESSION (Book #13)
THE PERFECT DECEIT (Book #14)
THE PERFECT MISTRESS (Book #15)
THE PERFECT IMAGE (Book #16)
THE PERFECT VEIL (Book #17)
THE PERFECT INDISCRETION (Book #18)
THE PERFECT RUMOR (Book #19)
THE PERFECT COUPLE (Book #20)
THE PERFECT MURDER (Book #21)
THE PERFECT HUSBAND (Book #22)
THE PERFECT SCANDAL (Book #23)
THE PERFECT MASK (Book #24)
THE PERFECT RUSE (Book #25)
THE PERFECT VENEER (Book #26)

CHLOE FINE PSYCHOLOGICAL SUSPENSE SERIES
NEXT DOOR (Book #1)
A NEIGHBOR'S LIE (Book #2)
CUL DE SAC (Book #3)
SILENT NEIGHBOR (Book #4)
HOMECOMING (Book #5)
TINTED WINDOWS (Book #6)

KATE WISE MYSTERY SERIES
IF SHE KNEW (Book #1)
IF SHE SAW (Book #2)
IF SHE RAN (Book #3)
IF SHE HID (Book #4)
IF SHE FLED (Book #5)
IF SHE FEARED (Book #6)
IF SHE HEARD (Book #7)

THE MAKING OF RILEY PAIGE SERIES

WATCHING (Book #1)
WAITING (Book #2)
LURING (Book #3)
TAKING (Book #4)
STALKING (Book #5)
KILLING (Book #6)

RILEY PAIGE MYSTERY SERIES
ONCE GONE (Book #1)
ONCE TAKEN (Book #2)
ONCE CRAVED (Book #3)
ONCE LURED (Book #4)
ONCE HUNTED (Book #5)
ONCE PINED (Book #6)
ONCE FORSAKEN (Book #7)
ONCE COLD (Book #8)
ONCE STALKED (Book #9)
ONCE LOST (Book #10)
ONCE BURIED (Book #11)
ONCE BOUND (Book #12)
ONCE TRAPPED (Book #13)
ONCE DORMANT (Book #14)
ONCE SHUNNED (Book #15)
ONCE MISSED (Book #16)
ONCE CHOSEN (Book #17)

MACKENZIE WHITE MYSTERY SERIES
BEFORE HE KILLS (Book #1)
BEFORE HE SEES (Book #2)
BEFORE HE COVETS (Book #3)
BEFORE HE TAKES (Book #4)
BEFORE HE NEEDS (Book #5)
BEFORE HE FEELS (Book #6)
BEFORE HE SINS (Book #7)
BEFORE HE HUNTS (Book #8)
BEFORE HE PREYS (Book #9)
BEFORE HE LONGS (Book #10)
BEFORE HE LAPSES (Book #11)
BEFORE HE ENVIES (Book #12)
BEFORE HE STALKS (Book #13)

BEFORE HE HARMS (Book #14)

AVERY BLACK MYSTERY SERIES
CAUSE TO KILL (Book #1)
CAUSE TO RUN (Book #2)
CAUSE TO HIDE (Book #3)
CAUSE TO FEAR (Book #4)
CAUSE TO SAVE (Book #5)
CAUSE TO DREAD (Book #6)

KERI LOCKE MYSTERY SERIES
A TRACE OF DEATH (Book #1)
A TRACE OF MURDER (Book #2)
A TRACE OF VICE (Book #3)
A TRACE OF CRIME (Book #4)
A TRACE OF HOPE (Book #5)

Made in United States
Troutdale, OR
02/09/2025